Using intricate, tightly-timed, surgically precise methods, Gunther and his international team of safecrackers, explosives and weapons experts, thieves, and assassins have stolen nearly three million dollars in a series of daring bank robberies. But they need more money. They need a really *big* score.

In New York City, an FBI and NYPD Joint Task Force on Terrorism is investigating several bombings by the Beirut Brigade, who are demanding to be paid $10 million to stop the terrorist attacks. No one's ever heard of the Brigade, but Jake Malloy, ex-Navy SEAL, currently a Captain in the NYPD, is determined to find them.

There is no Beirut Brigade—it's Gunther. In the next stage of his master plan, the Lincoln Tunnel is blocked at both ends with thousands of people trapped inside. The imminent disaster draws much of the Task Force away from tracking the ransom money. Malloy stays focused. Find the money. Find the terrorists. Save the city—*his* city.

DEA Agent Jo Velez is among those stuck in the tunnel. In the middle of a sting operation, Velez is riding with a Colombian drug smuggler. She has no idea that her cover's been blown and the drug dealer is trying to figure out the best way to kill her. Not that it would matter. Jo Velez, like her lover Jake Malloy, will do her job until she draws her last breath.

By Walter Wager
from Tom Doherty Associates

TUNNEL

WALTER WAGER

A TOM DOHERTY ASSOCIATES BOOK
NEW YORK

This is a work of fiction. All the characters and events portrayed in this book are either products of the author's imagination or are used fictitiously.

TUNNEL

Copyright © 2000 by Walter Wager

A Forge Book
Published by Tom Doherty Associates, LLC
175 Fifth Avenue
New York, NY 10010

www.tor.com

Forge® is a registered trademark of Tom Doherty Associates, LLC.

ISBN 0-812-56467-7

Library of Congress Catalog Card Number: 99-089059

First edition: April 2000
First mass market edition: September 2001

Printed in the United States of America

0 9 8 7 6 5 4 3 2 1

This book is dedicated to my wise and generous friend,
JAY BOTCHMAN

W.W.

TUNNEL

1

GUNTHER GLANCED at the clock in the blue sedan's dashboard.

It was 2:06 P.M. . . . they'd attack in eleven minutes.

The timing was crucial now.

All seven of them knew that.

They'd analyzed and weighed every step . . . considered anything that could possibly stop them . . . including human error.

Not theirs . . . someone else's.

They didn't make errors.

They were highly experienced and skilled, expert in armed robbery, safecracking, auto theft, several kinds of murder and related contemporary art forms. Physically and mentally tough, cool under pressure and ruthless, they were so efficient that none of them had ever been arrested. In their line of work, these six men and the dark-haired woman were among the best in the world.

So was their equipment. It included first-class automatic weapons, "cop killer" ammunition that pierced bulletproof vests, explosives to blast open vaults, and compact radio scanners.

The one held by the dark-haired woman seated beside Gunther continued to crackle orders to police cars. Two were to cope with "a 104 in progress" at Midway Liquors on Bell Avenue, one to intercept a stolen green van moving west on Front Street, another to investigate the report of a naked prowler in Grant Park.

The usual, Gunther judged silently.

Routine police business any day in scores of U.S. cities.

He nodded, guided the sedan right onto Oak Avenue, and eyed the dashboard clock again.

2:08 P.M. . . . exactly on schedule.

With specific criteria in mind, he'd chosen and scouted today's target carefully. They wouldn't be robbing it this breezy April afternoon if the bank wasn't independent, not part of a chain, likely to yield at least $500,000, located in America's heartland, in a mid-sized city with the transportation services this plan required.

Each of them knew precisely what to do . . . when . . . and how.

The same blitz tactics they'd used before.

Rip and run. Quick and fierce. Total coordination.

In and out in two and a half minutes . . . three *max*.

Anything more would be too dangerous, Gunther had told them, and they'd listened to him. They always did. It wasn't only because they were afraid of him. It wasn't just because he'd been here twice in the previous nine days to check and recheck the bank's guards and alarm systems, police communications procedures and patrol car response time, streets and highway routes, traffic and potential bottlenecks, and how the raiders would escape.

They always listened seriously to Gunther because he had a dirty talent for finding a weakness . . . or making one.

In a person or a system.

Or anything else.

Gunther enjoyed having that odd ability, and ignored the fact that he had several flaws himself. The largest, which he saw as a strength rather than a weakness, involved his morals.

He didn't have any.

Gunther had other things. A not quite handsome man of thirty-eight, he had a strong muscular body, a cunning computer-fast mind, clear glass spectacles that almost masked his merciless blue eyes, a variety of guns and razor-sharp knives, and no regrets about the nineteen people he'd killed so far.

Or the ones to come.

Now he drove on to the intersection of Oak and Ames, braking the car to a halt as the traffic light shone red.

At 2:11 P.M. . . . just as he'd timed it last week.

Six minutes until they raped the bank, he thought calmly.

Waiting for the light to change, he loosened the semi-auto pistol in his shoulder holster, looked left and right, then in the rearview mirrors, and listened intently to the new stream of police calls on the scanner.

A purse snatching, a mental patient with a knife screaming outside a church, a "domestic matter," a bloody nameless corpse in an alley.

More of the flowing garbage of urban life today.

The light turned green. As he moved the car forward, Gunther thought through his checklist once again. The others would be in position or approaching the bank. It was time for him to circle the objective again for a final reconnaissance of the perimeter. He'd served in the army, and still lived in military terms.

Gunther cruised the sedan through the area around their objective in a patrol pattern to detect any unusual traffic or police presence. He noticed neither, but he saw heavyset Arnold—skilled in both guns and explosives—step from the green station wagon with his dangerous briefcase a block west of the bank. Walking south toward it on Barbor Avenue came sandy-haired Scott with a pair of pistols, extra clips, and a quartet of gas grenades in a worn shoulder bag.

Gunther didn't even blink at either man. Each of them looked right through him too as he drove past. Seconds later he parked the sedan a block from the bank.

"Do it," Gunther told the woman as he clicked open his seat belt.

She took from the glove compartment a powerful little walkie-talkie.

"This is Doris," she said into it in a cozy Southern drawl. "This is Doris. One minute, please. One minute."

Her name wasn't really Doris, but the armed and violent men listening understood the message and walked faster.

She swiftly slid over behind the wheel as Gunther got out of the car. Though the temperature was only sixty-one degrees Fahrenheit he perspired as he walked toward the bank. The bulletproof vest he wore sealed in his body heat, and the weight of the submachine gun in the sling under his knee-length raincoat also contributed to the clammy warmth that embraced him.

Without slowing his stride, Gunther glanced at the big clock in the bank's wide front window as he approached the building. The sweep second hand showed less than half a minute to go. Gunther instantly reviewed his timetable. Howard, whose very strong hands had broken several necks and many more laws, would be ready to use his steel-jawed cutters just about . . . *now*.

Through the large window Gunther saw Arnold inside

pretending to fill out a deposit slip. Studying a poster promoting low rate loans, Scott was in position a dozen yards to the right near a paunchy uniformed guard. Off to the left, Clay stood at the other side of the spacious marble-floored chamber close to the desk of an earnest-faced bank "officer" who dealt with customers' daily problems.

There was a silent alarm button under that desk. Clay had a compact and extremely rapid-fire M-10 inside his unzipped tan windbreaker. If the "officer" made any move toward the button, Clay would immediately devastate him with eight or nine slugs in, literally, a second.

Half turning his head for a few moments, Gunther registered the sight of Casey seated behind the wheel of a gray van parked twenty yards from the bank entrance. His round face was set in that boyish smile he always had in danger. There'd be a sawed-off twelve-gauge with a score of extra shells in the Sears shopping bag on the seat beside him . . . as usual. The twelve-gauge was Casey's good-luck talisman.

At exactly 2:17 P.M. Gunther opened the door of the bank.

He wasn't sweating at all now. Like Casey, he was nourished by life-and-death risk and he felt cool and confident as he walked inside. This was his time. He had complete control.

Gunther advanced half a dozen steps into the bank, swiftly scanned the whole chamber, and took out his submachine gun. As he released the safety, the other thieves drew their weapons. Scott did more than that. In accord with Gunther's scenario, he used his twin pistols to shoot out the two security cameras.

Then he spun to jam the muzzle of one gun into the side of the uniformed guard. The astonished man's mouth opened in shock, and he began to make gurgling sounds.

Raw fear, Scott judged professionally and hoped that the man wouldn't vomit.

A terrified guard in another bank three states away had done that back in February. It had been very unpleasant.

With neither the time nor inclination to dwell on *that*, Scott now slammed his other handgun into the back of *this* guard's head and stepped aside as the unconscious man crumpled.

Before the guard hit the floor, Gunther spoke.

"One move and you're dead," he announced loudly to the bank's stunned customers and staff.

They looked at the weapons and the hard-faced men holding them.

No one moved.

"Go!" Gunther told the other bank robbers.

They went immediately. Two produced large green garbage bags as they raced around behind the tellers' cages to grab fistfuls of currency . . . nothing smaller than twenty-dollar bills. A third armed thief had followed right behind them. Protecting them with his submachine gun, he stood back against the nearby wall "covering" the tellers.

Each of the raiders was doing his job in accord with Gunther's plan.

In the main chamber Scott now reached down to complete the neutralization of the guard by taking the unconscious man's pistol from its holster.

Just in case.

A moment later Clay waved his rapid-fire weapon at the seated bank officer, gesturing for him to move away from the desk and the alarm button.

Just in case.

The threat succeeded immediately. The man retreated with his hands raised.

Clockwork, Gunther thought.

It was all going like clockwork again. He almost permitted himself the indulgence of a smile, but decided that might suggest weakness.

Strength . . . discipline . . . coordination were what mattered, he told himself again. The woman would be driving the blue sedan into the alley behind the bank within seconds . . . and Howard would be coming up from the basement with the cutters he'd used to sever the alarm cables.

"Vault!" Gunther called out sharply.

Having emptied the tellers' drawers of large bills, the two men with garbage bags sprinted back down the passage to the massive steel door. They knew where it was . . . and they knew it would be open. Gunther had, as usual, done his reconnaissance well.

Problem.

A balding assistant manager was coming out of the vault as the robbers approached. He saw their hard faces and the garbage bags and the guns, and he froze. He was right in their way, blocking the entrance. They couldn't spend ten or fifteen seconds to tell him to step aside . . . or anything else. Gunther's timetable was as tight and precise as his plan.

Solution.

Arnold raised his gun to blast the man out of the way with bullets to the kneecaps, but he didn't shoot him. He didn't get a chance. The terrified assistant manager simply collapsed. The thieves with the garbage bags hurried over his body into the huge metal safe, and began scooping up more large bills while Arnold pushed the dazed human obstacle aside from the doorway.

"One minute!" Gunther shouted.

The rest of the robbery only took forty-one seconds.

While Howard entered the sedan and the dark-haired woman drove it around to the front entrance, the men with the garbage bags hurried from the vault, ran past the body back to join the others in the main chamber, and looked out the front window.

Left—there was Casey starting the gray van.

Right—she pulled the sedan into position and Howard got out to open its rear right door.

"All clear," Scott reported.

Gunther scanned the large chamber again . . . just in case.

"We're leaving," he said in a strong cold voice, "and none of you is going to move—not an inch—for five minutes."

He swung the submachine gun in an arc to frighten them. Their faces and one woman's sobs signaled that he succeeded, but he knew that he couldn't expect a full five minutes. In most people fear didn't last any longer than courage, he reminded himself. He'd be satisfied to get a head start of three minutes.

He only needed two.

Clay and Arnold were the first out the door. They turned left and walked quickly to join Casey in the van. Scott and Gunther followed seconds later, striding ten yards right to the open doors of the blue sedan. They entered quickly, and the two vehicles moved off in opposite directions.

At legal speed. Not very far.

Six blocks west of the bank, the three men in the van transferred to a station wagon. Five blocks south and four east, Gunther, Howard, and the woman who wasn't Doris left the sedan in an alley and got into a minibus. Within twenty-five minutes, Clay was on a train to Indianapolis, Scott was settling into his seat on a Greyhound bus to Chicago, Arnold was boarding a feeder-line flight to Toledo, and Casey was driving onto the Interstate in a rented Avis car. Howard was cruising north in a sporty black Mustang he would drop off at the Hertz Company branch in Akron tomorrow.

Driving north on a secondary road less likely to get police roadblocks, Gunther and the woman listened carefully to local radio stations for reports on the bank robbery. It was nearly an hour before they were out of range of those transmitters. Ten minutes after that he saw the roadside telephone booth he was watching for and parked the minibus near it.

Then he looked at his wristwatch.

She didn't know why, and she didn't ask.

He disliked questions intensely. That was one of the things that could make him angry. She certainly didn't want to risk that.

Now he glanced at his watch again.

She wondered who he was going to call, and why it must be now. He didn't call anyone. As he was getting out of the vehicle three minutes later, she heard the telephone in the roadside booth ring. Someone was calling *him*.

He entered the booth, picked up the instrument, and turned his head so she couldn't read his lips. It didn't surprise the dark-haired woman that he didn't trust her. She knew that he didn't really trust anybody.

It wasn't a very long conversation.

Whoever it was who'd somehow known that they'd be at this nowhere booth at this time didn't have a lot to say. Gunther returned to the minibus in less than a minute. After the success of the bank robbery, he had been in reasonably cheerful spirits until he went to the phone booth. His eyes showed that he wasn't anymore.

"There *may* be a problem," he told her.

She waited for him to explain.

He didn't.

Without another word, he started the engine and drove north in total silence for three hours. When he finally did speak, he made no reference to the telephone call. That's how she knew it was important.

2

AN HOUR and a quarter later.

Some 780 miles east . . . and a bit north.

Carlos Corrientes looked down at New York City, and nodded. That week a lot of other people, including members of Congress and several comedians just as devoted to cheap-shot remarks that might help their careers, also looked down on New York City.

But not from 5,100 feet.

Corrientes was on an Avianca Airlines jet from Bogotá, a pleasant city of about five million and the capital of the Republic of Colombia. He was in fine spirits, for he was twenty-four years old today and this would be his first visit to the place some called The Big Apple.

This trip—all expenses paid—wasn't exactly a birthday present. A man in Cali, a Colombian community of 1,500,000, was financing the entire thing. Corrientes didn't know him, but another man who did said that Corrientes would go first class, stay in a quality hotel affiliated with a major chain such as Hilton or Sheraton, Corrientes could choose which, and be paid eighteen thousand dollars after he killed somebody in New York.

Since Corrientes had already murdered three people since Christmas in his capacity as a freelance assassin and had long wanted to experience cosmopolitan New York, the offer had been irresistible.

It didn't matter that the person to "hit" was a policeman.

Corrientes had "done" two other police officers in the past year, one the year before, all in Colombia.

Cops were the same everywhere, he told himself as a voice from the cabin's loudspeakers instructed passengers to fasten their seat belts. The landing was smooth and on time. With a doctored passport of the highest quality, the neatly dressed assassin went through the U.S. Immigration screening easily. As there was nothing illegal in his one suitcase, he had no problem with the Customs inspectors either.

They did search his bag very carefully, of course.

It was the drug thing, of course.

He'd heard that passengers on flights from Colombia got special attention as possible cocaine couriers. This wasn't entirely fair, Corrientes thought as he carried his suitcase through the crowded terminal. Only a small percentage of Colombians had any connection with the narcotics trade . . . and the gringos had created the whole situation *themselves* with their appetite for the white powder's instant pleasure.

In addition to his gift for homicide, Corrientes had a short attention span and the tastes of a macho high school dropout. By the time he got into the taxi, any negative thoughts had yielded to his confidence that he'd have a wonderful time in this country of great wealth and beautiful lustful women. He was in excellent spirits and high hormones when he checked into the lofty Hilton on the Avenida de las Americas, a street name that promised good luck.

That night Corrientes left the hotel at nine P.M. and, as ordered, walked four blocks to a public telephone. He dialed the number they'd made him memorize, spoke briefly in Spanish to an adult male named Jorge, and arranged for the delivery.

They met three-quarters of an hour later in a large Manhattan "club" where pretty young women—mostly tall and all with the bosoms Corrientes had dreamed of—wriggled, smiled, and danced with little or no clothes. Some wore nothing but shoes, the assassin noticed as his throat grew dry and his eyes wide.

The way these voluptuous females looked at him and licked their lips provocatively confirmed to Corrientes what he'd heard about American women. They were definitely wanton and animal, he thought and grinned in anticipation.

Jorge, who never offered a last name, recognized the look.

"*After* you do your work," he announced.

Corrientes nodded in assent. They watched the dozen women do their erotic work for almost half an hour, saw the shift change as another group of naked performers took over, and finally left. Jorge's car was parked around the corner. It was in that vehicle that he gave Corrientes the envelope and the package.

"Two things about this policeman," Jorge said. "First, he's still causing trouble so sooner would be better than later."

"What's the second thing?"

"Sooner doesn't mean rush. You can't rush with this man. He's tough and he's clever. You're only going to get one chance."

When he returned to his room, Corrientes opened the envelope first. It contained $2,300 in twenties and fifties . . . no hundreds. The hundred-dollar bill was the business card of the dope trade around the world. He found in the package his favorite model .32-caliber pistol with silencer, explosive bullets, a sheet of paper with the addresses of the target's home and workplace, and a photo of the policeman himself.

Corrientes looked at the picture for several seconds.

This policeman had a strong face, seemed to be thirty-five or forty, better-looking than any cop Corrientes knew. He didn't really seem to be that special. There was something odd in his eyes that Corrientes couldn't quite identify, but he knew that it was nothing he couldn't handle.

Corrientes rented a car, and followed the policeman for the next three days to establish his patterns and sched-ules. He did this prudently and expertly, applying the skills he'd honed over five years of stalking human tar-gets. He felt professional pride as he saw that the target had no idea he was being watched.

At eight A.M. on the fourth day, Corrientes was waiting in his rented car across the street from the apartment house on West Seventy-ninth Street in Manhattan where his target lived. The pistol with the silencer and explosive bullets was on the front seat beside Corrientes . . . the po-liceman would come out the front door of the building at any moment.

It was time to kill him.

Corrientes lowered the window beside the steering wheel, picked up the pistol, and thought for just a mo-ment about those big and busty blondes. Then he forced his focus back to the front door of the apartment house.

Three explosive bullets . . . all in the head.

Bits of skull and brain would be splattered over the

dirty sidewalk, the assassin told himself contentedly. He'd been told to make it gory to shake up the New York cops, and this would do it.

He was abruptly distracted by a noise behind him.

Door, his mind registered. Someone was opening the car door on the street side. As Corrientes turned he began to raise his gun. He didn't get to use it. He dropped it when the person who opened the door seized the wrist of Corrientes's gunhand . . . and broke it with a single swift twist.

In sudden terrible pain, the assassin began to scream.

He found that was impossible to do with a gun muzzle in his mouth. Shocked and gagging, he looked up into the face of his fierce assailant. It was the handsome policeman who Corrientes had thought wasn't special.

"Pay attention," the policeman said as he picked up the pistol the assassin had dropped. "I'll talk and you'll listen. Got that?"

Corrientes shook now in hurt and managed to nod.

Then he began to cry.

3

THE PRESS loved the story.

The mayor hated it.

"*What* did he say?" demanded the Honorable Philip F. Dowling who was up for reelection very soon and worried about everything.

Police Commissioner Alfred Jefferson, who had less hair but at least thirty pounds more girth than the telegenic mayor, managed to keep a straight face.

"Shall I read the *Times* piece again, Mr. Mayor?" he asked with careful politeness.

"What the fuck did the lunatic say?" Dowling pressed irately.

"According to the reporter, he pointed out to Captain Malloy that this attempt to kill him by what seems to be a professional Latino hit man might be related to that big drug ring the captain helped wreck three months ago."

The mayor shook his head.

"What did *Malloy* say to him?" he insisted.

"According to this reporter . . . and they do get things wrong sometimes, you know," Jefferson replied, "Captain

Malloy seemed to doubt that the head of the dope cartel in Cali would bother to come after him."

"The *exact* words. Give me the *exact* words," Dowling ordered grimly.

Here we go, thought Jefferson as he picked up the *Times*.

"He must have much more important things to do, Captain Malloy said," the police commissioner read aloud. "When asked what those might be, the captain said that there were some very unruly people in Cali and somebody like Eugenio Gomez, who is alleged to direct this major cocaine organization, might be more concerned about protecting his dear old mother and her nice four-bedroom house off the Plaza Bolivar."

"Jeezus Christ!" Mayor Dowling raged.

"He said *alleged*," Jefferson noted and hoped that the mayor would keep the cursing to a minimum. As the eldest son of a proper and dignified African-American minister, Jefferson didn't appreciate any form of swearing or misuse of the Lord's name.

"*Alleged*? That's not what I'm talking about, dammit! I'm talking about the fact that a captain in *my* police department has just used the *New York Times* to threaten this gangster's mother. That's the message this maniac sent, you know."

"You could read it that way," Jefferson admitted.

"What do *you* think of this mad dog message?" Dowling challenged.

The minister's son considered his answer carefully.

"I think that a major Cali dope operator would probably take this kind of message seriously," Jefferson replied. "Wiping out an enemy's entire family is routine in that crowd. It's supposed to scare the other side witless."

"But Captain Malloy isn't in that zoo. He's a law officer in my city. He's supposed to uphold the law and protect both people and property, not threaten them. Even though he wouldn't actually do these things," the mayor said as he peered into the plate glass that covered his imposing desk and straightened his striped silk tie, "we're going to look like goons."

He paused, frowned.

"He *wouldn't* . . . he *couldn't* do anything like this, right?" he tested warily.

Jefferson decided that this wasn't the time to tell a nervous politician that Jacob Malloy was a crack shot and explosives expert who'd been a much decorated member of a U.S. Navy elite SEAL team . . . who could do a lot of things. When he'd joined the NYPD, the Navy had made it clear that much of what Malloy's unit had done would never be declassified. He could probably blow up anything . . . or anyone.

What he would do was something else.

From what the commissioner knew about Malloy, he was almost too smart, highly principled, incorruptible, fair to his cops, and intolerant of any abuse of those who couldn't defend themselves. He wasn't going to attack anyone's mother. Of course, the drug tycoon didn't know this.

"Captain Malloy certainly wouldn't," Jefferson assured the mayor. "He comes from a very good family. You've probably met his mother."

"I don't think so."

"Judge Lisa Berg of the Court of Appeals. His father's a doctor, head of neurosurgery at Mt. Sinai."

Big league people, Dowling computed in a New York second. With powerful and dangerous connections. Money connections, media connections, legal and political connections . . . *no thanks.*

Dowling, who was basically a decent man who did the right thing on those occasions when he could figure out what it was, stood up and walked over to the sideboard. His eyes moved across the three tabloids.

The *Daily News* . . . the *Post* . . . *Newsday*.

Each had the same picture on the front page.

It was Captain Jacob Malloy. The headlines weren't *quite* identical, but they all included the phrase "Hero Cop."

No thanks.

"You know . . . it was very brave of Captain Malloy to disarm this professional killer," Dowling noted smoothly as he started back to his desk.

"That's what the *Daily News* and the *Post* said in editorials this morning," Jefferson reported.

"And he did it single-handed," the mayor pointed out as his rhetoric warmed. "He was fortunate that he spotted this assassin."

The police commissioner shrugged.

"The hit man was the fortunate one," he told Dowling. "Jake Malloy could have broken *both* his wrists and other things."

Now the mayor had an inspiration.

"Let's see what we can do to help your fine captain out of this complex situation," he proposed. "All this media attention must be distracting."

"He certainly didn't appreciate the five television stations' requests for interviews," Jefferson concurred. "Turned them all down . . . the BBC and some Japanese network too."

Dowling nodded in approval.

"We've got to get him out of the spotlight," he announced, "and this thing will blow over. How long has he been in your Narcotics Division?"

"Just under three years," the commissioner replied.
"Before that he was with the Terrorist Task Force. That's
a joint operation with the FBI out of 26 Federal Plaza."

"Low profile?" Dowling tested.

"*No* profile. Completely hush-hush."

Dowling beamed in pleasure.

"Perfect," he said. "Can you move him back there?"

Jefferson nodded.

"Timing's right," he declared. "Our senior guy on the
Task Force had a major heart attack four days ago. We
could use a replacement . . . and Malloy knows that
whole game."

"Give him a week's leave and an official commendation
for his outstanding work in the highest tradition of the
force," Dowling instructed. "By the time he gets back and
starts work with the Task Force, some poor drug addict
out in Brooklyn will grab all the media attention by killing
her daughter and everyone will forget about Malloy."

The mayor's cynical prediction was only partially correct.

It was a male coke freak out in Queens who dismem-
bered his son *and* his daughter *and* a psychiatric social
worker who rang his doorbell by mistake. The rest of
Dowling's estimate came to pass.

The next eight days saw a number of sensational stories and colorful distractions—lewd and bloody episodes
that broadcast and print media celebrated with unseemly
enthusiasm. By the ninth day what Captain Jacob Malloy
had done and said was a dim memory. New chills and
new thrills had pushed him offstage like an understudy
no longer needed.

Malloy didn't mind. He'd sent his message to Cali, and
that was what mattered to him. It mattered to Eugenio

Gomez too. The whole thing was a damned affront to his dignity.

He had to do something or nobody would respect him anymore.

He had to do it soon.

4

AT LEAST half a million newspaper and magazine columnists, songwriters, and other maudlin philosophers around the world have declared that everything changes.

That isn't entirely true.

Not in and around the Russian city named Moscow.

Colonel Andrei Belkov, a sharp-eyed and barrel-chested man of fifty-one who'd worked diligently and deviously at KGB headquarters in the Soviet capital for over a decade, saw himself as living proof of that. He was still doing the same job with the same goals under the command of the same sort of hard self-serving people.

A number of things *were* different now, Belkov admitted to himself as he left his office at four P.M. the day after Malloy was transferred. There was no more Soviet Union. Now Moscow was the center of a new and smaller state, one of fifteen in an odd and uneasy confederation. Belkov no longer worked for the KGB, the widely feared Committee for State Security. Instead he was employed by an almost invisible young entity called the SVR, Sluzba Vneshneie Razvedki, the Foreign Intelligence Service.

SVR headquarters wasn't in the great historic city. With its tall structures visible above the trees, the SVR operated from a heavily guarded complex of modern buildings outside Moscow in semirural Yasnevo. Belkov and many other espionage veterans in nearby offices thought that it was ironic how much Russia's key spy center resembled CIA headquarters at Langley outside Washington.

No one at the SVR ever said so, of course.

Even in the new Russia it wouldn't be prudent.

Despite all the publicized changes, the SVR quietly kept many of the old ways and KGB careerists who enjoyed them. These careful professionals still thrived in good jobs with significant powers because they'd mastered certain practical skills in both "cold" wars . . . the fierce global one and the other brutal conflict that destroyed so many inside the Soviet empire. These survival skills included the oily arts of always agreeing with the more powerful.

Or their friends, Belkov reflected as he walked to the elevator.

That hadn't changed.

It remained an endless show-and-tell ritual, he thought and pressed the DOWN button. You still had to show your total loyalty by telling them what they wanted to hear. That barred comments about Russia's ambitious Foreign Intelligence Service possibly copying anything done by its arch adversary, the American CIA.

Political theories had nothing to do with it, the husky colonel told himself as he entered the elevator. The leaders of this powerful espionage organization had been beyond ideology for a long time. Belkov had seen it happen over the years. They had budgets and egos, personal domains and careers to protect. With those priorities clear, they did what they had to do.

They were pragmatic men, he thought. They had no heroes and no dreams. The elevator stopped, and he stepped into the imposing lobby. The armed and uniformed sentries at the front door of the twenty-two-story tower stiffened to attention when they saw him. Belkov walked from the building, sniffed the crisp late-afternoon air, and nodded to the driver of his car. Minutes later it rolled down the Moscow Ring Road toward the heart of the capital.

Colonel Andrei Belkov, third in command of the cloak-and-dagger organization's American directorate for half a decade, looked out at the budding trees calmly. Then he glanced at the rearview mirror. It didn't bother him that he was being followed by an SVR surveillance team, or that this car and his office were bugged. He understood all that went with this delicate and complex operation.

He eyed the trees again, and felt the microfilm cartridge in his pocket. Belkov knew that sooner or later someone would probably die for these pictures, but that didn't disturb him either.

What did trouble him was that *they* were covertly scrutinizing his files. It could be a routine spot check because nobody was considered totally trustworthy. "I don't trust anyone, including myself," paranoid but cunning Stalin had said . . . and the same rules survived.

It might also be a security probe initiated by the new head of the First Directorate to get Belkov's job for a crony.

Or it could relate to Omar.

Government policies were shifting unpredictably in the not so stable new Russia. Today Omar could get Belkov into very serious trouble. There wasn't a word about

Omar left in the files Belkov had sanitized so thoroughly, but it might be different in what had been East Berlin.

There the Stasi, East Germany's big internal and external spy service, had for decades filled warehouses with millions of bulging files and wiretaps on everyone and everything. It was an obsession of Stasi, which was completely loyal to and linked to the KGB. Just before the Wall and East Germany itself collapsed, a Stasi general had promised Belkov to purge all records and signal logs of any mention of Omar.

But within days it was desperation time . . . every man for himself. Who could predict what the West German authorities might do to senior Stasi officers? Who'd risk waiting around to find out? Things had been chaotic as the Stasi chiefs, fearing the worst, abruptly fled.

Could Belkov *really* be sure they'd paused to wipe out all traces of Omar?

The methodical Germans were so damned organized and fanatical about paperwork and other records that they might have duplicates or even triplicates of everything, Belkov told himself again and shook his head. He'd been concerned about this for some time. This worry had become much more urgent in the six days since he'd heard that specialists from Bonn's counterespionage *apparat* and the CIA were searching the Stasi records of covert operations against the United States.

They'd go through every file, page, photo, tape, disk.

Unlike the Stasi general rushing to flee to avoid arrest, they'd have unlimited time.

If there was anything left about Omar, how much time did Belkov have? And where could he run?

Now the car was entering Moscow. There were more and more passenger vehicles and small trucks in the capital these days, and it seemed as if the drivers were less or-

derly each week. The swollen traffic was as noisy and tur-
bulent as Moscow itself, the colonel thought as his boxy
limousine slowly crawled toward the center of the city.

Red Square . . . not so red anymore.

Beyond the far end of the famous square, facing toward the colorful onion domes of St. Basil's and the walls
of the Kremlin, was the bulky and fairly modern Hotel
Rossiya. At the main entrance Belkov got out of his car,
told the driver to park and wait, and entered the building
in a covey of earnest Japanese tourists.

The colonel knew this lobby. He looked around as if
he didn't before he made his way to the hard currency
gift shop. He glanced at his wristwatch. Both the CIA
and SVR were quite rigid about time . . . and a lot of
other things, he reflected. To be on schedule, Belkov
spent a few minutes surveying the cognac, Scotch
whiskey, cigarettes, and dolls before he left the Rossiya
by a rear door.

Then he walked to the always busy and crowded old
GUM department store, a high-ceilinged artifact of the
distant past. Sometimes the rendezvous was here . . .
other times at the Tretyakov Gallery. Belkov looked
around "casually" . . . hoped it would go smoothly again.

At the appointed counter—at the agreed time—he saw
the American courier he'd come to meet. This thin
woman in her mid-thirties had been identified months
ago by SVR as a CIA agent listed on U.S. Embassy rolls
as an administrative assistant with full diplomatic immu-
nity. She ignored Belkov as they both scanned the
mediocre sweaters on the counter.

Then, for a few seconds, they studied each other's
hands.

If either Belkov or the woman gave the closed fist danger signal, they'd abort the transfer. It would be delayed

until the day after tomorrow. Since this was May they'd use one of the pre-set blind drops behind Moscow's newest Tex-Mex restaurant.

There was no signal.

All clear.

Seconds later the exchange was made swiftly and smoothly with a standard "brush pass" . . . a routine tactic taught in the training programs at spy schools in many countries. Her execution was flawless.

Tradecraft One, Belkov thought cynically.

She'd probably been at the top of her class, he told himself and pushed the envelope she'd delivered deeper into his pocket. He knew what was in the envelope but he didn't open it. *They* would do that themselves.

They did some forty minutes later at SVR headquarters. They—General Strelski, who commanded the First Directorate, and a colonel who was his deputy—handled that. Strelski didn't trust Belkov to open it because Belkov *might* steal something for himself. The deputy was present to be a witness that Strelski hadn't done that either.

The general counted the money twice.

Nine thousand dollars in used hundred-deutsche mark notes. Somebody at Langley had the bizarre idea that using foreign currency might increase the deniability if the operation was blown.

It had been going on since the Americans finally woke up to CIA veteran Ames's betrayal, and began increased efforts to "turn" someone in the SVR. When they'd approached Belkov, they were quite professional and wary. They realized that his hints about discontent and financial problems might be a trap, but that suspicion slowly faded by the end of the first year.

He was delivering quality information.

Carefully "cooked" by the SVR, which had baited this

classic deception operation, these "hot" secrets were a clever blend of truths that could be checked and falsehoods that couldn't. It had gone well for over two years now. Both sides were satisfied.

The CIA was pleased that the plan to get even and achieve a high-level penetration of the SVR was so productive.

The SVR was delighted that its double-deception plan to trick the foolish CIA was such a success.

There were two things that neither intelligence organization knew.

They had no suspicion that their presumed pawn—Colonel Andrei Belkov—had a rather extraordinary plan of his own.

And they'd never heard of Omar.

5

"**I DON'T** like it," Gunther announced bitterly.

"Maybe next month," the woman who'd helped him rob half a dozen banks began.

She didn't finish.

"I don't like *maybes* either," he broke in with the grace of a hit-and-run driver.

They were sitting in a clean and utterly drab motel room nine miles south of Dayton, Ohio. Now she looked again at the colored pieces of paper in neat stacks on the Formica-topped desk. They were *it*, the reason for his anger.

This was the loot from the latest bank raid. There'd be no point in telling him that $397,800 wasn't a bad take, she thought. That sum simply wasn't good enough for Gunther. After living with this obsessive and dominating man for almost three years, she knew that he had his own math.

He even had a personal number.

Eight million.

That was the magic figure. He'd created it, and it would save them all. With eight million they'd be out of the country, completely anonymous, equipped with the best false identity documents and enough money so they'd never need to steal any again. No police—city, state, or federal; U.S. or foreign—would even be aware that they existed. This invisibility had been a key objective from the beginning. It was the reason he'd spread the robberies over many months and various states to minimize the chance that law enforcement people might realize the crimes were related.

If there was no visible connection, no one would search for a group. If the banks hit weren't too big or part of larger chains, there was less likely to be pressure on the cops from some business with financial or political muscle to launch a major effort to find and cage them.

Gunther had calculated every aspect of the scheme. He'd figured on a million for each of the seven, plus an additional million for contingencies. He'd worked out a timetable, picked the banks, and studied them with all his professional expertise. It had started well. The second bank had actually yielded close to six hundred thousand, but then the take from the next three had dropped to about four hundred thousand each.

It was going to take longer than he planned to reach the magic number, but it still could be done.

He might not have time to do it though.

Something not under his control was threatening them all.

The phone call he'd received at the booth by the highway made it clear that his schedule, his plan, perhaps his very survival might be in serious danger. Operating patiently and unobtrusively, they had—after expenses—just a bit less than two and three-quarters million dollars.

About a third of the magical eight.

A lot of money . . . but far from enough.

Anything less than his magic number couldn't provide enough income so none of the seven bank robbers need steal again. If even one did, Gunther thought grimly, his entire effort—so masterfully planned and perfectly executed *thus far*—would be for nothing. It hardly mattered who did it or where the theft took place. Once the police there started searching for the criminal, his invisibility would be gone.

None of them would be safe anymore.

Anymore was the rest of his life, Gunther told himself, and there was no way he'd accept the idea of looking over his shoulder for years . . . decades. The possibility that he'd be some cops' prey, that he'd be stalked and hunted, caught and caged like an animal, flooded his consciousness with anger.

And fear. Gunther wasn't afraid of anybody because he knew that he was more clever . . . simply *better*. The only thing that frightened him, viscerally and indescribably, was being confined in a small space. Sometimes he thought this dread had roots in the many times his harsh stepfather had locked him for hours in the choking blackness of that unlit closet. Sometimes he couldn't think at all . . . just hate.

He hadn't told the bank robbers or anyone else of this blind terror. Gunther wouldn't—couldn't—show any sign of weakness, for then they wouldn't fear him. He didn't forgive or forget either. After his first professional murder, he had returned to his hometown to deal with his stepfather. Gunther didn't lock him in an inky, stuffy, steamy closet. Taking care and pleasure in leaving a half-inch air hole so his enemy wouldn't perish too soon, Gunther walled him up in an empty house's basement toilet where the man would have water, no food, and time to die very slowly as his body consumed itself.

Now Gunther smiled as he relived it in his mind.

He could still see the horror in the man's eyes before the last cinder block was sealed into place.

He could still hear the screams.

The woman with the Southern accent saw Gunther's grin, but didn't consider asking what was amusing him. He wasn't thinking of telling her. This was *his* secret, and his mind had already moved on to something else anyway.

The threatening news in the telephone call hadn't been expected but, as Gunther often boasted, he survived—free and invisible—because he expected the unexpected. He'd known that something like this could happen. He was ready for it.

If the threat became a reality—if there wouldn't be time to complete his program of perfect bank raids—he'd prepared another totally different program. In one attack it would raise all the money they needed. A single assault—daring and shocking, high-tech and even higher in emotional impact on people—would do it.

Gunther had already picked the rich target, located the high ground to watch and dominate the battlefield. Some of the basic equipment he'd use was already in place. It would take only a few weeks to complete the preparations.

Two hours more for the raid.

Big stakes, big score, the magic number and they'd be gone.

Gunther took a small notebook from his jacket pocket, thumbed the pages to the communications schedule. Mentally translating the jumbled numbers and letters, he found the telephone number and time to reach Arnold.

The leader of the bank robbers didn't call from the motel room, of course. Somebody might be listening or tapping, and Gunther didn't want his female lover-accomplice-subordinate to hear the conversation either. If she was captured by the cops, she couldn't tell them what she didn't know, he reasoned realistically.

He was quite realistic for a career criminal and multiple murderer. His cunning and paranoia were actually helpful. They certainly contributed to his ongoing success in breaking laws and people without getting caught.

An hour and a quarter after they checked out of the motel—a bit more than two days after Belkov passed the microfilm to the American courier in the GUM store—Gunther stood at a pay phone in a gas station at the edge of a small town. With seven quarters in his left hand, he dialed with his right.

Three rings . . . hang up.

Redial.

Arnold was *there*, as he was supposed to be.

You could count on Arnold, Gunther thought as he heard the familiar voice. He was a serious person, very responsible. He was not only expert with a variety of standard explosives but also deft in making his own from products used on farms or in homes. That ability to "live off the land" and improvise could be vital, Gunther knew. Federal law enforced by the Alcohol, Tobacco & Firearms Bureau of the Treasury Department barred the sale of explosives to anyone who didn't have a license to buy them.

Gunther and his backup plan needed explosives, but not the risks of seeking a license with forged papers under false pretenses. Even if they succeeded, there'd be a paper trail.

No more invisibility. No way.

"How's it going, buddy?" Gunther began.

"Everything's cool. What's up with you?"

"I'm calling about the surprise party for Uncle Phil. I think you'd better pick up the decorations," Gunther replied.

"Now?"

"Why not? We want to do it right. If you can't find nice things at one shop, try a couple."

"No problem," Arnold assured him.

"See you on Monday," Gunther reminded.

At the next bank robbery.

Gunther didn't have to say that. Arnold understood.

"Bet on it," the explosives expert answered.

Gunther hung up the phone, walked back to the green sedan he'd rented after turning in the minibus.

"Radio says it might rain," she told him calmly.

Gunther smiled benignly. *Louisiana*, he thought as he listened to her soft Dixie drawl and tried to remember if she'd ever been there. It didn't matter, he decided. She had the speech down perfectly.

6

ARNOLD, A bulky methodical man who earnestly enjoyed being on time and never wasted any, was on the highway in a rented van thirty-nine minutes later. He'd gone over this part of the plan, in detail, twice, with Gunther months earlier. The explosives specialist knew exactly where to go.

East.

Some 510 miles . . . and he also knew where to get the "party decorations" on the way.

He'd prepared for all this half a year before. Arnold had gone to the extensive periodicals collection at the New York Public Library in mid-Manhattan, scanned several magazines devoted to the construction and demolition industries, and found a number of advertisements for major producers of explosives. Now he had their corporate names and telephone numbers on a card in his shirt pocket.

On the seat beside him were several road maps covering routes to his destination. When he stopped at a gasoline station to refill the van's fuel tank, Arnold studied these highway charts again. Yes, he'd steal the "decorations," the explosives, in three cities on the way. In each he'd take only a few cases of dynamite.

Not enough to give local police any acute concern.

Not enough to generate headlines that might "red flag" federal explosives monitors at ATF headquarters in Washington.

Youngstown, Ohio.

Scranton, Pennsylvania.

Hartford, Connecticut.

These were his choices for the thefts. He telephoned four different explosives firms to get the names of their local vendors. Each call from a different booth, from a "contractor" with another fake name in one of the target cities, the usual precautions.

There must be no connection . . . maximum diversion and confusion. Everything went well in Youngstown. He disabled the alarm system at 2:05 A.M., and drove off sixteen minutes later with three cases of dynamite.

And a desktop computer. He also emptied several drawers to reinforce the image of a common standard thief . . . perhaps a local addict trying to raise money for a drug "fix." There was no problem in Scranton either the next night when he repeated the process. This time he took a fax machine. Arnold dropped both pieces of office equipment into a river 160 miles farther east.

He knew he had to do it, but he didn't like it.

He couldn't stand waste.

What happened in Hartford was much more disturbing, even though it certainly wasn't Arnold's fault. Arnold, who read newspapers conscientiously because it was his duty to keep up with the state of the nation and the world, knew that Connecticut still had some unemployment. There was, however, no way he could know that a homeless man would wander up behind the warehouse as Arnold emerged from the rear door. He'd already loaded the dynamite into the van. Now he was carrying out two small items whose theft was to divert some attention from the explosives.

He had a cellular telephone in each hand.

And almost no time. The homeless man had seen Arnold's face, and could describe him and the van to the police. He *probably* wouldn't. He *probably* shunned the police, but Arnold knew beyond any doubt that *probably* wouldn't do.

Five seconds.

That was all the time the explosives expert had for decision.

It was also all the time that the homeless man had before he began to die. Arnold swiftly considered how to kill him. No gun or knife. No garrote either. Nothing that would say "weapon" or "murder" to a cop or coroner examining the corpse. It had to look like an accident or some fight between alcoholic street people.

There was one more restriction.

Not here.

The body had to be found somewhere else so the police wouldn't connect the death to this break-in. A simple burglary would be one thing. A burglary-homicide wouldn't be simple at all. It would be much more important . . . get more investigation and publicity. All this went through Arnold's mind in the five seconds.

As Arnold stepped forward he could smell that the rheumy-eyed homeless man hadn't bathed in weeks. This situation was unjust, Arnold thought as he raised the twin cell phones. Terror twisted the poor man's features a moment before Arnold smashed a phone onto each side of the victim's head. Arnold immediately crashed the phones against the man's ears twice more, battering him into blinding pain and the black void of unconsciousness.

The explosives specialist studied the limp body at his feet for several seconds. Then he carefully picked it up and put in on a plastic sheet inside the van's cargo compartment. Arnold glanced down for any drops of blood. He saw two crimson stains and matching smears on the telephones.

Gunther wouldn't leave any blood that might alert the cops there had been violence here, Arnold thought. He had to get rid of or hide the red drops. Yes, he'd do what Gunther would do. Gunther always did what was necessary . . . necessary and simple. He excelled at problem solving, Arnold reflected.

Arnold looked at the street littered with crushed cigarette butts, empty matchbooks, newspaper scraps, dog feces, and beer cans. He knew what Gunther would do. It was simple and it worked. After Arnold urinated on the red droplets they were invisible in the yellow puddle. There'd be no homicide investigation here.

There really couldn't be, Arnold thought as he drove across town looking for a suitable place to unload his human cargo. After all, the man wasn't dead yet. His life didn't actually end until the van stopped in a dark alley across town a dozen minutes later. It was in that poor and visibly run-down neighborhood that the explosives professional shattered the man's skull against a wall . . . again and again until he stopped breathing.

Deception time.

Arnold knew he must make this crime look like something else.

He swiftly decided that it would be a routine mugging, one nameless street person robbing and killing another. Since both would be nobodies, nobody would care a lot.

The overburdened police wouldn't put much effort into such a nothing case, he reasoned.

Arnold turned the dead man's pockets inside out, scooped up the meager contents. A quarter, a dime, and two squares of paper. Then he took the corpse's half-ruined shoes. When the coolly lethal explosives expert was eighteen miles down highway I-95 en route south, he stopped to bury the smelly footwear in the contents of a trash can at a closed gas station.

Next he drove farther south for another half hour to check into a motel for the night. Before going to bed, he burned in an ashtray the greasy Social Security card and dog-eared photo of a plump woman that he'd taken from the dead man's pocket. For a moment Arnold wondered who she might be. Then he washed his hands very carefully and went to sleep.

No nightmares.

No dreams at all.

Arnold was a placid pragmatic man who functioned without emotional crises or uncertainties. Life was simple, and guilt a total stranger. When he awoke the next morning, he wasn't thinking about the dead man. His attention was on what he had to do before he could deliver the dynamite.

He went over a mental checklist as he enjoyed a hot shower. When he got back in the van to resume his journey, he went over each item again. The route, the timing, what to buy in the store he'd found in the local telephone directory at the motel, the Kendall key, *that* was it.

Rolling south at fifty miles an hour near Fairfield, Arnold saw what the phone book had promised. Entering the large branch of the Staples office supplies chain, he nodded in admiration of the vast array of products. He paid cash for the cardboard transfer files, duct tape, jet-black Magic Marker, and box cutter. Nine miles down the highway, he stopped off the wide road to prepare the dynamite for unloading later.

He used the Magic Marker to cover the word EXPLO-SIVES and the manufacturer's name on each crate. After he assembled the transfer files, he put one box of dyna-mite into each of those eleven cardboard cases before sealing them with brown duct tape. He reached into his trouser pocket, fingered the Kendall key on the "chain" with the others.

Now he could deliver the explosives.

In midmorning. That was important. He wanted to ar-rive in heavy traffic after the business day had begun. There was less chance that anyone would notice or pay any attention to him or his camouflaged cargo.

He saw the first New York City sign shortly before ten o'clock. Three-quarters of an hour and some dense met-ropolitan traffic later, Arnold steered the van into the basement driveway of a twelve-story building at Thirty-sixth Street and Eleventh Avenue. It was a drab func-tional edifice filled with an assortment of small graphics, printing, design, data processing, paper, and computer marketing firms. The plain and commercial building had no charm, but rents were attractive because it was out of the prestigious midtown area.

The low rent wasn't what had brought Gunther here.

Gunther had no interest in scenic beauty, but he'd found the view from the two-room suite on the top floor irresistible.

Now Arnold stepped from the van to speak to the porter in overalls who was sneaking a smoke in the driveway.

"Kendall . . . 1206 . . . delivery," Arnold said.

"Uh-huh," the swarthy porter replied sincerely and took another puff on the cigarette.

"Got a dolly?"

"Uh-huh," the man answered and pointed at the doorway into the building.

Arnold thanked him with a thumbs-up gesture before going to get the dolly. He rolled it to the back of the van, and loaded onto it the eleven transfer files. Then inside to the left to the freight elevator . . . Arnold knew the way. He'd made deliveries here twice before.

Five boxes were already stacked neatly in a locked closet in Suite 1206. There was another closet a few yards away. After locking the door to the corridor behind him, Arnold carefully stacked the transfer cases in the closet. He didn't worry whether the floor could carry the weight. Another reason that Gunther had picked this building was because it was semi-industrial with extra and very strong steel beams to support heavier loads.

Now he locked this closet. Then his eyes moved automatically to examine a pair of steel filing cabinets that held no files. Protected by combination locks, they were filled with expensive and sophisticated radio equipment. Each piece was new, compact, and designed for high-speed operation.

The bottom drawer of one of these cabinets housed a pair of metal containers with additional hacksaw-proof combination locks of their own. They looked like large tool kits.

One box concealed a score of the finest small timing devices.

The other housed the same number of state-of-the-art electronic detonators.

There were three desks, each with a swivel chair and a

telephone plugged into a black box. The bills for these lines, paid every month within a week of receipt, showed additional charges for conference calls and call-forwarding services. All fed into an answering machine that could be completely remote-controlled if you knew the right number sequence. It wasn't the one that the manufacturer had installed.

The two bigger desks were in the larger inner office, flanked by an American Airlines calendar on one wall and a framed color photo of a factory on another. There was a sign that said KENDALL on top of the plant and a U.S. flag flying from a tall pole on the lawn.

The third desk—smaller and obviously for a receptionist or secretary—was in the antechamber near the corridor. Half a dozen trade magazines relating to the gift and costume jewelry worlds lay on the floor near the mail slot in the door. Arnold had pushed them aside with his foot when he entered. Now he picked them up and put two in the gray-metal IN basket on each desk.

It was more than ritual neatness.

Arnold had an orderly mind, and he *knew* that the IN basket was where such material *belonged* in any properly run office.

There was one more thing that he had to do. He walked to the corner window in the rear office to look down at the view that made Gunther sign the lease eight months ago. It was a wide impressive panorama of the broad Hudson River plus both the New York and New Jersey shores.

"Perfect" was what Gunther had exulted.

He was right, Arnold thought soberly.

For more than a minute he let himself enjoy the soothing experience of watching the large and small vessels—a ferry, a Circle Line sight-seeing craft circling Manhattan island with a load of tourists, a couple of speedboats, and several other small craft—going up and down and across the historic river. Even the ships at docks on the New York side, the elegant *Queen Elizabeth 2* and a decommissioned World War II aircraft carrier with combat planes crouched on its deck, pleased him.

The husky bank robber was smiling as he left Suite 1206 with the dolly and locked the door. Being a responsible person who didn't want to be remembered, he returned the dolly to the porter and thanked him. This time the porter didn't even say "uh-huh." Arnold, a career lawbreaker who blasted and killed for a living, didn't comment on the rudeness, but he shook his head in annoyance.

Half an hour later he dropped off the van at the rental firm's Fifty-third Street branch. Glad to get rid of the vehicle, he felt lighter and free as he strode out carrying the one small suitcase into the lively, noisy, surging bustle of New York. Traffic was heavy in this part of midtown, but Arnold didn't worry as he flagged down a taxi. His plane didn't take off from the airport with the Italian name for another two hours. La Guardia wasn't as grand a name as Paris's Charles de Gaulle, Arnold reflected, but it suited this dynamic and earthy urban center well.

Surviving an almost grim chicken salad sandwich at an airport snack bar, the explosives expert was relieved when he heard his flight being called over the grating speaker system. As he walked to the gate in a stream of shuffling passengers, he found himself thinking about what had happened.

He'd acquired and delivered the dynamite—both in a reasonable manner not likely to arouse local or federal police.

And it wasn't his fault that some mindless vagrant had wandered into the last theft by sheer bad luck . . . and had to be killed.

Now Arnold told himself that no one would connect that final robbery and the missing explosives with the shoeless corpse of some unwashed street person found more than a mile away.

Even though it certainly wasn't Arnold's fault, the unavoidable incident might bother, even anger, Gunther. Gunther was very intelligent but had a bad temper, Arnold thought. He was just a bit afraid of Gunther who had no tolerance for any deviation from his plan. Rationalizing that they couldn't be linked to the death of the homeless man . . . so there was no *real* reason to tell Gunther, Arnold decided not to mention it.

Now he felt better, and put it from his mind.

He had other important things to think about anyway.

First, the next bank robbery . . . and then Gunther's ingenious and remarkable Plan B. They'd go on to it swiftly if the robberies didn't produce the money or if something threatened that entire program. Arnold would be crucial in the backup plan, he told himself as he walked to the airliner. Explosives would play a key role.

His part wouldn't be easy.

After all, Plan B presented no ordinary target.

8,006 feet long . . . thousands of tons of concrete and metal . . . overengineered and overbuilt for survival . . . a huge and massive thing.

Arnold had never blown up anything like it before.

He probably wouldn't have to now, Gunther had said. The threat itself would make them pay. It would if it was made clear and terrifying, Gunther had said in that calm logical way. You had to respect Gunther's logic, the explosives expert reflected.

To be terrifying the threat had to be absolutely real. That part of Gunther's plan was entirely logical too. Arnold had figured out both parts of the plan, determined where the charges should be, how big and how many, how to detonate them. He'd explained all this to Gunther. Arnold wanted him to know that he wasn't going to let him down.

If Gunther said that it was necessary, Arnold would destroy the target . . . and all the people in it.

At least six hundred, Gunther had estimated.

He was probably right, Arnold thought as a trim blond flight attendant flashed on and off a strobe-light smile. Gunther had a valuable gift for numbers. He definitely seemed to like them better than people, Arnold judged.

He'd never killed any numbers.

7

HER NAME was Jo, and she was naked.

Her lovely face was framed in a silky mane of long jet-black hair. She was visibly in excellent health, six or seven pounds overweight by some standard charts but she didn't mind. Joanne Velez, her full name, was a glowing clear-minded woman with her own standards.

She was also almost five feet four inches tall, exactly twenty-nine years, eleven months, and two days old, more intelligent than ninety-three percent of the population of the western hemisphere, and very close to Captain Jacob Malloy of the New York Police Department.

He was five inches away.

Warm . . . naked . . . smiling. She was smiling too.

It was a quarter to seven on the morning after Arnold flew back to the Midwest to rejoin Gunther and the others. The policeman and Joanne Velez had been together, very much together, for nearly a year. In tastes and mind and body they meshed effortlessly and totally. They were so utterly in tune that they even awoke each morning at the same time—ten minutes before the alarm clock sounded.

They didn't waste a minute of it. They usually awakened, eyed each other in silent delight, and made love again before the clattering clock broke the spell. It was the same magic this morning. Their hearts were still pounding and they glistened with the sweet perspiration of passion when the jarring alarm buzzer called them to that other world where so many people wander alone in unseeing crowds.

They kissed again, and sighed. With faces flushed and eyes beaming, they rose from bed, embraced once more. Then they both studied the full-length mirror on the wall beside the framed Polish circus poster.

"You're *very* good-looking," she declared.

"That's *my* line," he protested affectionately and kissed her neck until she shivered in his arms.

Now they glanced at the clock, nodded as one, started toward the bathroom. After showering together in hot soapy intimacy, they toweled each other dry and began to dress swiftly.

"Can't be late," he said in half jest. "First day on a new job."

"Wear a power tie," she advised slyly as she opened her lingerie drawer.

This was her apartment. His was next door. He'd kept several shirts, ties, and other clothes here—where he spent so many nights and nearly every weekend—almost since that evening they'd met in the elevator. As she deftly sheathed her woman curves in brassiere and bikini panties, Malloy controlled an impulse to embrace her again. Instead he reached for a white button-down shirt, paused to consider a rich red tie adorned with small golden dragons.

He thought about the FBI agents on the Joint Task Force.

Always in dark conservative attire. It had been dogma

since the days of tight-lipped J. Edgar Hoover, the Bureau's legendary and autocratic icon-parent.

Malloy studied the eye-catching red silk tie again.

"Could be too much for the low-key federal folk," he judged.

Brushing her long tresses, she looked at her lover and shook her head. It wasn't that he was wrong. He was probably right. He was also probably going to bother the FBI people in one way or another before the week was out.

"Make the coffee," she said.

"You give great hair," he told her admiringly.

"*Coffee*," she insisted.

He put the water up to boil, ground the dark Colombian beans. Then he attended to his shirt and tie, a neat Irish tweed, before he donned light gray flannel pants. After he strapped on the shoulder holster, he took his Glock nine-millimeter pistol from a drawer. Malloy checked the safety before he slid the weapon in and out of the holster twice to make sure it would draw easily.

"Expecting trouble?" she asked.

"I'm expecting *everything*," he evaded effortlessly. "I've a very positive personality . . . and I make great coffee."

They were drinking it half a minute later. It was excellent.

"You're thinking about that son of a bitch down in Cali," she said after a few sips.

"*What* son of a bitch down in Cali?" he asked calmly as he savored the rich strong brew.

"The one who sent the goddam hit man up here to kill you!" she replied fiercely.

"Oh, *that* son of a bitch," he responded pleasantly and took another sip of the fine coffee. "There are a number of sons of bitches down in Cali. Just a tiny percent of the population, of course, but they give that swell town a bad name."

"*Were* you thinking about him?" she challenged between sips.

"You've got it—if you'll pardon the rude language—ass backward," Malloy said. "The real question is whether that creep is thinking of me."

"We both know that crowd, Jake," she said as she finished her coffee and rose. "You've embarrassed him publicly. He's got to be thinking of you."

"Big mistake," Malloy thought aloud and drained his cup. "He should be concentrating on at least seven other creeps in his own business, in his own neighborhood, who're probably planning to eat him for brunch next week."

"He's a *macho schmuck*," she concurred and took her nine-millimeter Sig. Sauer semiautomatic from a drawer. "And damn dangerous," she added.

Malloy watched as she put on her shoulder holster.

Then he tapped his own weapon.

"Mine has sixteen rounds. You've only got fourteen. Don't worry. I'll protect you," he promised with a smile.

She shook her head.

"Jake, I know I shouldn't worry because you're very good at what you do . . . and I know you're smarter than any man I ever met . . . and I'm sure you know how to take care of yourself . . . but I worry. I worry a *lot* because I care about you."

"So do I," he told her, "and about you too."

She eased the Sig. Sauer into the holster . . . then did what he'd done two minutes earlier. She moved the weapon in and out, making sure that she could draw it instantly.

"What are *you* expecting?" he teased.

"No jokes," she appealed.

She wasn't likely to get any, he thought. She knew a good deal about the son of a bitch in Cali . . . and his head. There was little doubt that she understood she might be in terrible danger too. Raping or killing a lover or relative of an enemy was standard operating procedure for the cocaine kings.

Malloy decided not to remind her now. He tapped his wristwatch instead. It was moments later when they put their coffee cups in the kitchen sink that something else bothered her.

"Juice," she remembered. "I forgot the damn juice."

Squeezing fresh orange juice each morning was her job . . . or that was how she saw it.

"So did I," he soothed. "We'll have some before dinner, with champagne. Healthy drink, right? Let's go."

They left the apartment "on automatic," as thousands of other couples were doing. Double-lock the door, scoop up the daily newspaper waiting outside, pause at the mirrors beside the elevator doors to recheck hair or tie or whatever. Regular New York stuff.

Down in the elevator, nods to people whose faces they knew but not the names, through the lobby to the door to the street.

Here, now, for a few seconds, they deviated from the normal New York routine. Despite what second-rate comics and third-rate politicians said on television, most residents of this dynamic, independent, and do-it-my-way city didn't hesitate at their front doors to scan the streets for killers.

Joanne Velez and Jacob Malloy didn't ordinarily do that either. Today they were being wary . . . and neither of them liked it. She swore softly in Spanish. She spoke the tongue perfectly, having spent six years of her childhood in Venezuela and Colombia when her father was an engineer for a U.S. petrochemical company.

"Feeling better?" Malloy asked after she cursed.

"Not really," she admitted.

"Then you're in just the right mood to go to work," he told her cheerfully.

They proceeded downtown together as far as Twenty-third Street and Broadway. Then they separated, and she made her way to a dull-looking nine-story building on Tenth Avenue between Eighteenth and Nineteenth Streets. There was no sign on the outside of the yellow structure, but there was one on the door of the office she entered three minutes later.

U.S. Drug Enforcement Administration.

Malloy continued south on Broadway alone to the area near Foley Square where various city, state, and federal courts and agencies resided in stately proximity. He went to a massive building that dwarfed all of them. Named after a dead U.S. senator, it loomed forty-one floors tall. Housing the New York and regional headquarters of an assortment of federal agencies, the Javits Building—aka 26 Federal Plaza—had been recognized by Washington as a possible target even before those home-grown terrorists murdered so many people in another large federal center in Oklahoma City.

Visitors had been screened here for a long time.

Armed guards, metal detectors, a whole security system was in place and working at both entrances to the wide and busy lobby. Everyone's ID was checked. Malloy showed his police department employment card with his badge as he approached the metal detector.

A tall husky guard studied both.

"You have a weapon, Captain?"

"As authorized," Malloy replied and tapped his blazer where it masked the Glock in the shoulder holster.

A minute later Malloy ascended by elevator to a floor where there was more security. He showed his credentials again, and said whom he'd come to see.

"Please take a seat, Captain," the receptionist replied.

In a short while a neatly dressed man of about thirty came to show him the way. Visitors were not allowed to walk these corridors without a security escort. Malloy's escort made no small talk as they walked. He didn't say a word, and neither did any sign on the door to which he guided Malloy.

There was no sign.

Just a number.

People who got this far were supposed to know what was inside.

8

FRANK B. BRIGGS was five feet ten inches tall, a solid 179 pounds, and forty-three years old. He had a full head of brown hair, teeth that showed what semi-annual dental care could accomplish, wary gray eyes, and a logical orderly mind. A responsible person, he worried more about making a mistake than about facing an armed enemy.

He was armed himself . . . with a powerful weapon.

The large-caliber handgun most used by American criminals and cops alike was a nine-millimeter pistol. Briggs's gun was even bigger, a ten-millimeter Smith & Wesson. It threw a heavier slug that could knock down a man or an ox. He hadn't chosen this weapon. Some people in another city had made that decision.

That didn't trouble Frank B. Briggs.

He was a sensible and disciplined organization man.

He'd been a loyal and effective employee of the Federal Bureau of Investigation for nearly two decades. During the past three and a half years he'd been the SAC, Special Agent in Charge, of the federal half of the Joint Terrorist Task Force in New York City. Those above him on the

FBI food and command chain respected him as a compe-
tent professional.

Briggs felt almost the same way about Jacob Malloy.

He respected the police captain's professional skills and
how much he got done. What Malloy did wasn't the
problem. It was *how* he did those things that made the
SAC uneasy. Having worked earlier with Malloy on the
Task Force for fourteen months, Briggs didn't even trust
the way the ex-SEAL commando thought.

It wasn't quite *linear*, and it was supposed to be.

It wasn't predictable either.

A bit too intuitive, a bit too improvisational, a bit too
bold.

That had bothered Briggs during their previous collab-
oration when Malloy commanded the city police on the
Task Force. It still did.

Malloy saw that uneasiness in his eyes on entering the
SAC's compact office.

Mending fences time, Jacob Malloy thought instantly.

He'd be working closely with Briggs in the dangerous
shadow world of terrorism for at least a year . . . probably
more. It was hard enough to blend the methods and cul-
tures of the by-the-book, white-bread federal agents with
those of the more earthy, urban, and street-smart, bagel
and pizza cops of the NYPD. Friction at the top would
make it even more difficult.

Malloy couldn't afford that if he wanted to.

He didn't.

The meticulously trained FBI people were good investigators. What's more, they had the hardware, the latest,
the best, the highest tech surveillance and communications stuff so cutting edge that they wouldn't talk about
these devices by their real names. One other thing they
didn't discuss was the rumors that much of this sophisti-

cated big-dollar gear had been developed by "another agency of the government"—long Washington's preposterous euphemism for the enthusiastically secretive Central Intelligence Agency. While the fierce Cold War was over in most—not all—ways, the mean rivalry between the Bureau and the CIA remained fit and active like a peppy vampire who wouldn't or couldn't die.

Malloy wouldn't speak about the hardware or the CIA today.

He'd be affable, polite, and very careful.

That might reassure Briggs *a bit.*

At most. The sensible and experienced SAC knew the game of office talk and bureaucratic correctness too.

"Good to see you, Frank," Malloy began briskly. "Lost a few pounds?"

"Wish I did," Briggs responded evenly to the implicit flattery as they shook hands.

The words hardly mattered. The two men might have been speaking Uzbek or Martian. This was just a ritual coming—not quite—together, and they both understood that.

"What's happening?" Malloy asked.

"The usual," Briggs answered cautiously.

"*That* bad, huh?" the ex-SEAL said and he was only half joking.

For this unit, "the usual" was a multi-ethnic horror show. Terrorists came in all colors and creeds, ages and nationalities. All sorts of people—ranging from tough and weapons-wise former soldiers to hyperventilating young extremists to self-styled patriots and devout religious folk from lands most Americans could not even spell—were out there in a rage.

That was the common denominator.

Boiling rage . . . simmering sizzling rage . . . icy rage.

Grandparents and teens, men and women, people with graduate degrees and illiterates.

All furious, all deadly, all hateful toward the American people for something the U.S. government did or didn't do or should have done, all seething to express their rage in violence against the world's greatest power by violence in its most famous metropolis.

World center . . . world target, Malloy thought.

A very strange world, but the only one he had.

"No improvement at all?" he tested hopefully.

"The IRA crowd and the Kurds seem to have calmed down . . . for now," Briggs admitted.

"The IRA never did anything here but buy weapons," Malloy reminded. "How about our main customers?"

The SAC shook his head.

"No good news there," he reported. "Two new Arab outfits and an African group tied to one of the U.N. missions. There's a splinter Armenian faction that may be planning to take out the Turkish consulate."

"What about our home boys, Frank?"

"You mean blacks? Just some hot rhetoric in a student group in Brooklyn."

"I didn't mean that. I meant militias and other native-born gun bunnies."

"*Maybe*," the SAC said very carefully. "We've got a surveillance operation on some people at the edge of Queens."

Surveillance and investigation were the Task Force's two main programs. In both, each city cop had a federal agent as a partner, pooling skills and information. With inter-agency rivalries and bureaucratic bitchery so common this shouldn't have worked. It did.

"We've added some new faces since you left, Jacob," the SAC continued. "I'll walk you around to meet them."

Some executives would summon an employee to their office, Malloy thought as he strode down the corridor with Briggs. This SAC knew better. For the Task Force's coleaders to go to the cubicles where the pairs of partners worked would show that the supervisors respected the men on the firing line.

And the women too.

While neither the NYPD nor the FBI had an abundance of female investigators yet, that was changing *slowly*. One of the "new faces" among the city police on the Task Force was street-wise Carla Hunt, a clear-eyed African American with a practical gift for tracking bad guys—the gold shield of a detective to prove it—a brown belt in karate, and a dazzling smile.

"Heard about you, Captain," she said when Briggs introduced them.

"It's not true," he fenced amiably.

"That's too bad," she said and flashed that smile again.

It was different with Donna Olsen.

Courteous and correct rather than flirtatious, she was earnest, intelligent, proper, and a good shot—as an FBI agent should be. She was also pleasant-looking and fluent in Arabic. While that was the tongue of millions of law-abiding people, a number of Arabic-speakers felt that Western society's injustices obliged them to destroy people and property in various countries, the skies, and the high and low seas.

This sincere and violent minority made (1) bombs (2) corpses (3) Donna Olsen's command of Arabic useful to the Task Force. There were, of course, many other terrorists of different nationalities, beliefs, and languages. Seven of these languages were spoken by one or more members of the Task Force, which also maintained a computer file of city or federal police who "worked" other tongues.

Detective Judy Fong's family had made sure that her Cantonese was as good as her English. Detective Abraham Diaz grew up speaking Spanish in Puerto Rico before moving to the Big Apple's crowded Bronx. Sergeant Peter Rocco, a burly son of Little Italy in lower Manhattan, was fluent in the speech of Sicily before he built a working command of Russian in the streets of Brighton Beach in Brooklyn's Six-Oh precinct. That was where he'd met Malloy.

Rocco grunted before he spoke.

"You shoulda whacked that guy, Cap," he began.

"Do I get three guesses?" Malloy asked coolly.

"The one who came from Cali to whack you. It's not just my idea," Rocco announced. "I know twenty cops who say the same thing."

"I know *forty*," Malloy replied. "How's everything with Giuseppe?"

Rocco beamed. It pleased him that the captain remembered his passion for collecting recordings of the compositions of Giuseppe Verdi. *Aida, Rigoletto, Traviata,* and Verdi's other elegant operas. Some four hundred tapes, cassettes, and assorted records, they were his pride and joy as well as his private place—his refuge from what he saw every day.

"Perfect . . . always perfect," the sergeant replied happily and then introduced his new partner to the captain. Square-faced and soft-spoken Bernard Gill was a thirty-five-year-old FBI special agent from Memphis who'd come to New York only two months earlier from the Boston office where he'd learned something about illegal arms exports.

He was courteous, careful, and curious.

When the SAC led Malloy on to meet two more "new faces" to complete the "new faces" tour, Gill turned to Rocco with an unspoken question in his eyes.

"He's a cop and a half," Rocco assured him, "and that's not all. He once sat at the same table at a fund-raising dinner with *the great Leontyne Price*!"

Gill's face showed no reaction.

"Leontyne Price!" Rocco insisted. "As fine an Aida as I ever heard!"

Still nothing. Rocco turned away to hide his distress, stunned by the possibility his partner hadn't heard of Aida either. Maybe Gill was just putting him on, the Verdi lover speculated. He was still wondering when the two coleaders of the Joint Task Force returned to the SAC's office where Briggs began to brief Malloy on the current investigations in progress.

Another briefing, the next morning at 8:40, far away.

SVR headquarters near Moscow.

The weekly briefing on operations in NATO nations was almost over when General Strelski paused . . . and abruptly uttered *the* word.

"Omar," he said, looking directly into Belkov's eyes.

The startled colonel blinked . . . absorbed the impact.

"Yes, General?" he responded mechanically.

"Tell me about Omar."

His face impassive and heart pounding, Belkov pretended to reflect for several seconds before he shook his head.

"I don't think I've heard of Omar," he lied slowly.

"The CIA and German security people have," Strelski said in a cold harsh voice. "They've been strip-mining the old Stasi records. According to one of our sources in Berlin, they found Omar in those files . . . and they're really bothered."

He paused again to light a dark Cuban corona.

The general still had sources in Havana as well as Berlin.

"*I'm* bothered too," he continued and puffed on the cigar. "You dealt with the Stasi on U.S. operations, didn't you?"

"For several years. What is it that's bothering you?"

"Omar," he said bluntly. "Omar's bothering me a lot. The Stasi sent Omar to the U.S. on a mission thirteen months before East Germany disappeared . . . and apparently *forgot* to clear it with us. There's no damn record of any clearance in the Stasi files, and we don't seem to have a file on Omar at all. How could that be?"

"I don't know, General."

"There's more," Strelski announced. "The CIA and the Germans want to talk to Omar about that mission, but they have a problem. They can't locate Omar. In fact, they can't even find any record that Omar *ever* came back. Do you know what that means?"

Belkov realized that this might be a trap.

He also recognized that he had to play the hand.

"General, it could mean that their records—" he began.

"*Maybe,*" Strelski interrupted impatiently, "or it could mean Omar's still in place in the States . . . still operating there."

"You think that's possible?" Belkov asked.

The general took another puff on the cigar, grunted.

"Not without support," he answered soberly, "and who'd support such an operation?"

"And why?" the colonel added.

Strelski nodded.

"*Very* good, Belkov," he said. "That's the key question. I'm confident that the Americans and Germans are asking it too, so I'd like to get the answer first."

"They've probably started looking already," the colonel

thought aloud. "If the CIA is talking to the FBI this month, there should be a major search on now."

"Alert *our* people in the States too," Strelski ordered. "All of them, Zerkalo first."

Zerkalo was Russian for "mirror." The code name had been chosen for this first-class deep-cover agent because people who looked at Zerkalo saw what they expected to see and suspected nothing . . . while Zerkalo saw and reflected everything back to Russia.

"Please move on this immediately," the general told Belkov curtly. "We must find Omar before the Americans do."

"We'll start looking *at once*," Belkov promised. "It would help to have a photo, a physical description. Some facts on Omar's mission would also be useful. One more thing. Omar's a code name, right?"

"Of course."

"What's his real name?"

A crafty smile bloomed briefly on the general's face.

It vanished in seconds.

"Why do you say *his* real name?" Strelski asked. "How do you know Omar is a *him*?"

"I simply assumed . . . is Omar a female?" Belkov blurted.

That sly look blooomed again . . . and disappeared into the recesses of the general's conspiratorial and complex mind.

"Our source in Berlin is trying to get the answers to those questions," Strelski said slowly.

He was picking his words carefully, Belkov realized. He wasn't giving the slightest hint about the sex or identity of the source in Berlin.

Very professional, very cautious, very dangerous.

"There's one more thing I ought to mention," the general continued. "It is possible—there is some evidence that might be so interpreted—that Omar is more than a single individual."

"A team? Two agents? Three?"

The general shrugged and puffed on the cigar.

"It's being investigated," he said blandly. "I'll let you know. Meanwhile we ought to do some investigating right here. If Omar's mission was in the States, we *ought* to have a file on it. Why don't we? If there's something, or someone, wrong in our system, we must identify and eliminate the problem."

"Absolutely," Belkov agreed quickly.

He had no choice. Any other response would be highly hazardous.

"A comprehensive in-depth investigation," he urged. "I'll give instructions to our security people right away."

"I've already done that," Strelski told him and moved on to the last item on the agenda. It didn't take long. The report on the latest French missile was completed in less than three minutes.

The briefing adjourned. Walking back to his office, Belkov felt the small ball of knotted fear in his stomach. It was justified, he thought, but he didn't have to panic. He didn't. He was a veteran cloak-and-dagger operator . . . a pragmatic one. Fear was no stranger. He knew how to use it to survive.

He'd do everything that the general had ordered . . . and more.

The *more* would save his life.

He'd get word to Omar swiftly. Being clever, practical, and professional, Omar would have a plan for this kind of contingency. Belkov had his own plan . . . actually two. He was confident that they were good plans.

He hadn't expected to use them quite so soon.

A week . . . two at the most. More could be fatal.

Having made his decision, Colonel Andrei Belkov entered his office and drafted the message to be coded and sent to Mirror. Mirror would know what to do. Having operated with significant success inside the American government for well over a decade, Mirror was as good as they came. To protect Mirror, the deep-cover agent's sole supervisor in the SVR was Belkov. The general and a few other senior officers knew who and where Mirror was, but all communications flowed via Belkov.

That was going to be important.

9

IT WAS twelve degrees warmer than Moscow.

Tenth and Pennsylvania.

In the northwest section of the capital city of the United States.

A large bulky building, constructed with modest grace at great cost, named after a famous dead man whom a number of politicians had admired or dreaded.

That's the way governments do things.

Tenth Street and Pennsylvania Avenue Northwest is a busy intersection near a cluster of federal agencies in big and quite official-looking edifices. This one—global headquarters of the Federal Bureau of Investigation—is the J. Edgar Hoover Building.

Since it's the nerve center of U.S. law enforcement, a lot of important people had offices there. Leon Feist wasn't part of that prestigious group. While his FBI colleagues respected him, he wasn't considered *that* important. He was just a conscientious and capable midlevel analyst in the unit designated Violent Crimes—Major Offenders.

Feist's job for the past seven years was to keep track

of things and look for patterns. He scrutinized reports from FBI offices, state and city police across the country, considered and compared them, and tried to identify people or gangs whose violent crimes deserved the Bureau's immediate attention. Day in and day out, he earned his $42,300 a year salary by diligently applying a special talent.

In this high-tech era, he used an old-fashioned human gift.

Feist had very good judgment.

The Bureau's computers helped him organize the information, of course, but the judgment was his alone. He was correct so often that he was taken seriously by the few senior FBI executives who knew his name. That and his pride in achievement were enough for Leon Feist.

This Wednesday morning he rechecked a small pile of printouts on bank robberies in Midwestern states. He'd culled these reports from a larger heap describing armed thefts of at least $100,000 each during the previous year. Three-quarters of these involved banks. As far back as the violent era of such hoodlums as John Dillinger, Pretty Boy Floyd, and the Barker gang, the FBI had always paid particular attention to raids on banks. The Bureau initially made its reputation by taking down those criminals.

Now Feist considered the selected printouts again.

There was something special here. The reports came from a variety of cities and states but they had something in common. He looked at them again, tried to pinpoint it, and then decided to test his estimate by broadening the sample. He reached for the computer keyboard.

The printer began to sound scant moments later. Dozens more printouts emerged, and it took him half the morning to scan them. It was almost noon by the time Feist told his supervisor what he'd discovered.

"A new gang of bank robbers," he began. "Five or six men, and a woman driver—working the Midwest. No, *harvesting* it."

"They're that good?" the supervisor asked.

"The best I've come across in seven years," Feist told him. "First-class planning and flawless execution. Slick and fast. In and out, and they vanish like smoke."

The supervisor shook his head in disagreement.

"*Nobody* vanishes like smoke," he said. "There's always some clue . . . some trail. That's what the Bureau is all about. Now what is your new crew of thieves about?"

"About three million dollars. That's what they've scored in eight very efficient bank jobs."

"Who are they?"

"No one has any idea," Feist reported. "No prints, no leads, not a word from any informers. Nobody's heard of them."

"How about bank cameras?" the supervisor challenged. "These people are professionals, so they must have criminal records. That means mug shots we can compare to the security camera pictures."

"They're professional," the analyst said. "They're so professional they blitz the alarms just before they hit, and shoot out the cameras right after that."

"What about pictures taken when they entered the banks?"

Now it was Feist who shook his head.

"They obviously knew where the cameras were," he answered. "They came in with their heads half turned. There are a few barely mediocre pictures, and no names to go with the faces."

Now the frustrated supervisor leaned forward in his chair.

"There must be *something*," he insisted. "How about patterns? You're very good at patterns. Did you find any?"

Feist nodded and almost smiled.

"*Fridays*," he said with quiet pride. "They only hit medium-sized and independent banks, and only on Fridays. Only banks in five Midwestern states, and none in the biggest cities. *That's* their pattern."

"Excellent! Anything else?"

"Frequency cycle," the analyst replied. "On the basis of their past performance they should be hitting another bank in between eight and nineteen days."

"We'll be waiting for them!" the supervisor vowed. "Wall to wall stakeouts with lots of firepower. We'll alert our own bank robbery squads in those states, and they'll tie in the local police."

"You might warn them to be *extremely* careful," Feist said in a matter-of-fact voice. "This gang is like some kind of commando team—heavily armed, very well coordinated, and highly skilled with both guns and explosives."

At the word "explosives" the supervisor glanced down at the latest fax memorandum on his desk from the Bureau of Alcohol, Tobacco & Firearms about very recent thefts of blasting materials.

An instant later he saw in his mind's eye the horror of the federal office building in Oklahoma being blown into rubble. Images of the rows of corpses followed immediately.

The question erupted from his mouth.

"*Militia?* Some crew of right-wing militia?" he blurted.

It was a legitimate question, Feist thought. The supervisor was usually calm and controlled—and the analyst was comfortable with that—but the whole Bureau was seriously concerned about the threat of paramilitary and paranoid extremists who had knowledge of explosives and automatic weapons. The self-styled militia with their earnest and bizarre beliefs in conspiracies, black United Nations helicopters, and anti-Christian plots troubled a lot of people in several branches of the government.

Feist considered the urgent question carefully.

"*Maybe*," he replied cautiously, "but they could just be a group of very sophisticated and intelligent bank robbers. Or they might be something else."

"What else?"

"I don't know. What I do know is that they seem superior and more purposeful than the typical gang doing bank jobs," he said.

"From the patterns or anything else, do you have any idea of what the purpose might be?"

Feist shook his head.

"I'll think about it," he promised.

After he left, the supervisor took a deep breath and began drafting the "stakeout" alert. Up till now these clever bank robbers had had the initiative. Now it was time for the FBI to strike back hard . . . to stop them dead in their tracks. Their little crime wave was an affront to the Bureau, the inspector thought.

Whoever they were, whatever their purpose, they had to go.

10

ANOTHER FRIDAY afternoon.

Another independent bank in a medium-sized city in the American heartland.

Gunther began to circle the block once more.

He saw his people moving into position as he drove by slowly in the gray Buick. Their faces and body language showed no sign of worry. That wasn't surprising, for he hadn't told them yet about the message he'd received three and a half hours earlier.

It might bother them.

Right now they had to focus fully on his plan and the raid. They couldn't afford the slightest distraction, he thought as he parked the car near the intersection of Jeffries and Pemberton. Even a moment's hesitation or delay could be disastrous.

Turning off the motor, he nodded to the woman beside him. This time she wore a different wig, and when she spoke into the walkie-talkie she didn't call herself Doris. She changed names for each bank robbery. She'd explained to Gunther that you could never tell "what nut with a scanner" might overhear her brief message.

"Morton, this here is Judy," she drawled. "You listenin', Morton? Ah'll be there in two minutes, so get out the six-pack."

Gunther smiled. Well, his eyes did anyway. He enjoyed her creative human touches—and the fact that she respectfully cleared them with him. It was almost too bad that he'd probably have to kill her in the not-too-distant future.

Gunther picked up the large cardboard box from the seat, and scanned the street before he got out of the sedan. He began walking toward the bank. Every twenty-five or thirty steps he slowed or paused to look into some shop window while checking for any sign he might be watched.

No one . . . nothing.

A realistic sort of obsessive, Gunther knew that he'd been in acute and mortal danger for years. That was only half of it, of course. So long as he was alive, Gunther thought, *they* were in deadly danger too.

All of them . . . whoever and wherever they might be.

He felt strong, ready for them all as he continued toward today's target. His eyes searched the street in both directions twice more before his wristwatch showed 1:54 P.M. and he entered the bank right on time.

Each of his attack team was in position. Gunther produced his submachine gun from the florist's box just before Scott pulled his twin pistols and shot out two security cameras. Then the expert marksman turned to blast another pair of them.

The robbery went forward smoothly, as usual, according to plan. Once the uniformed guard was disarmed and clubbed to the marble floor unconscious the other bank employees and assorted customers cooperated fully. That was quite sensible from a medical point of view, for Gunther and his group were prepared to kill . . . one person or a score . . . instantly.

Now Clay and Arnold were behind the teller's counter menacing the cowed clerks, moving swiftly to fill the large garbage bags with bills of twenty dollars or more. Then they hurried to rape the open currency section of the vault. Everything proceeded perfectly. Some two minutes and thirty-one seconds after they'd drawn their guns they were heading for the door.

It was their best time yet.

The bulging green plastic sacks indicated that they'd seized even more cash than usual, Gunther noted.

He nodded in silent approval. Clay grinned in response.

"Stay on the floor and stay alive," Gunther told the people sprawled facedown under the threat of the raiders' guns. "Five minutes. Nobody moves for *five minutes*."

Three would be plenty, he thought as he led the robbers out of the bank to the waiting vehicles.

Nineteen seconds wasn't nearly enough, however.

As the last of them, Clay, was coming out the door, a boyish-looking man in an inexpensive brown suit approached the bank. He was coming to deposit his paycheck. He was twenty-eight years old, and he'd just been promoted from street cop to plainclothes duty after seven years on the force.

Last week he'd read a routine alert about bank robbers who carried their loot out in garbage bags. Suddenly he recognized what he was seeing, and he reacted automatically. He wasn't trying to be a hero . . . just to do what he'd been trained to do.

"Halt!" he shouted and pointed his .38-caliber pistol at Clay.

The thief didn't even consider obeying. He had a bulletproof vest and a compact M-10 that could spray out over seven hundred rounds a minute—plenty to deal with this one man holding a handgun. Clay drew the automatic weapon in a single smooth motion.

Then the plainclothes cop fired two shots. One bullet was stopped by the body armor, but the other ripped a terrible hole in Clay's throat. The policeman began to aim his pistol at Arnold.

That was when Casey, seated at the wheel of one of the getaway cars, raised the sawed-off shotgun and blew half his face off with a pair of twelve-gauge shells. There was blood all over the place, spouting from the tottering plainclothes officer's ruined visage, gushing from the awful wound in Clay's throat.

Gunther erupted from the Buick, fired five shots into the cop as a matter of principle, and dragged Clay and his bag of money into the sedan. As the woman drove them away to where they'd change to other vehicles, Gunther coolly turned Clay so that none of his blood would stain any of the others in the car.

It was obvious that the man was dying.

Now the immediate issue was damage control—how to protect the rest of the group. All of them had false Social Security cards and other identity papers, top quality. None of them had their fingerprints or pictures in the files of any law enforcement agency in the country. There were no laundry marks or clothing store labels on any of their garb.

There was no question of getting Clay to a doctor.

No one could save the bleeding man, and Gunther had neither the time, the resources, nor the will to do anything to keep Clay alive. If he died he couldn't be persuaded, tortured, or tricked into telling anything about the others. Alive Clay was dangerous. He had to die.

They didn't absolutely need him for Plan B, Gunther thought.

They could carry it off without him.

When they reached the place where the other cars were waiting, the woman stopped the Buick. She saw a sewer grating, and dropped the keys down into it. Gunther nodded in agreement. That would make it more difficult for the police to move the vehicle for any comprehensive inspection. It could buy the robbers some time.

Now she pointed at the mortally wounded man.

Gunther shook his head.

"We can't take him," he said as he got out of the sedan and brushed the bag of money against Clay's trouser leg to get rid of the splashed blood.

Crimson bubbles were oozing from the bullet wound, and Clay was trying to say something. No words came out, but that didn't matter for the look in his eyes said it all. He was shocked, in great pain, desperate with the awareness that his life was nearly over.

"Silencer," Gunther said to her.

She opened her purse, took out a small .32-caliber pistol and a silencer that she screwed onto it. Gunther gestured. She gave him the weapon that he aimed between Clay's hurt-filled eyes.

Gunther paused.

"Get his wallet," he told her and she obeyed. There was no reason to leave even the false ID for the police.

Now the dying man tried again to speak . . . failed.

"I'll say it for you," Gunther announced. "See you in hell!"

He stepped aside and back to avoid being splattered by bits of bone or brain before he squeezed the trigger twice.

Then, without a word, he led her to one of the getaway cars.

"Plan B . . . *now*," he said to Arnold. "We'll rendezvous with you and Casey at Place One at noon on Monday."

The explosives specialist knew what Plan B was, but the others didn't. They all stared at Gunther, wondering whether to ask.

"Tell them," he ordered Arnold.

"The Lincoln Tunnel," Arnold said bluntly. "The one between Manhattan and New Jersey. We're going to hijack the Lincoln Tunnel for eight million dollars."

They looked stunned at first. Then they smiled at the audacity and brilliance of the idea. Casey flashed their leader a thumbs-up salute.

"Thank you," Gunther acknowledged.

They entered their vehicles, each moving in a different direction five miles an hour below the speed limit. They were some distance from the city when the Buick with the dead man in blood-soaked clothes was noticed by a public-spirited citizen who called the police. They came quickly, for corpses with gunshot wounds weren't an everyday occurrence in this part of the country.

Bodies with two different caliber slugs in them were even more unusual, the local sheriff thought when he eyed the coroner's report the next afternoon. Sheriff Garfield Bryan was no fool. After careful consideration, this veteran and overweight law enforcement professional came to the conclusion that the dead man with no identification might be connected with the violent bank robbery on the previous day.

Sipping his Diet Pepsi, the sheriff pondered the "alert" on some high-powered gang of bank busters that had come in from the FBI last week. The Bureau liked it when local police asked for help, he reasoned, and he couldn't look bad if he turned it over to them.

He had two more years to a pension.

He certainly didn't want to look bad now.

Sheriff Bryan was humming as he reached for his telephone to call the FBI for assistance. He'd never done that before, but he'd seen a lot of movies and a television series about the Bureau.

No doubt about it, he told himself.

They'd know exactly what to do.

11

... 6:10 P.M. ... Manhattan.

A small apartment in a large building on the sort of cool and fashionable Upper West Side of the crowded island.

This was the residence of a trim, attractive, and with-it young woman who had an exceptional mind and reflexes to match. Wearing electric-blue panties and a frown of concentration, she was putting clothes into a suitcase on the double bed when she heard the sound.

She didn't hesitate. Her semiautomatic pistol was in a holster beside the suitcase. She immediately drew the gun and spun to point it at a man in the doorway behind her.

"Was it something I said?" he asked archly.

"You're early," Joanne Velez told Malloy. "I wasn't expecting you now."

"You did that *very* well," he complimented with a smile.

She didn't smile back.

"No wisecracks, Jake," she admonished as she slid the

gun into its holster. "I'm a little tense, and I have a reason to be."

"Someone out to get you?"

"Not me. *You*. We both know there'll be another hit man coming up from Cali . . . maybe three of them."

"Hope not," Malloy replied with mock sincerity. "I hate violence."

"That's not funny, Jake. They're planning to *kill* you."

"I've got a plan too," he said and then pointed at the suitcase in silent question.

"I told you I might go out of town on an undercover deal," she reminded as she resumed packing. "I got the word this afternoon."

"Where?"

"A place I'm not known. That's all I can say."

Suddenly too warm, he took off his jacket and hung it on a doorknob as bachelors do.

"How long will you be gone?" Malloy tested.

She looked up, studied the jacket for a few moments. Remembering that she disliked garments on doorknobs, he now draped it over the back of a chair.

"Thanks, Jake."

"You're welcome. How long?" he pressed.

"I don't know," she admitted. "Don't say *be careful*. I'm always careful."

He didn't ask if her assignment was dangerous.

They both understood completely that it was.

Malloy stepped closer and took her in his arms.

"I don't like this," he announced and kissed her passionately.

She should have felt safe in his embrace, but she knew she wasn't. Or wouldn't be the moment she left. Now she kissed her lover urgently, and then again, before she stepped free. She swallowed, sighed, and resumed the packing.

"Why don't they send Bruce Willis on this?" Malloy demanded bitterly.

She didn't smile.

"He's having a really bad hair week," she answered. "No more jokes, Jake. Okay?"

Malloy shook his head.

"I don't like this *a lot*," he announced.

Her well-educated and sophisticated lover looked as if he wanted to hit somebody, she thought.

He did, but he didn't know whom.

He shook his head again angrily.

"Aren't you going to say *it sucks*?" she asked as she finished folding a silk blouse.

"It *definitely* sucks," he insisted.

She carefully placed the blouse in the suitcase, and zipped it shut.

"Feel better now?" she asked.

"Not a bit. Is this absolutely necessary?" Malloy challenged.

"Just doing my job, Captain," she replied.

Then she saw that look in his eyes.

"I've got an idea," he told her.

"I know," she replied, "and you're going to miss me."

It wasn't that bad an idea, she thought as she took off the panties. Even if he had that all too common male problem of not saying those dangerous words of emotional commitment, he'd shown her how much he cared. She smiled as they went to bed, and she was smiling when they rose to dress sixteen minutes later.

She was ready to leave. She picked up her gun and holster. They were standard Drug Enforcement Administration issue that could buy her a bullet—no, a dozen bullets—in the face. The highly professional cocaine dealers in the quick-to-murder group she meant to infiltrate would recognize the federal tools in seconds.

Bringing the gun and holster was unthinkable.

Under DEA rules she couldn't leave them in her empty apartment either.

She handed them to Malloy.

"Take care of these for me," she said and he nodded.

"I'll water your plants too," he promised.

"I'll be back before you know it," she told her lover.

"No, you won't," he thought aloud candidly.

After he put down the gun and holster they kissed once more at the door. He opened it, watched her walk down the corridor with her suitcase. Even after she turned left to the elevators and was out of sight he kept staring and listening. He didn't stop until he heard the elevator door open . . . then close.

He shut the door to her apartment, looked around the living room, and decided he'd do the plants tomorrow. He found a plastic shopping bag in the kitchen. It wouldn't do to be seen in the corridor with her nine-millimeter and the holster, Malloy thought grimly. He put her gun and holster in the shopping bag, picked up his jacket, and checked the windows.

Weather report had predicted it might rain.

She wouldn't like it if her rugs got wet.

Double-locking the door behind him, he left and walked a dozen steps to his apartment. Once inside with the portal double-locked and the security chain "up" in the great New York tradition of urban paranoia, he put her Sig. Sauer and its sheath behind half a dozen other shopping bags in the storage space under the sink.

Then he hung his jacket on the bedroom doorknob.

He didn't feel the least bit guilty. The emotion that fully dominated his consciousness was a brew of angers. He was bitter that she was moving swiftly into mortal danger, that he couldn't do anything about it, that she was right about the threat of additional professional attempts on his life.

Irish whiskey, he thought.

That would help him with his plan, Malloy decided.

He poured three fingers of Bushmill's smooth Black Bush, the top of the line single malt brew from the world's oldest licensed whiskey distillery. This was his father's favorite drink for special occasions—a powerful male link to their Hibernian roots.

Malloy dropped in an ice cube before he put one of his Brazilian jazz disks into the CD player. The surge of pulsing music and rhythm was as smooth as the Black Bush. Before he finished the eighty-proof pleasure, he knew what he must do.

She probably wouldn't like his plan at all.

The mayor would hate it, but it was actually the only practical plan. Confident that he knew how to do it, Jacob Malloy listened to the end of the Brazilian CD and then put on one with the big swaggering saxophone of Stan Getz and the brute power of his cool bold band. It was an old recording that still worked, Malloy thought.

What he had to do was get rid of the man down in Cali.

Either Malloy would do it or he'd get rival drug lords to move against him.

Now the ex-SEAL began considering how he might maneuver them into doing the job. Sipping the Irish whiskey, several interesting ideas came to mind in minutes. Malloy knew that he had more than minutes to perfect his plan.

The question was how much more.

12

GUNTHER WASN'T wasting any time either.

He realized that might be extremely dangerous.

He also knew that he couldn't rush things. While his Plan B prepared months earlier was much more complex than the scheme Malloy was considering, Gunther was fully aware that his plan must be carried out swiftly with professional skill and precision.

They had to strike expertly and *now*, while they were still invisible, before any U.S. police or intelligence organization discovered that they existed. Gunther had told his force again and again that their only chance was to execute the plan perfectly. He'd repeated that four times more to Arnold before sending the burly blasting specialist ahead to start the attack.

Some three and a half days after Joanne Velez left on her undercover mission, Arnold arrived in New York's bustling Pennsylvania Station on a train from Cleveland. He'd come by rail instead of by air because there were no metal or explosives detectors or searches for guns or bombs in train terminals.

Arnold's hard-sided suitcase contained two freshly

oiled semiautomatic pistols, a dozen thirteen-round clips of ammunition, four U.S. Army antipersonnel hand grenades, a high-quality walkie-talkie equipped with a scrambler and three Ziploc plastic bags.

Each contained an envelope addressed to the mayor of New York—with the right stamp for domestic first-class mail. There was also a letter—a different one in each plastic bag—that Gunther had made by cutting out letters and words from a newspaper. Even though there was no reason to believe that any U.S. or NATO nation police agency had a file on any of their team, Gunther had made certain that there wasn't a single fingerprint on the letters, envelopes, or plastic bags.

All these things were carefully wrapped and placed under a covering layer of Arnold's well-worn and nondescript clothes. He was not a "sharp" dresser. He had no interest in impressing women with either his appearance or charm. Though he was endowed with what social workers, psychiatrists, and most film critics might consider normal heterosexual attitudes, the female half of the planet's population often left him feeling uneasy or ignored.

That was all right for Arnold.

He was an earnest modest man who didn't want to be noticed.

Gunther found these qualities as admirable as Arnold's gifts with explosives and indifference to human life. He could be counted on to do without question what he was told. He was doing that now as he walked out of the teeming rail terminal. He followed the instructions he'd memorized—one, two, three.

First, he checked into the third-rate hotel in the east twenties where he'd reserved a room by phone. Then he took the subway out to the initial target in mid Brooklyn. He walked around the large building with the dramatic windows twice before he strolled through the immediate neighborhood to make the essential area reconnaissance. He'd done this before—months earlier—on Gunther's instructions. It was a standard operating procedure, and Gunther was quite strict about those.

Arnold had the letter that Gunther had designated Number One with him. The explosives specialist rode the subway back to Manhattan, getting off at a stop two miles north of his hotel. He found a mailbox, looked around to see that no one was paying any attention to him, and warily opened the Ziploc so he might extract the letter without leaving his own fingerprints on the envelope.

Gunther had predicted that it would reach City Hall on Tuesday. He'd studied U.S. postal schedules as part of his thorough preparation for this operation. Letter Number One actually arrived in the historic old building on Monday but didn't get the attention of the Office of Correspondence for a day and a half.

No reason it should.

The envelope wasn't marked as a declaration of war.

That was the message inside.

It wasn't that clear. Gunther had deliberately written it that way. He wanted to puzzle them first for an uncertain enemy is much more vulnerable. *They* had taught him that as one of the elementary rules of clandestine operations. *They* were gone, but he'd tested the principle so he knew it was true.

The letter was very brief.

First, a date. The following Wednesday.

Then the word "Morning."

Beneath that simply "Brooklyn."

It was signed "The Beirut Brigade."

The American public had a vague and widespread fear

of Arab terrorists, Gunther had reasoned, and this might create a false identity and trail to distract police from any investigation that could affect his team. He was buying time. That was crucial.

The somewhat jaded civil servants in the not-too-exciting Office of Correspondence were annoyed rather than confused. It took them a few minutes to decide to direct this letter—most likely the work of "a head case"—to the police. After all, the word "Beirut" had the effect that Gunther expected. It was enough to get the letter directed to the special intelligence unit that the N.Y. Police Department maintained in City Hall.

Following its common sense and its routine, the intelligence unit sent a short memo about the message from "The Beirut Brigade" to the mayor's chief of staff while a courier was carrying the letter and its envelope the three blocks to the Javits Building offices of the Joint Task Force dedicated to fighting terrorism.

Within minutes after he received the two items, Inspector Frank Briggs did what any well-trained and experienced FBI supervisor would do. He ran a computer check and called a meeting. It wasn't a big one—just himself and his opposite number from the city police.

"What do you think, Jake?" Briggs tested as Malloy studied the letter and its envelope.

"I don't like it."

"There's no real threat here," Briggs pointed out quickly.

"That's what I don't like the most. There's something creepy about how nonspecific it is. It's not like the usual nut letter City Hall sends us."

Briggs nodded.

"Anything else you don't like?" he asked.

"You said there were no prints on this stuff from any-one but a guy in the mayor's office. That's *pro*—big time. Creepy and pro—I hate it."

"You haven't asked about The Beirut Brigade," Briggs said.

"I never heard of it," Malloy answered.

"Neither did anyone else in the entire U.S. and NATO *intelligence community*."

Malloy winced when government officials or journal-ists who had masters' degrees and a tendency to show off used that phrase, but this wasn't the time to debate lan-guage inflation.

"It may be that there isn't any Beirut Brigade," he told Briggs.

"You think so?"

"I wouldn't be surprised," Malloy declared, "but we'd be idiots if we didn't go looking. Let's check with the Mossad and the Brits, and put the word out on the back streets in Cairo and Istanbul, Athens, Rome, and Karachi. Hell, let's even try Beirut. Probably a waste of time, but it'll look good to our lords and masters."

"What do you think they'll do next Wednesday in Brooklyn?" Briggs worried aloud.

"They'll give us a clue as to who they are and what they want," Malloy predicted. "It's going to be nasty, Frank. Creepy and pro and playing name games? It's got to be nasty."

Gunther and the rest of his group reached New York two days later. They took up their assigned positions in the individual locations and housing Gunther had pre-pared. Early on Thursday morning Arnold and Casey loaded half a case of dynamite and the timing device into the dirty blue van Casey had stolen off a street in SoHo thirty-eight minutes earlier.

Following instructions, Arnold set the timer for eight A.M. and locked the rear of the van as Casey hurried out of sight around the corner. Then Arnold drove to that place in Brooklyn to park the van just across the street from the big building with the fine stained-glass windows.

There weren't many people in the streets as he walked to the subway station. He was back in his hotel room in Manhattan, listening to an all-news radio station, when the van exploded. The blast hurled chunks of metal in a wide arc, and chunks of flaming debris and burning spouts of gasoline spattered everything for over a hundred yards.

The whole front of the synagogue—the big building with the stained-glass windows—collapsed as if hit by a giant hammer. Some fourteen cars parked nearby were smashed or set ablaze, leading to more explosions as their fuel tanks blew up with force that devastated nineteen houses. Now there were other fires.

And fire engines.

And polices cars in swarms.

Ambulances with screaming sirens for the seven dead and thirty-one injured.

The Joint Task Force had its routines too.

As in a military command post, there was always a supervisor in the office "to implement emergency procedures" for "rapid response."

Malloy got his call at 8:14, and was in the office twenty-five minutes later. So was the rest of the unit, Briggs and everyone else. The small television set facing Briggs's desk was tuned to the round-the-clock news network that was CNN. Police, journalists, and disaster fans around the world knew that CNN could be relied upon to be Johnny-on-the-spot for major crises or carnage. The crews were quick and efficient with little fear and a professional gift for covering the sensational life-and-death things the public couldn't resist.

Of course, very few people anywhere tried.

No one in Briggs's office was making the slightest effort to. They were all staring at the burning buildings and vehicles, the devastated synagogue and the smashed ruins that had been human beings now being zipped into body bags.

The stink of charred flesh and death was in the air there.

Malloy couldn't smell it for he was miles away, but he knew it filled that Brooklyn street.

"Wednesday morning—just as they said," Briggs said grimly.

Malloy nodded.

"What do you think comes next?" the FBI inspector asked.

"The usual," Malloy replied. "Come on, we all know the routine. First, the fucking letter."

He saw the FBI inspector wince at the obscenity.

"Then the massacre," Malloy continued harshly. "After that, it's good old CNN to help the world share the gory thrills. The other networks pile in as fast as they can. People have a right to see the corpses. It's electronic democracy."

"You going to make one of your speeches?" Briggs asked.

Malloy shook his head.

"That's not the routine," he declared. "The mayor makes the speech. Wherever and whenever one of these damn things happens, the local mayor calls a press conference and makes a terrific speech. I wouldn't be surprised if all the mayors make the same speech. Very humanitarian but righteous—and absolutely correct."

Briggs decided not to try to stop him.

You didn't interrupt a man like Malloy when he was furious.

"Those mayors are always correct—in every language including Indonesian and Eskimo, and they all *share the pain* of the victims' families. The speech must have something about prayers. That's a must. And the mayors say something about the Lord—whoever their Lord is—and *solemnly* promise that the bad guys will be *brought to justice.*"

Briggs opened his mouth to speak.

Malloy pointed at the television screen first.

It was the mayor who'd just arrived at the scene of Gunther's first target in New York City. Malloy reached forward to turn up the sound. It was the usual speech as he'd predicted, and *correct* in every detail. He even left out what Malloy thought he would, for the omissions were standard too. When he called in the regulation finale for the perpetrators to be *brought to justice*, he didn't mention two things.

He didn't specify who had the dirty and dangerous job of tracking down the armed and homicidal fanatics who'd done this.

And he didn't explain that the *justice* he really had in mind didn't involve any long and expensive court proceedings. He was hoping the city could save all that money if the Joint Task Force or other police shot the perpetrators down in the street like rabid dogs—blew them away swiftly and economically.

The mayor didn't need to say any of that.

Jacob Malloy and everyone else in the room knew it.

"Let's go," Briggs said as he flicked on the VCR that

would tape what followed as they left. He didn't mind that Malloy was behind the wheel as they started the trip to the bombing. Driving was one of the things the ex-SEAL did very well.

13

THE SMELL of charred flesh still hung in the Brooklyn air when Malloy, Briggs, and four of their two-man teams reached the place where Gunther had struck. To keep the record straight, one team included a pretty woman—the clever black detective who liked to flirt with Jacob Malloy.

She wasn't flirting with anyone this morning.

She kept staring at the nightmare and saying "son of a bitch" over and over.

The vehicles in which the Joint Task Force members arrived were unmarked, so at first the antiterrorist specialists were waved away by "uniforms"—regular cops from the local precinct who didn't want sight-seeing civilians to pollute the evidence or contaminate the crime scene in any way.

The Task Force professionals didn't argue or explain. They simply held their badges and other ID out the windows of their drab sedans. One of the Emergency Service cops walking by recognized Malloy.

"It's a fuckin' mess, Cap," he told Malloy.

"Always is," Malloy said and for a few seconds his eyes

wandered to a bearded rabbi coming out of the smoldering synagogue. He was coughing from the smoke. The
rabbi held—very carefully—something about three feet
long encased in a velvet sack.

"We told him not to go in there," an Emergency Services cop in full flak jacket grumbled. "That thing could
come crashing down at any second, but he charged in before we could stop him."

"*Had* to," the black woman said. "That's a Torah, man.
It's holy. Right, Captain?"

Malloy wondered how she knew that, but he didn't
say so.

He simply nodded.

"Wholly what?" the puzzled EMS cop asked.

"A holy *scroll*," Detective Carla Hunt replied. "Heavy
duty . . . the heaviest. Where are you from, Jack? Nebraska?"

"Don't knock Nebraska," Malloy broke in and pointed
at the tangle of police cars and fire trucks clogging the
street.

"Where can we park?" he said.

Around the corner behind a supermarket was a lot for
shoppers' vehicles. That's where they left the unmarked
Task Force sedan. Walking back to the crime scene, she
speculated silently on why Malloy hadn't gotten out of
the car at the ruined synagogue. There had to be a reason, she realized. This man didn't do things without a
reason.

Captain Jacob Malloy was simply doing what Gunther
had ordered the bomber to do. Having mastered the assault tactics of special operations teams in his years with
the rip-and-run SEAL commandos, he was reconnoiter-
ing the strike area. He was seeking something that might
tell him more about the enemy.

His instincts said this was the work of professionals, so he wasn't likely to find anything. Professionals almost never left any souvenirs beside corpses, bits of a detonator, and a gram or two of explosive for laboratory technicians to study. The odds were against Malloy this morning, but he knew that he had to look—left and right, up and down—on the undoubtedly remote chance of some carelessness or human error.

Not today.

Malloy found no shred of evidence, but he wasn't surprised. When they reached the smoldering synagogue they saw eight FBI members of the Task Force slowly and warily putting little bits of things into the plastic bags they always carried along with sterile tweezers. Methodical and careful, the meticulously trained federal agents were highly skilled in handling evidence. That was one of the things at which they excelled, the former SEAL thought. As a person who did a lot of other things extremely well, he had no desire to be like them but he respected the FBI agents and made sure the city cops he led knew it.

He'd spelled it out to them the day he rejoined the Task Force.

Malloy's rules.

Mutual respect and a totally unified effort—or you're gone.

No competition, no jokes about Washington, no bullshit, and no argument. None was necessary. There was an unspoken authority in this captain that the street-wise cops recognized and welcomed.

When Malloy and the woman detective reached the blasted temple they saw the tall rabbi still dazed, still defiant, still holding the holy scroll. Malloy went to him immediately. The rabbi coughed, and the two police officers could smell the smoke in his clothes.

"I know you," the rabbi announced and coughed again. "Saw your picture in the paper. You're the judge's boy."

"I'm Captain Malloy," the ex-SEAL confirmed correctly.

"*Jake* Malloy," the rabbi remembered.

"I think you'd better see a doctor," Malloy said truthfully.

The rabbi shook his head.

"I'm all right," he announced. "I saved the Torah and that's what matters."

Malloy gestured to a white uniformed ambulance aide ten yards away, pointed to the rabbi.

"I'm not going anywhere," the rabbi insisted. "I'm staying here with my Torah and my temple. *That's* what I'm doing, Jake. Now what are you going to do?"

"I'm going to identify and arrest the people who did this . . . my job under the law," Malloy said grimly.

Gesturing again to the ambulance attendant to look after the rabbi, Malloy then walked to the senior FBI agent to get an update on what the federal agents had found. They were doing their job their way—a proper start to the investigation.

"I'll get out of your way," Malloy said and started back to the supermarket lot. The woman detective walking beside him saw his frown, and didn't speak till they were halfway there.

"Mind if I ask you something, Captain?"

"What?"

"Why didn't you tell the rabbi the rest of it?" she challenged.

"What are you talking about?" Malloy said.

"Don't get mad, Captain, but I can see it in your eyes. You've got more than the laws of New York in mind."

"All that damn cappuccino's getting to you," he replied without breaking stride.

"You're going for that biblical thing," she predicted. "The Old Testament number. The eye and tooth thing. It's okay with me. I won't say a word to anyone."

"Why don't you take a day off?" Malloy suggested.

"I told you—it's okay with me. Just be careful, will you?" she urged.

"Take *two* days off," he evaded as the parking lot came into sight.

Next to their sedan was a small green station wagon.

Beside the driver's window of the wagon a large swarthy male was leaning forward. He was also reaching inside his blue plastic zipper jacket. In a nicer world it might have been for a lovely floral birthday card. Neither Jacob Malloy nor Detective Carla Hunt thought this world was quite that nice.

In an instant, they decided that the overweight man in the blue jacket might not be nice either. Something in his body language seemed to suggest that to the pair of police officers who took body language seriously. They both knew of cops who had not and died.

The sixty-something-year-old woman behind the wheel was not that familiar with body language, but she recognized the shiny metal object suddenly drawn from the zipper jacket. So did Malloy and the already wired female detective with him. He didn't say anything to her. The sight of the gun made it unnecessary.

Carjack.

The two police knew what to do.

They both drew their pistols, and Malloy pointed to direct her to circle around to a flanking-blocking position.

This carjacker wasn't going anywhere.

Now he was pointing his weapon into the wagon, ordering the terrified driver to slide over on the seat so he could take the wheel.

And take her hostage. That was the standard drill these days, Malloy thought as he walked closer. The carjacker would dump her out—dead or alive—a dozen or more miles away. Malloy was holding his heavy Glock flat against the outside of his right leg as he approached the carjacker. The thief was opening the station wagon door as Malloy reached him.

"Excuse me," Malloy said calmly.

The carjacker spun and waved his gun in menace.

"Back off," he ordered harshly. "Back off or I'll hurt you."

He hadn't noticed the Glock. He did when Malloy swiftly swung it up and smashed it against the thief's wrist, sending the silver .32 flying like some toy. The frantic carjacker began to raise his right foot to ram a steel-tipped boot into Malloy's knee or groin or other vulnerable body part. The thief abruptly forgot about that idea when the ex-SEAL hit him on the left temple with the Glock.

The carjacker made some animal sound, staggered, and crumpled to his knees as Detective Carla Hunt reached him.

"Cuff him and talk to him," Malloy instructed her.

Trying to avoid smears or droplets of the blood seeping from the thief's battered head, she handcuffed him with professional expertise. Then she carefully recited to the half-conscious criminal all his relevant rights in this matter under the U.S. Constitution. Articulating clearly, she mentioned that every citizen was entitled to a lawyer and could remain silent until an attorney arrived.

The man seemed to have no interest in either the Miranda case decision on a defendant's rights, or how either the Supreme Court or the overall democratic process worked in this country. He kept cursing and bleeding and groaning.

"I'm not sure he understands what's going on," she thought aloud.

"Tell him," Malloy suggested.

"You're under arrest for attempted carjacking, resisting a police officer, and at least four other felonies," she said.

"Probably six," Malloy speculated. "Look out. He may vomit."

The gasping, raging, cursing man didn't but he did call her a bitch and spewed out racist obscenities even cable television talk shows wouldn't use. The damaged hoodlum was adding nothing to the national debate on public morality or better health care, Malloy judged and turned to Detective Hunt to get rid of this thug.

"Better call for a couple of RPMs," Malloy advised.

She used the radio in the neaby Task Force sedan. Three of the RPMs—radio patrol motorized in New York cop talk for patrol cars—were there in a few minutes. Five of the newly arrived officers got out of their vehicles, surveyed the scene.

"I'm on the job," Malloy said as he showed them his NYPD badge in the traditional self-identification ritual of plainclothes cops here. "I'm Captain Jacob Malloy."

The patrol car cops nodded in recognition.

"You should've burned that perp, Cap," one of them volunteered fraternally in reference to the Cali assassin. Malloy decided to ignore the remark, hoping the incident would be forgotten in another month or two—and knowing that was unlikely. New York street cops had extraordinary memories—especially about their mortal enemies.

"The guy who tried to pop you a month ago," the officer from the blue and white RPM continued to make it clear he wasn't speaking about the handcuffed carjacker six yards away.

"What happened here, Cap?" another cop asked.

"Detective Carla Hunt," Malloy said in introduction. "She can tell you the whole thing. It's *her* collar."

Aware that it wouldn't do to call her superior a liar, she began to describe the attempted carjacking while Malloy walked to the station wagon. He'd heard the sobbing, and he knew what he had to do. He showed his badge again to the shaking owner of the vehicle, asked her permission to sit beside her, and devoted several minutes to helping her regain control of her emotions.

Then he got out and waved to a radio car cop.

"I wonder if you've got time to do me two favors," Malloy began. He pointed to the hoodlum's gun, then into the station wagon.

"That silver piece on the ground was the perp's. Take it with you to the precinct when you book him. That's *one*," Malloy said. "*Two* is that the woman in the wagon is still shaky. I want someone to drive her home. Do the cops are warm and human bit, okay?"

Malloy started walking back to join Hunt at their sedan. A stream of shoppers carrying bags of groceries was flowing from the back doors of the supermarket. Other people just arriving were clutching lists of things to buy as they parked their vehicles. Both groups stopped to stare at the uniformed police, the blue and white patrol cars, and the handcuffed prisoner being nudged into one of them.

"What happened?" asked a neatly dressed white-haired woman who looked like a sweet grandma in an oatmeal advertisement.

"Bad guy," Malone replied and nodded toward the carjacker. "Stuck a gun into the face of the lady in that green wagon and tried to steal it. Then he tried to shoot a cop."

The neo-grandma, who could also have made a living in toothpaste commercials, studied his face for a moment.

"You the cop?" she guessed as Carla Hunt walked toward them.

"Yes, ma'am."

"What kind of cop?" the older shopper challenged.

"He's a captain cop," Hunt volunteered while pulling out her own gold shield, "and I'm a detective cop."

Malloy was amused by the deadpan irony in her response. The white-haired woman didn't quite notice it. She knew that she really ought to say something now because everybody had a snappy answer in all the cop shows on television, but she was uncomfortably stuck for a few seconds.

Then it came to her.

Not great, but it would do.

"Have a *real* nice day," she declared firmly with a fixed and sort-of-friendly smile and started toward her car.

"You too, ma'am," Malloy acknowledged with equal insincerity and an excellent imitation of politeness.

A dozen minutes later he was silently driving the Task Force sedan onto the bridge to Manhattan. On the other side of the island in the office overlooking the wide Hudson River, Gunther was listening intently to an all-news radio station's graphic updates on the deaths and destruction at the blasted synagogue.

This was more fun than a major railway disaster, he thought.

Of course, it ought to be.

He'd caused this carnage himself, and it was just the beginning.

He couldn't help grinning as he told himself that he had just declared war on New York City and its millions of people.

A great deal of blood would be shed.

There would be a lot more corpses before the great metropolis surrendered. That was absolutely certain. It was part of his plan.

14

THE NEXT day . . . ten minutes past noon . . . more than an ocean away.

The sun was shining over downtown Moscow as Colonel Belkov stared across the heavy flow of vehicles moving through the famous square. Without thinking he looked toward the big metal statue of the ruthless Hero of the Soviet Union for whom this place had been named more than half a century ago.

Feliks Dzerzhinsky had been the fierce founder of the Cheka, the steely secret police organization whose name changed several times before it became the KGB. For decades that large building across the square housed KGB headquarters, a notorious place where so many "enemies of the State" had been tortured and executed.

In the years after his death in 1926, government publicity made Dzerzhinsky into a saint to Soviet security professionals and a terror to many other citizens who feared even the dreaded statue. People fell silent as they entered *his* square.

Until a few years ago.

The statue wasn't there anymore. One wild night a

roaring and near hysterical crowd of Muscovites was overwhelmed by the new freedom, and they'd pulled down the statue by brute force. It was an historic event seen on television across the entire country and around the world. Now the broken remains of St. Feliks rusted in a bizarre graveyard for Communist monuments on the edge of the city.

No one went there.

No one was sure just what to do with this wreckage of Soviet history.

Now the terror was only a gut-knotting memory, but Belkov still couldn't help looking into the square for the ghost statue. It was a foolish thing to do, he thought and sighed. He had to break this habit, Belkov told himself as he walked toward another large and ornate building on the square renamed Lubyanka.

This was a much cheerier place than the grim old KGB center it faced.

It had no subterranean cells where awful pain had been inflicted day and night and blood flowed in dreadful profusion.

There were no silent echoes of screams here, no miasmic memories of death, no nearly palpable hate or horror in the air.

This was Detsky Mir—Children's World. This large and very popular department store was well known for its toys and games, clothes and furniture sized for boys and girls. Long a Moscow tradition and a celebrated magnet for shoppers, Detsky Mir had survived the grimmest days of the Soviet tyranny as a unique oasis of life and laughter.

That hadn't changed. Children were giggling and their parents smiling as Belkov walked into the store. He began to smile himself until he thought of Strelski's agents following him. Belkov didn't see them but he knew they were watching and taking pictures. That was all right, for the watchers were part of his plan.

All *four* of his plans.

For over a year he'd been prepared for various eventualities.

Strelski's surveillance teams were good, but he was better than them—and better than the CIA people too. Belkov was icily aware that he had to be for he had no one to help him.

It was soothing to be alone and without illusions.

He counted on no one, and no one could betray him.

From a professional point of view, this combination was oddly liberating and made him focus. Focus and a cool head were the keys to survival in this gory game that had never had any rules. The no rules made it all the more interesting, Belkov reflected as he saw the female American courier at the doll counter.

Once again Belkov thought that the persistent CIA fondness for contacts in department stores was an error. He recognized that the crowds in these establishments offered some cover, but any repetition in tactics would eventually be noticed as a pattern. Patterns were dangerous. The CIA's setting every fifth or sixth rendezvous in some busy and popular museum wasn't really enough of a change.

Now she picked up one puffy doll to consider it, put it down, let her eyes range "casually" to scan for her contact or watchers or both. She noticed Belkov, and he noticed that she wasn't carrying any package or folded newspaper.

No brush pass for the exchange this time.

At least they'd changed that, he thought.

How would it be done?

She raised another doll from the counter, studied it intently, nodded, then placed it among the others in the display for just a moment before she raised the stuffed thing to eye level and nodded twice more.

It was an almost too simple system of signals.

Three nods meant blind drop number three. There were a few blind drops near each meeting place. *This* one was less than a hundred yards away in the classically elegant Hotel Savoy. While she was paying for the doll, Belkov circled to an exit and walked briskly to the grand little boutique hotel. Built for the affluent in Czarist times, it had fallen into gloom and grunge until a joint venture of Finnair and the Moscow government tourist office refurbished it into a first-class operation with luxurious decor, excellent food, and all modern conveniences.

When it was reborn to serve foreign visitors who paid in hard currency, the Savoy stunned the Soviet capital by offering round-the-clock uncensored reporting via a Cable News Network satellite dish. Hotel guests could see it all on the sets in their rooms or on the big screen TV on the bar in the Savoy's version of a British pub where dozens of journalists gathered.

Now a dozen hotels in the capital were equipped with CNN dishes, but Belkov was committed to the Savoy's pub this day. Blind drop three was in a booth in the men's room there. That location was considered safe because nobody outside the booth could see an agent open the panel in the wall, remove the package, and close up the hidden compartment that some CIA technician installed covertly forty-one months earlier.

Blind drops were frequently used when something bigger than a sheet of paper with some microdots was to be transferred. Today Belkov was dealing with a package some seven inches long, three inches wide, and nearly two and a half inches high. He opened it carefully and expertly. There was a letter that he knew included one or more microdots with instructions.

There was also forty-eight thousand dollars in British fifty-pound notes. As was his custom, he coolly stole a third of the cash for his own emergency fund before re-sealing the packet with meticulous skill that reflected a lot of experience.

His next moves were by the book. He left the hand-some hotel, walked six blocks to where his unmarked of-ficial car waited with plainclothes driver, and said nothing as the vehicle rolled off to the intelligence organization's headquarters outside Moscow.

"More than thirty thousand dollars of those stupid Americans' cash!" Strelski exulted as the funds were counted and heaped on his desk.

He handed the sheet of paper to an aide who immedi-ately put it in a microdot enlarger-projecter. There were five separate instructions for Belkov, with each calling for information on a different subject.

A nuclear submarine base near Vladivostok.

Current status of a nerve gas depot in the Urals.

Negotiations to sell medium-range missiles to Iran or Iraq.

The full "order of battle" of Russia's spy team in the Washington embassy.

And complete information about the who-what-where and what the hell is going on today with somebody or something code-named Omar.

Information in sweeps of Stasi files—highest classifica-tion—convinced both the CIA and German security exec-utives that Omar was important and should be addressed at once. It was a priority project.

General Strelski banged his right fist on the desk in triumph.

"I knew it!" he said triumphantly. "I was right! I have terrific instincts, you know. From the first time I heard about this damn Omar I was sure that it deserved immediate attention. I told you that, didn't I?"

"You certainly did, General," the colonel agreed with a very good imitation of sincerity. "You've got great instincts all right."

"Born with them," Strelski boasted. "This must be big and dangerous. Belkov, we're going to get the answers first. I don't care what you have to do, what it costs, who you have to smash. Do it, Belkov! Do it!"

"I won't let you down," the colonel lied earnestly. "I know what has to be done, and I'll do it!"

Belkov had spoken truthfully.

With both the Russian and American intelligence organizations aware of the long secret Omar, the pressure would build swiftly.

Trapped between them, Belkov would be crushed.

As he walked from the general's office, he realized that he had very little time. With both sides bitter and vengeful about his hiding Omar for his own schemes, he was in enormous danger. Even with the Cold War over, both sides would be furious that he'd made fools of them in the big game that never made much sense anyway. Humiliated and rushing to cover up the embarrassing mistakes as they always did, they'd want to bury this whole thing.

Every trace of it.

Every person who knew of it and might talk.

They'd want to bury Belkov.

Yes, the odds were excellent that they'd kill him.

He was ready for something like this, and knew what he must do.

The time had come.

He had to run.

15

THOUGH NEW York City is widely considered by distant strangers to be a community of the hard-boiled and more than jaded, it really doesn't take *that* much to cause a sensation there.

Almost any well-armed psychopath could probably do it.

Blow up a house of worship ... burn, maim, or kill a number of unarmed civilians ... leave some large fires ... and destroy over a dozen cars in a tranquil residential area ... and plenty of people will take notice.

Quite a few will talk about it—big time.

Energetic reporters and ambitious social critics in all the local media, print and electronic, subway, bus, and sidewalk graffiti, lavatory walls and mosh pits, bingo clubs and poetry slams, all took what had happened in Brooklyn seriously and personally. A flash of fear joined with the liberating spontaneity of not knowing most of the facts to encourage many individuals to vent instantly, loudly, and negatively.

How else would you get noticed?

Furious, caring, and insecure in equal portions, they

indignantly hurled questions and ungrammatical accusations, fiercely denounced the police, local public schools, and diverse neighbors of other beliefs, haircuts, or clothing styles, doubled their own consumption of alcoholic beverages and carcinogenic tobacco products, and turned off their minds as they turned on radio's least rational talk shows.

They also clicked enthusiastically to the most preposterous "interview" programs on television. The shaken citizens of the republic knew what to expect, so they felt safe. It was comforting to gorge on well paid and furious blamers chatting up the publicity hungry, morally challenged, and earnestly irresponsible—the familiar outpatients of today's media world.

It was a zoo and a half.

Malloy, whose talents included a gift for ignoring the senseless, paid almost no attention to this diverse outcry. He would not comment on any of the predictable outrage hosed out by elected officials, and urged journalists seeking interviews to speak with the FBI executive who was co-chief of the Joint Task Force.

This was noticed and approved in City Hall.

"I'm glad Malloy's keeping out of the spotlight," Mayor Dowling told New York's wary-eyed police commissioner. "Guess he's learned his lesson."

"Won't argue with that," Jefferson replied with bureaucratic tact.

Jefferson totally doubted the mayor's estimate, but wasn't surprised by the flawed diagnosis. Self-important and convinced he had the shrewdness and power to get anyone to do what he wanted the person to do, the Honorable Philip F. Dowling had no idea as to who Jacob Malloy really was.

Or what he could do . . . or had done.

Jefferson had tried to learn about Malloy's activities in the no-holds-barred SEALS. No one who knew would say a word. Even now, years after he returned to civilian life, the Navy blandly claimed he'd merely been a training officer. Last month Jefferson had met at a high-level security conference a rear admiral from Naval Intelligence. A little curious and compulsive, Jefferson made another attempt and asked if he knew Jacob Malloy.

It happened very quickly . . . just for a second.

There was a strange gleam in the admiral's eyes before the naval officer could control it.

Then the admiral had smiled and shrugged.

"It's a common name," he said and walked away before Jefferson could continue the conversation.

The police commissioner found himself thinking about that gleam again as he left the mayor's office. It had been admiring but cold and hard like iron. More than any words it said that in the top secret and violent world of special operations Jacob Malloy himself had been special, and was remembered.

For what?

What could Malloy have done to stand out in—to shock—the fierce jungle world that no one in the Pentagon would admit existed? Suddenly Jefferson's focus shifted to a more immediate and urgent question as the commissioner reached the elevator.

What was well-educated and dangerous Jacob Malloy doing and planning at this moment?

All the commissioner's instincts warned him that it would be very different from what other police captains—the capable and careful careerists who cared about promotions and pensions—would do. As Jefferson left City

Hall, he decided that it might be time to speak with Malloy, perhaps to ask about the latest reports from the FBI laboratories on the bombing.

That would justify some wary questioning. There was nothing wrong with that, Jefferson told himself as he reached his car. It was wholly appropriate for the head of the police department to seek an update on the status of a major investigation from the cop in charge of the case.

Jefferson called the Task Force on his car phone . . . grunted.

Malloy wasn't at his office in the towering Javits Building.

He was down in the basement of One Police Plaza, which housed the NYPD headquarters, Jefferson's own suite, and a lot of offices for senior administrators. Special facilities included a well-built underground firing range.

That's where Jefferson found Jacob Malloy, wearing "earmuffs" to muffle the blasts, crouched in classic shooter's pose, firing his regulation handgun. Methodically, efficiently, very accurately, he fired, reloaded, and fired again. Squeezing off round after round, bull's-eye after bull's-eye, every slug in a killing zone, he paused only—and briefly—to reload.

He wasn't even breathing hard, Jefferson noticed.

He wasn't squinting, and there was no bead of perspiration on Malloy's face as he accurately fired a final clip and took off the protective "earmuffs." A moment later he turned and saw Jefferson.

They both played the game.

As grown men do so often, they pretended that they were meeting by accident and neither had a motive or scheme.

"Nice to see you, Commissioner," Malloy greeted coolly.

"Nice shooting," Jefferson fenced and complimented in a single phrase. "Getting ready for the nationals next month?"

The ex-SEAL shrugged at the reference to the six gold marksmanship medals he'd already won in so many state competitions.

"I'm getting ready to shoot somebody," he replied truthfully.

Jefferson blinked. Malloy's calculated candor bothered a lot of senior police officers. Others found it admirable but startling. The commissioner was usually but not always one of the latter. As he opened his mouth to speak he noticed the full clip of ammunition Malloy had just taken out of a pocket.

"That's not standard load, is it?" Jefferson tested.

"Standard armor-piercing," Malloy answered. "The people I'm planning to shoot may be wearing body armor. I think they're pros."

Now he explained to the commissioner about the estimate in the FBI laboratory report that the Brooklyn synagogue bomb was the work of an explosives expert with experience.

"In my book that makes him a pro," Malloy said.

"When did this report come in?"

"About thirty-five minutes ago. There should be a copy on your desk when you go upstairs," Malloy assured him and inserted the clip.

Jefferson considered and analyzed swiftly.

"You said *people*," he pointed out as Malloy slid the gun into its holster. "You think there's more than *one*?"

"I think pros work in teams."

"What kind of pros?" the commissioner pressed.

Malloy shrugged.

"I'll let you know," he promised.

Jefferson shook his head and frowned.

"As soon as possible," he said. "The mayor is *very* concerned."

It was time to address the other reason he'd come down here.

"By the way," he began in a casual tone that immediately alerted Malloy to be careful, "I was at an interagency security meeting and ran into an admiral you might know. Name of Doherty. ONI, I think."

"Tom Doherty? Very sharp? A tall guy?" Malloy responded.

The commissioner nodded.

"I don't know anyone like that," Malloy said with a straight face.

"How did you know his name's Tom?" Jefferson blurted.

"It's a common name," the ex-SEAL replied.

"That's what *he* said when I asked if he knew *you*," Jefferson reported wryly a second before his beeper sounded. Moments after that the two policemen went on their separate ways.

Malloy was back on the firing range the next morning.

He was shooting when Gunther's second message reached City Hall and ruined the mayor's whole day.

16

THIS MESSAGE was as curt and blunt as the first one.

It began with the month and numbered day . . . then named it.

Thursday . . . that was the day after tomorrow.

There was one word on the next line . . . Afternoon.

Below that was the place . . . the borough in New York City . . . The Bronx.

Like the previous warning, this was signed The Beirut Brigade.

That name wasn't much help. While federal experts were intently using state-of-various-arts gear to study the original of the message, Malloy and his FBI coleader of the Task Force stared at an excellent Xerox copy and wondered why repeated and diverse computer scans had found no mention of the Brigade.

CIA . . . FBI . . . NSA which eavesdropped all over the world . . . negative.

NATO . . . zip. The Russians . . . zero.

Even the Israelis who were so well informed on terrorist groups had nothing.

"Forget the name for now," Malloy urged. "Maybe we can find something else in the rest of the text."

Briggs nodded.

"Let's take it from the top again," he said. "Why do you think they gave us this much advance warning?"

Malloy shook his head . . . pointed at the large map of New York City on the wall.

"So we'd have time to sweat," he replied grimly. "The Bronx is something like forty-four square miles . . . about 1,200,000 people and God knows how many possible targets."

"Many synagogues?"

"Plenty. There were more thirty or forty years ago before half the Jewish population moved out to the suburbs and Latinos came in, but there are still a bunch of shuls up there."

He saw the question in the FBI man's eyes.

"Shuls . . . synagogues," Malloy translated. "Big ones, small ones that have lost most of their congregations, orthodox, conservative, and reform. All kinds . . . all over the place. Check the Yellow Pages."

Briggs was trained to think in terms of process and tactics.

That's what he did now.

"Can we put a cop or two at each . . . shul?" he asked.

"And an unmarked car with a couple of plainclothes guys," Malloy added. "We'll have to alert all the rabbis too."

"Can we suggest they suspend religious activities at noon—maybe an hour before that—and keep everyone out till six?"

"Suggest? That should be okay," Malloy reasoned aloud. "Rabbis don't like being *told* what to do, especially by secular folks. Rabbis are used to telling other people about big moral and spiritual things. Of course, rabbis are practical too. They wouldn't risk the lives of their congregations. They won't like this though."

Briggs shook his head.

"I don't really care whether they *like* it, Jake. For God's sake, will they close the shuls?"

Malloy nodded.

"Yes, Frank. For God's sake—and other good reasons—they'll do it," he answered. "We've also got to notify the precinct commanders right now because we'll need their troops round the clock. Not tomorrow. As of five minutes ago."

"We've got to tell them this whole thing is secret," the federal agent said. "We don't want the bad guys to know what we're doing, and we certainly don't want the public up there to panic. Not a word to the media, right?"

"Sure," Malloy answered. "They don't need to know, but they will about nine minutes after our uniforms show up outside the synagogues. People in The Bronx notice things, and they'll talk about it. Hell, some of them will dump it into chat rooms on the Internet. Reporters in Puerto Rico, Tel Aviv, and Tokyo will be phoning in with questions an hour after our cops move into position."

"No comment?" Briggs tested.

"No way," Malloy disagreed. "No comment is history. Nobody buys it anymore. *We* don't have to say anything because we do secret stuff. We'll tell the mayor to say this is just a standard security precaution. By the time they figure out that it isn't the media folk will be busy with something else more important."

He saw the question in Briggs's eyes.

"Don't ask me what that might be," Malloy advised. "If

we're very lucky it won't be fifty-seven people bombed into bits."

The ex-SEAL paused . . . shook his head.

"About security for the shuls," he thought aloud, "one uniform and a couple of plainclothes in an unmarked car won't do it. If my hunch is right and there's more than a single hood in this Brigade, we should have two cops in front and another pair covering the back. At least one unmarked car at both sides of the building."

"Police chopper overhead on criss-cross patrol?" Briggs proposed.

"Two."

"You think that should do it?" the FBI supervisor tested.

Malloy shrugged.

"Answer me, Jake," Briggs pressed. "Say something."

"You want to know whether the shuls will be safe?"

Briggs nodded.

"Frank, I have no idea. I'm not convinced that the next target is going to be a shul," Malloy answered candidly.

It wasn't.

17

NOBODY WAS guarding the second target.

It was 2:58 P.M. the next afternoon.

Thursday.

There wasn't a uniformed cop in sight, or any nearby parked vehicle with a couple of husky men that could be an unmarked police car.

The bomber had been trained to check for these things, and he was good at unobtrusive reconnaissance. Arnold drove the stolen car carefully past the target once again, listening to the radio news announcer talk in crisp dramatic tones about how Bronx synagogues were being protected.

Arnold managed to stifle a smile. He'd been trained to do that too. He couldn't do anything that might cause someone to remember him, and he must not leave any trace of his identity. Just before he took this Nissan seventy minutes earlier he'd covered each of his fingertips with two applications of nail polish.

There'd be no prints that way, Gunther said.

Even though Arnold's fingerprints weren't in any computer in North America, Gunther pointed out there was no point in giving the enemy anything.

Gunther was very smart, Arnold thought contentedly as he heard the radio voice say it would be three o'clock in one minute. Arnold circled the block again to the small parking lot behind the target. None of the four cars there was large or new. Arnold guessed that these vehicles belonged to the modestly paid people who worked here at Saint Agatha's.

The target was a Catholic high school for girls.

Arnold's assignment was to kill some of them . . . not all of them. Gunther was raising the ante in corpses with each bombing, combining homicide with mounting fear to prepare the city for eventual surrender.

The next attack would slaughter even more people.

After that would come the final assault . . . and then the money.

Arnold parked the car, closed the windows, got out, and locked the doors. He glanced at his wristwatch, which showed three o'clock. The first of the girls would be coming out the front door in a few minutes. The last of them wouldn't come out at all until the body bags arrived.

Arnold had studied the traffic flow from Saint Agatha's on the four previous afternoons. On the basis of what he'd seen, most of the teenaged girls would leave the building by a quarter after three. About eighty would come out after that.

He'd set the bomb for a quarter after three.

Gunther had said that eighty corpses would be enough this time.

Without glancing back, Arnold walked five and a half blocks to the bus stop. He paid his fare with six quarters, and sat down as the driver closed the door and continued south. Some minute and a half after the door closed the time bomb exploded.

It was exactly 3:15 P.M. when the back of Saint Agatha's vanished.

A hailstorm of deadly debris, broken glass, spears of metal window frames, chunks of brick and masonry, jagged pieces of electrical fixtures and twisted ruins of pipes scythed out from and into the building in the first of two blasts.

To add some horror Arnold had built a second and different bomb that he'd rigged to go off just after the first massive explosion. It had been Gunther's suggestion, but all the credit for making the napalm belonged to Arnold. The four containers of jellied petroleum flew through the opening that the dynamite had made.

Then the small charges on the napalm weapons exploded.

Bits and spouts of burning napalm splattered out in wide arcs, attaching themselves to anyone and anything they hit. Schoolgirls and nuns, male teachers and custodial staff, began to scream.

The school was burning and the people were burning. First created by agricultural researchers just before World War II, napalm was invented to incinerate weeds. Then some clever defense scientists reasoned that it might also incinerate human flesh. That's what it was doing at 3:16 P.M. at Saint Agatha's.

It was doing its job very conscientiously.

It was burning through the flesh right down to the bone.

That's why so many of those still alive and conscious in the parochial school were running and jumping, rolling on the floors and screaming. And screaming . . . and howling too. Agony does that to animals, and napalm turns human beings into animals.

The building was ablaze in a score of places, pouring

smoke from the fires and dazed injured teenagers and adults from the front door and other exits. People were jumping from windows. Two girls and a nun leaped with their hair on fire. Neighbors tried to beat out the flames with jackets . . . then rushed from adjacent homes with pitchers of water.

The screaming continued.

So did the dying.

Sirens . . . lots of sirens.

Police sirens, ambulance sirens, Emergency Medical Service sirens filled the air in a clashing atonal symphony.

The vehicles from the morgue came with no loud mechanical warning. They didn't need sirens to part the traffic and save time. The men in the hearses—there were a few women too—had all the time in the world. Knowing that the corpses didn't have any, the morgue teams drove carefully.

Ambulance crews watched impatiently as the firemen extinguished the fires, then chafed as bomb squad professionals checked to see whether there might be other explosive devices or booby traps or delayed-action weapons. Some terrorist groups—a few extremists in the anti-abortion underground among other righteous friends of violence—liked to leave time bombs to maim medics or firemen who showed up after the first blast.

The ambulance crews were frustrated and afraid.

There might be students or adults bleeding to death inside, but the rules were plain and absolute. No one could go in until the fire and bomb professionals said it was safe to do so.

By the time Malloy and Briggs arrived with five of their antiterrorist specialists the ambulance teams were cursing—and a few of the EMS people were crying. With more siren-armed vehicles still rolling up and fill-ing the air with sound, it was difficult for the conscientious radio and television newsers to tape the anguished obscenities.

They kept trying.

They knew they'd be in trouble with their highly competitive employers whose mantra was what bleeds leads— the first story on each newscast should be the most violent. This gruesome massacre of young girls in a religious school fit that cynical bill perfectly, Malloy thought as he instructed a dozen "uniforms" to move the bustling throng of journalists back fifty feet.

"For their own safety," Malloy lied.

"They won't like it," one veteran patrolman predicted.

They didn't, but that didn't bother Jacob Malloy for a second.

"They can complain *later*," he said coldly. "Freedom of the press. They've got a right to complain. That's what makes America great . . . that and baseball."

Briggs heard him, and shook his head.

"They may not buy that, Jake," he warned.

"They don't have to . . . we're giving it away."

They didn't buy it, and made that clear both vocally and with hostile hand gestures to the sergeant who delivered the message. Some of the more emotional media people spoke rudely to the sergeant.

"Your mother," he replied sincerely.

Minutes later the bomb squad specialists came out of the smoking building, coughed a lot, and reported that the medical teams could enter.

"Is it bad in there?" Briggs asked.

"Worse than that," the head of the bomb squad answered bitterly.

Then the ambulance crews began removing the living and the dead. Some of the survivors were sobbing, others dazed and mute, more than a score bloodied, burned, and unconscious. The medical teams moved swiftly to deal with the living. The men from the hearses were a little slower in putting the corpses into the body bags.

There were rows and rows of dead.

Arnold tried to count the bags. Once back in his room, immediately he'd turned on the television set. He had no difficulty in finding extensive reports—some "live" ones still coming in from the scene—of the bombing.

"Forty-one . . . forty-two . . . forty-three," he counted aloud before the earnest reporter announced that the total was eighty-three, and there might be one or two more fatalities before morning as several of those taken to area hospitals were in critical condition.

"City police and FBI agents from the Joint Antiterrorist Task Force continue their inch-by-inch search of the ruined school," the newsperson continued briskly.

He had very good teeth, the bomber noticed.

The half-gutted school behind him looked a lot worse.

Arnold flicked the remote control.

"Law enforcement teams are seeking physical evidence that might lead to the perpetrators," a female reporter on another network was saying. "They continue to look for any additional survivors, but there's not much hope for that."

Jump cut.

Close-up of fire chief's soot-stained face.

Very determined.

"We know what the odds are," he said firmly, "but we don't give up that easily."

"Neither do we," said Gunther who was monitoring the same torrent of television reports on the set in his mid-Manhattan "safe house."

They would learn that soon enough, he thought as he

reluctantly turned off the electronic window on the world. He had to stop watching and listening because it was time to leave. Gunther checked the street "casually" and carefully before he started the seven-block walk to the telephone booth where he'd get the call.

Gunther knew that the timing was crucial.

That was exactly what Colonel Andrei Belkov was thinking several thousand miles east.

Twenty-seven miles north of Moscow to be precise. Precision was especially important today, he realized as he drove toward the rendezvous with the CIA courier. He was driving the car himself for, as he'd explained to the general, the Americans had specified that.

"No problem," the general had assured him. "Any word on the Omar situation?"

"I hope to have something soon," Belkov had replied.

He drove carefully, always aware that one—perhaps two—surveillance units were trailing him. There'd be a listening device in his car, of course, and this time there was probably a radio beacon to transmit the vehicle's location.

Other teams of watchers with long-range microphones and advanced photo gear were already in place near . . . not too near . . . the meeting place. Though the general had no way of knowing that Belkov meant to run, another concealed listening device had appeared in the colonel's apartment a week ago.

For a moment Belkov wondered if there might be a mole in the CIA's station in Moscow. Now he turned his attention to concentrate on the driving. He was four miles from the rendezvous, and the twisting road ran under a roof of trees. He nodded as he saw the tight curve, and swung the sedan around the corner.

The first surveillance team was some 120 yards behind

him. Just as it reached the curve the watchers heard an explosion, saw a spout of flame. With the surface of the road still wet from the early morning downpour, the driver of the lead car trailing Belkov took the curve carefully.

Then he began to swear.

As he slammed on the brakes, he knew he was in trouble.

General Strelski would be furious.

This wasn't supposed to happen.

Fire and smoke . . . terrible heat. Belkov's sedan was barely visible. Belkov's car had slid off the wet road. The impact of smashing into a big tree had crushed the front of the car. It hadn't done the colonel any good either. His body was slumped over the wheel, shrouded in fire.

The lieutenant who commanded the surveillance team knew what he had to do, and he was scared. Any sane person would be, he thought as he jumped out of his vehicle. He was swearing and sweating—not just from the heat of the burning car—as he forced himself to run to the burning sedan.

Belkov didn't have much face left, no hair on his head at all. The damned door beside the dead driver was jammed. Now the lieutenant roared a command to the others in his unit. They raced forward, hesitated, and half stiff with fear themselves struggled to manhandle the ruined corpse out the window on the driver's side.

The smell was awful, but they knew what the general would do might be much worse. Trying not to throw up, they managed to drag the charred thing some forty yards before the fuel tank on Belkov's car erupted in a final blast. Gasping and shaking, they paused for some two minutes . . . unable to speak.

The lieutenant spoke for them three hours later.

"It's him all right, General," he told Strelski. "His

hands were too charred for fingerprints, but our best people checked the teeth. Teeth don't lie, General."

Strelski's eyes narrowed.

"All you have is the teeth?" he tested.

"No, General. Everything else confirms the identification. The clothes, shoes, watch, plates on the car. I'm afraid Colonel Belkov's dead."

Strelski thought for a moment before he shrugged.

Then he saw the worry in the lieutenant's face.

"It's all right," the general announced. "I'm not blaming you. I never really liked Belkov anyway. There was something *funny* about him . . . no, *guarded*. Too bad the bastard had to die now though."

"In the middle of the double game with the Americans?"

The general nodded.

"That and Omar," he replied.

"I'm sorry, General," the puzzled junior officer apologized. "Who's Omar?"

"I don't know either," Strelski said angrily, "but I'm going to find out . . . Don't mention Omar to anyone."

The lieutenant obeyed for medical reasons.

Everyone in this command was aware that it could be extremely unhealthy not to follow General Strelski's orders to the letter. It could be fatal.

18

"THEY'RE PRETTY good," Malloy judged.

"I'd say they're *terrible*," Donna Olsen disagreed. "In fact," the female FBI agent who spoke Arabic continued, "I'd say they're the *worst*."

"I mean they're good at terrible things," Malloy explained as he picked up the laboratory report. "These bastards made their own napalm from scratch. That's not like baking brownies, you know."

Monday morning briefing session.

Joint Task Force . . . full staff.

Daily updates were standard procedure now. Malloy and Briggs had decided that everyone had to know everything as soon as possible. That was why the additional phone on Briggs's desk was a direct secure line to the head of the FBI's antiterrorist division in Washington. It was also the reason the television set in Malloy's office across the hall was on and tuned to the all-news CNN channel . . . around the clock.

"About this napalm," Briggs began.

He paused when a bell began to ring.

"We've got mail," Malloy thought aloud. Then he pointed at the black woman detective standing beside the door.

"Please?"

She returned in seconds with the fax message.

"Thanks," he said as she handed it to him.

Good manners . . . and good-looking, she thought.

"Anytime, Captain," she replied with half a smile.

Malloy scanned the fax swiftly before he gave it to Briggs.

FBI agents across the nation were checking on recent buyers of the chemicals used to make the napalm.

That could take more time than New York might have, Malloy computed silently.

The second part of the fax announced that Washington was sending up an additional fifty agents with special skills to help.

When Briggs read this aloud several of the New York cops were visibly unimpressed.

"Listen, it can't hurt," Malloy told them.

Now he saw the mayor and police commissioner blossom on the television set across the corridor. The ex-SEAL pointed again . . . this time at the twenty-one-inch screen. The whole unit followed him and Briggs to watch and hear the press conference.

Mayor Dowling did what Malloy had hoped he wouldn't.

His Earnest Honor announced that there had been threats from a group that called itself The Beirut Brigade. Then Dowling asked the public to share any information it might have about that organization.

"Here we go," Malloy said bitterly.

"Maybe not," Briggs replied.

"Every damn head case in the U.S.—and all the other lucky countries blessed by CNN—will check in before morning," Malloy predicted.

It was obvious the ex-SEAL had never completed a course in stress management, Briggs realized. The FBI supervisor had taken such training in Washington, so he understood that the mayor believed he had to do something—anything—to reassure the frightened public that the authorities were actively seeking to end the threat.

No, Briggs decided.

The look on Malloy's face made it clear this wasn't the time to discuss stress management. Changing the subject might be more realistic.

Malloy did it first.

"No point in sitting around waiting for the armies of cranks and legions of brilliant media people to clog our phone lines," he said crisply. "Let's do what *we* can do . . . but do it better."

With Briggs's approval, four Task Force members went to the firing ranges each hour to improve their marksmanship. The cops took their weapons to the NYPD range, while the federal agents went downstairs in the building in which the Task Force lived to shoot in the FBI range beside the garage.

When Malloy returned to his apartment that night, he tossed his jacket on the couch and loosened his gun holster before he sat down in his favorite armchair. He stared at the framed photo of his lover for a dozen seconds . . . sighed.

Where was she?

Was she safe?

Was she alive at all?

Urgently wanting to hold her, he told himself that she

was careful and smart . . . professional and strong. She didn't scare, he thought, but that wasn't enough. Was she still *lucky*, he wondered. He remembered two incidents when she had been. She must be now.

She'd sweated about him and some hit man from Cali, but she was in much greater danger.

Every day . . . every minute.

Malloy knew there was almost nothing more hazardous than trying to infiltrate a cocaine ring. Why the hell would she do this? Did she think she was better than everyone else, he asked himself angrily.

This was crazy.

And there was nothing he could do to help her.

It was too warm in the room. He opened both windows, lit a Don Diego corona, and turned on his television set to escape. Even a cop on an antiterrorist team had a good chance most nights of finding on the news reports something worse than his daily life. For a few moments—maybe as much as two minutes—you could flee from your own reality into these horrors, Malloy thought as the first pictures of the ferry disaster in Asia filled the screen.

Death in living color . . . big numbers.

Hundreds had drowned. Even more than in last year's ferry sinking in Bangladesh . . . now there was a network reporter standing in front of the United Nations building over on First Avenue. A dozen chiefs of Middle Eastern and other Muslim missions had denounced the bombers who'd killed so many children in The Bronx, but the king of Saudi Arabia had done more than that.

A million dollars.

The monarch was offering a reward of one million dollars for information leading to the arrest and conviction of those who had carried out the massacre at the school.

Damn good idea, the ex-SEAL approved and puffed on his cigar.

Politically good, morally good, and good public relations. There had been speculation that some Muslim nation might fund this Beirut Brigade, but the sensible king was making it clear that it wasn't his.

The well-coiffed anchorperson—one of nature's noble folk who never had a bad hair day—was starting to speak about tomorrow's memorial service for the Saint Agatha victims when Malloy's ringing telephone broke the spell.

"You weren't exactly off target on the reaction to the mayor's talk about the Brigade," reported Briggs who was still at the Task Force headquarters.

"The *alleged* Brigade," Malloy responded.

"There have been something like 204 telephone calls, fax messages, and e-mails to the mayor's office, your police commissioner, FBI headquarters in Washington, the FBI bureau here, and our Task Force," Briggs said.

"No cakes?" the ex-SEAL asked.

"I'm too tired for jokes, Jake."

"There'll be messages coming inside cakes, in water pistols and rosaries, letters, postcards, FedEx envelopes, and maybe boxes of dried fruit. The tapes will start to arrive tomorrow . . . in a nice assortment of languages," Malloy told him.

"For God's sake, Jake," the senior FBI supervisor reproved.

"For all the gods' sakes and the saints too. Now how about the bad guys?" Malloy asked. "Any leads?"

"Maybe," Briggs replied cautiously. "Three of the 204 messages apparently came from terrorist outfits who're in our computer bank—and there were five more from other groups that also claim responsibility—but nobody knows who they are."

Malloy blew a smoke ring before he answered.

"No reason to believe any of the eight, right?" he guessed.

"Not yet. Jake, I've been thinking about what you said about the *alleged* Brigade. Was that just careful lawyer talk?"

"Hell, no. You and I know the rules of this game, Frank. Terrorists make specific demands or at least clearly identify their politics. They want us to know who they are and what their goals are."

He paused to glance at the news broadcast.

A picture of the White House filled Malloy's television screen.

"The people who blew up the synagogue and the high school aren't playing by the rules," the ex-SEAL said bluntly, "so they're not professionals. But every damn thing they do—their tradecraft—is professional. There's something wrong, something phony, here. It doesn't make sense to scare the crap out of the city with two ex-pertly executed—*professionally* executed—bombings and not say why."

"Red flag?" the federal agent asked.

"Very red," Malloy agreed.

Red flag was trade talk . . . the shorthand phrase for something suspicious that might be a diversion or decep-tion.

"Whoever these people are," Malloy continued, "I very much doubt that they really have any connection with Beirut or the whole Arab number. If I'm right, they're lay-ing a false trail so we won't track them down later."

"When does *later* start?" Briggs wondered aloud.

"After their next attack . . . or the one after that. After they make their demands," Malloy predicted.

"How soon would that be?"

Jacob Malloy didn't answer.

He was watching and listening to the White House press secretary announce that the president would be in The Bronx the next afternoon to attend the memorial service for the eighty-five who had succumbed to the bombing.

"Two more died?" he asked.

"A sophomore and a math teacher," Briggs answered. "We just got word half an hour ago. It's going to be an interfaith service. The student was a Jewish girl whose parents had sent her to Saint Agatha's because of the quality of the education."

"*Eighty-five* dead? Any more good news?"

"Maybe, Jake. Our agents tracking the buyers of the two chemicals used in the homemade napalm can identify one guy who made two cash purchases about ten weeks ago."

"Separate suppliers . . . different states, right?"

"How did you know?"

"A little vulture told me," Malloy said. "Just gallows humor, Frank," he explained. "I didn't know about these buys. All I knew was that's how people in our weird trade would operate. More rules of this peculiar game. Lie and run. Move fast and move often. Don't stay anywhere more than a couple of weeks, and change your look and ID in each new place. Then you can stop and kill children or buildings or airplanes . . . and go somewhere else."

"Jake," Briggs began.

"I'd call that sick," Malloy interrupted. "Wouldn't you say there's a mental health problem here?"

The ex-SEAL sounded very tired.

"Jake, we have descriptions of the guy who bought the chemicals so we're developing a composite to send out. We know what he looks like," Briggs reported in an encouraging tone.

Malloy wasn't encouraged.

"You know what he *used* to look like," he corrected. "By now he's changed the color of his hair, added or subtracted glasses or a mustache, and modified how he dresses. That's how they play it, Frank. Remember?"

Suddenly sensible Frank Briggs found himself thinking that he wouldn't mind if Malloy wasn't right all the time.

"I'll get back to you," Briggs said and hung up the telephone.

Some two miles south of Malloy's apartment, Gunther turned his rented car toward the Lincoln Tunnel. As he saw the entrance directly ahead, he slowed the sedan and thought about the woman with the skillfully fake Southern accent. She'd been an effective member of the group as well as an excellent sexual partner. She'd been very conscientious with lots of imagination, few inhibitions, and a cheerful willingness to do whatever he wanted without any hesitation or complaint.

Gunther could see why she'd been at the top of her class.

Her loyalty and commitment were admirable, he reflected as his car neared the toll booth. It was unfortunate that both they and she were now becoming too costly. He didn't need any unecessary expenses or baggage.

Nothing personal, of course.

Gunther was very rarely personal.

This was a professional matter. It didn't make sense to give her the million dollars planned when he could add it to the money he was taking for himself anyway. There would or could be one more risk to all their futures if she survived. It was quite unlikely that she'd get caught or betray them if she was seized, but unlikely wasn't really good enough.

There was the toll booth ten yards ahead.

No one was in it, for collections at the New York end had ceased in order to reduce costs.

Cutting costs was always logical, Gunther told himself as he drove on into the tunnel. He'd cut his costs by a million dollars and reduce his personal danger . . . what the Wall Street crowd called downside exposure. He smiled as he contemplated the phrase "downside exposure" . . . it was so American.

So he'd kill her.

It would pull less police attention if her death looked like an accident . . . and if her remains couldn't be identified. He considered that as he carefully guided the sedan under the river toward New Jersey. Both ends of the tunnel and the escape routes had to be checked and rechecked.

Deciding exactly how and when to kill her would be no problem, Gunther thought as he saw daylight ahead. He was totally confident about this. As he had demonstrated so many times, killing people was probably his greatest talent.

Nobody did it better. The target didn't matter, he reflected, for it was the technique and timing that counted. He hadn't been relating to this woman as an individual anyway. Gunther didn't take women seriously, didn't really respect them as a group. He wasn't the least bit embarrassed as he faced that and looked out at New Jersey.

After all, he didn't respect men either.

19

WHEN THE president of the United States stepped from Air Force One at the New York airport named for a murdered predecessor, he was surrounded by a score of wary-eyed Secret Service agents who escorted him to the nearby helicopter that would fly him into Manhattan. He would proceed by armored limousine to the memorial service in The Bronx.

Standard procedures.

At the moment he boarded the helicopter, another important person was landing in a four-engined U.S. military cargo plane at Andrews Air Force Base near Washington. The rear ramp was lowered, and five enlisted men in coveralls came aboard to start feeding bags of mail and assorted packages onto the unloading machine that two other airmen in identical attire moved into position.

Standard procedures . . . scheduled flight . . . nothing to draw anyone's attention or questions.

Unless a suspicious observer counted.

Five men in coveralls came aboard . . . and *six* left the big jet some forty minutes later. When they got to the hangar the sixth man, a husky and taciturn person who hadn't said a word during the unloading, wandered off toward the rear of the large building. The toilets were back there, so the rest of the unloaders understood that he was off on kidney patrol and would be back soon.

It didn't work out that way.

A blond-haired fellow in the uniform of a first lieutenant stepped out from behind a small tractor and waved.

"Johnson," he said and pointed to a side door.

The sixth man—whose dog tags identified him as Airman Alfred Johnson—followed the lieutenant out the door. The blond officer wasn't a member of the U.S. Air Force at all, and the sixth man's name wasn't Alfred Johnson. He had no connection with the armed forces of the United States of America, though he knew a good deal about them.

The fake lieutenant and the man who wasn't Alfred Johnson got into the back of a waiting van that apparently belonged to Potomac Electric. That's what the sign painted on the side of the vehicle said, but that was a lie too.

The people who'd organized this whole thing were rather compulsive about deception, and with a lot of practice they were quite good at it. In the closed rear compartment of the van the sixth man took off his coveralls to change into civilian clothes that fit him perfectly. The garments and the shoes—the whole outfit—didn't look new. Someone had actually worn them for days, and nights, so they wouldn't be noticed.

The same people who were running this had sent ahead the measurements of the sixth man. He assumed that there would be additional clothing—worn and in his sizes—where the van was going. He didn't know where that was, and with no windows in the cargo compartment of the van he couldn't see any landmarks or street signs.

He wasn't troubled by this, for he understood that this was the way such things were done. The fake lieutenant and the driver in the uniform of Potomac Electric probably didn't even know who he was, he reasoned.

He was right.

He was a "priority package" to them, and to the armed men in the cars that preceded and followed the van. They had their orders and their machine guns. The escorts didn't know his name either, only that he was "hot" and must be protected at all costs.

It was all standard, the man who wasn't Alfred Johnson reflected. He felt entirely comfortable with these procedures, but he wasn't wholly free of tension about what lay ahead. Though they were committed to his safety, he knew he was in acute danger.

Many kinds of danger.

He couldn't trust these people who were his protectors, and they certainly didn't trust him. They'd be very pleasant but they'd be wondering about him . . . as they should. They would be testing and probing with a lot of questions . . . some of them apparently casual and innocuous but all purposeful.

There might be drugs in the tasty and ample food they'd serve him. He was a guest, so he could order any dish he wanted. What they wanted was first to ascertain whether he was a well-trained, expert, and ruthless liar . . . as skilled in deception as they were. Then they'd get to substantive questions that might be life-or-death matters for other people.

Hypnosis? Yes, his hosts might use that. Lie detector sessions were certain though his hosts still wouldn't be sure. It might be nice if they tried women and drink, the man who wasn't Alfred Johnson mused. He smiled for a moment. It might be interesting if they provided a tall female with long red hair. He'd dreamed about such a person several times over the years.

Now the van turned left sharply.

There was still a distance to go, he reasoned. The place where they were taking him would be miles from the military air base that was Andrews, he estimated correctly as the van rolled on at moderate speed. They wouldn't do anything that might attract attention. They would be careful.

Up in New York City, another person with a false name was being careful too. This individual with several identities was listed in the most guarded files of Russian foreign intelligence under the code name Mirror. Colonel Belkov had assigned it to the agent in a touch of irony, for Mirror was to offer a view of the inner workings of the U.S. security and intelligence community.

Mirror looked up at the nearby television set for a brief glimpse of the president at the memorial service, then turned to the computer that came with the spy's "day job." Mirror's mind wasn't on the screen but on the message Moscow had blitz-radioed last night.

Mirror would no longer be "run" by Dagger—code name for Belkov—who'd died. Future orders would come from Coachman. That was General Strelski himself, commander of the entire First Directorate of the SVR. The second part of the signal was a renewed request for any data about Omar. Mirror didn't understand this reference to a previous request. Mirror didn't know that Colonel Belkov had never sent it.

There was something else that Mirror didn't know about this situation.

Moscow's most effective deep-cover agent in the United States hadn't heard anything about the man who wasn't Alfred Johnson . . . didn't even know he existed let alone where he was or why.

The mole had no warning that things were swiftly growing more complex—and moving out of control. Unaware of these changes, Mirror decided to address the Omar question first. Having survived for years by caution, the deep-cover operative decided to speak to the leader of the Omar team before replying to Moscow's "renewed" request.

Gunther would supply all the information needed, Mirror thought. The mole wasn't aware that there was one matter Gunther would keep back. It involved murdering a lot more people and extorting millions of dollars before Omar disappeared.

Vanished into thin air like smoke.

When this happened, Moscow might blame the deep-cover agent for not reporting years earlier that Belkov and Omar had been running a totally unauthorized and utterly improper rogue operation. The general would never believe that Mirror, the communications link, hadn't known it was completely criminal.

Now Mirror paused to look again at the live television report from the memorial service. The expert mole wondered who might be responsible for these bloody bombings. Mirror didn't know that either. Gunther had never even mentioned them. He'd gone by the book. This was his operation, and he was quite certain that Mirror had no need to know.

It was better that the deep-cover agent didn't know.

That way it probably wouldn't be necessary for Gunther to kill Mirror too.

Probably.

20

LATE THAT afternoon the president of the U.S.A. went home to the White House in Washington.

Several hours after that Gunther's explosives expert left mid-Manhattan to go to a movie theater in an adjacent borough named Queens. Arnold didn't travel there because the sixty-four-million-dollar action film being shown had good reviews and even better special effects. Though a significant number of thirteen-year-olds and adults with tastes that were just as childlike found the picture a satisfactory distraction, Arnold didn't make his way to the movie house in Queens for the same reason they did.

They wanted to kill time.

His purpose was to kill people.

More precisely, it was to recheck certain aspects of his plan to kill people . . . in ninety-seven hours.

Gunther had set the time table, and Arnold hadn't asked for the reason. There were many times when Gunther didn't like questions, the bomber knew. This seemed to be one of them, so Arnold simply took the subway for his fourth visit to the theater in Queens, a borough some two and a half times as large as The Bronx where Saint Agatha's was.

The bomber wasn't aware of the size difference, or the fact that an autocratic Dutch bureaucrat who didn't care much for Native Americans—called Indians then—had bought most of today's Queens from the Rockaway tribe in 1639. The Rockaways were long gone—today just a name on a beach—but the borough was now home to some other Indians. And Pakistanis and Chinese, descendants of Eastern European Jews and a fair number of immigrants from ten other countries.

In large part a bedroom community for Manhattan, quite international, a population closing in on two million.

Soon that population would be smaller when Arnold executed the next phase of Gunther's plan. Arnold rode the subway one stop past the one closest to the movie house, got off the train, and ascended to the wide street. Lots of traffic, many vehicles, numerous pedestrians, easy for Arnold to stroll back to the theater without attracting any attention.

There was a line of people in front of the theater.

Arnold did not join them.

Instead he walked around to the back of the four-story office building next to the movie house. Making sure that no one was watching, he picked the lock on the rear door. Six minutes later he was on the roof of the theater.

Now Arnold took from his well-worn shoulder bag— the one with the insignia of the Mets baseball team so popular in Queens—an infrared flashlight and special glasses that let him see what the infrared beam illuminated. He knew where to look. Gunther had acquired the building plans for the theater. Knowing how to find which public agency had such important papers and how to get copies was a skill Arnold admired.

He scanned the roof, especially the four corners, very slowly and carefully. Next Arnold picked the lock that offered access to the interior of the movie house. He moved slowly, cautiously, silently, as he reexamined the top-floor offices and computer space near the projector room.

There'd be just one person here at this hour. The modern projector was automated, so the operator felt free to sneak out for a trip to the toilet or an illicit smoke on the roof for a ten-minute break. This projectionist and many others believed that if they needed a break, they were entitled to it.

No harm done, and no one would notice.

In a bit over ninety-six hours a lot of people would notice, Arnold told himself silently as he finished rechecking what he had to be absolutely sure about in this plan. Gunther wanted more bodies this time, a key factor in picking this target. The plans for the theater showed it had 362 seats.

And the film being offered was drawing well.

That ought to do it, Arnold thought and left the building through the door to the roof. When he got to the street he walked to the other side of the busy avenue, then on to a subway stop closer to Manhattan.

At 9:54 P.M.—exactly on schedule—he called the phone booth where Gunther was waiting.

"Bob," the bomber said, "I just saw your sister. She asked me to say hello."

"She feeling better?" Gunther tested.

"Absolutely fine. She's expecting you for dinner on Saturday," Arnold replied with the agreed code phrase.

"I wouldn't miss it for anything," Gunther said.

It had to be perfect, he thought as he walked from the booth seconds later. That meant he must recheck every detail of the preparations himself. In a deliberate imitation of a man who was simply strolling in the night, he made his way seven blocks north. He paused now and then to study shop windows and restaurant menus, using these "covers" to mask his search for possible followers.

As he reached the next phone booth on his route and timetable, he eyed his wristwatch. He was pleased that he was two minutes early . . . as usual. The extra time would give an additional opportunity to scan the battlefield. From Gunther's point of view, every place he went now could be the site of an ambush. He had to be ready—at all times—for a surprise attack. In a basic sense Gunther had been at war for years.

He dialed the number.

Scott picked up on the third ring as instructed.

"Vic?" he tested.

"Who else? How about lunch tomorrow?"

"Sorry I can't make it," Scott said. "Just got my new bike, and I'm breaking it in."

The "bike" was a powerful Harley . . . part of Gunther's plan.

"Smooth ride?"

"Great. I hacked out to Barry's on this baby, and it flew," Scott enthused.

"Glad to hear it. Let's try for lunch next week. Chinese okay?"

"Or Mexican," Scott answered to end the exchange.

It was supposed to sound like routine small talk between two typical New Yorkers who had no foreign accents or anything else to alert anyone who might be listening. Or even hear accidentally through a crossed wire. Gunther was devoted to these precautions, which might sound a bit paranoid to some people.

Paranoia had worked well for him and Omar so far.

He saw no reason to change his comfortable lifestyle now.

He walked on five blocks to the next phone booth on his schedule. He started toward the instrument when he heard a hissing sound behind him. Gunther turned to face a sort of young woman in a low-cut tight green blouse, black leather miniskirt, and an excess of slutty makeup that suggested she was either a prostitute or a with-it "club kid."

She moved quickly between him and the booth.

She obviously wanted his attention, and got it.

He realized that he had very little time, a bit more than a minute.

"Excuse me," he said. "I've got to make a call."

She didn't step aside. She opened her mouth and licked her overpainted lips.

"You'll have more fun with me, baby," she replied in a husky voice. "I make dreams come true. Fifty bucks?"

She moved her hips but not her feet. She was still blocking the booth, grinning in a trashy way that added fuel to Gunther's anger. He swiftly considered his options. The street was too well lit for him to do what he wanted to—crush her skull against the sidewalk. Breaking her arm wouldn't be practical either, for she'd be able to identify him.

He took the third option.

"Can't do it," he said as he shook his head. "I'm HIV positive."

The threat of the savage AIDS virus did the job. Without uttering a word of compassion, she hurried away as if she feared his breath might contaminate her. When she was twenty-five yards away Gunther looked up and down the street before dialing the number of the telephone where Casey waited.

He'd bought a bike too, a Fat Boy with lots of power. He'd driven it south to Princeton to see his grandfather. Good ride, good visit. Princeton was down in New Jersey, Gunther calculated, so Casey had probably gone through the tunnel twice. Probably? No, surely.

Those had been his orders.

Check out the tunnel and the high ground that Gunther had scouted himself many weeks earlier. They'd test the radios the next afternoon, then again two days later. It was all going well, Gunther told himself.

Some nineteen miles from Andrews Air Force Base, the man who wasn't Alfred Johnson was also feeling guardedly positive. *They* had been treating him with professional respect. No leggy young women with long red hair *yet*, but the food and drink were superior and the tone of the questioning was correct thus far. They were actually quite good in this whole operation, he thought as he puffed on a Cuban cigar that was illegal in the rest of the country.

It didn't surprise him that the Central Intelligence Agency could put their hands on the best Cuban coronas . . . or anything else. After all, they had done an impressive job in acquiring an appropriate corpse, putting in dental work that precisely matched Belkov's, and even delivering the body in exactly the same car, garb, and watch model the colonel had worn on the day of the expertly staged car crash.

Even though the idea of faking Belkov's death had been his own, the CIA had shaped and executed the plan very well. No one was hunting him, the Russian colonel thought. He'd have to pay for his safety, of course. The questioning would go wider, be more intense.

The CIA would want to know everything about any

and all Russian intelligence operations—past and present. Codes, gear, communications procedures, and people. They'd be very insistent about the people. They'd want to know a lot more about Russian spies than Belkov had reported while he was feeding information in Moscow.

They'd want him to prove his loyalty to the U.S. cause by coming up with the identities, contacts, blind drops, signal systems, and targets of important agents. He could stall for a while to make himself and the information more important, but—sooner or later—he'd have to give them some of what they wanted.

What was that American expression?

No such thing as a free lunch.

Yes, he'd have to betray someone . . . probably in the next few days.

Looking across the table at the CIA interrogation specialist who called himself Major Wilson, Belkov smiled and relit the fine cigar. Then the veteran Russian intelligence officer silently went over the list he'd prepared a week ago in anticipation of just such a situation.

The list was still valid, he decided.

He knew whom he'd betray first.

That would be a down payment, of course.

He might well have to give them more later.

21

QUEENS—2.

"What does *that* mean?" Briggs wondered.

"Do I get three guesses?" Jacob Malloy fenced and stared at the copy of the latest threat.

"As many as you want," the FBI supervisor replied.

The rest of the new note . . . Friday . . . night . . . was clear enough, but the number that followed the name of the target borough was puzzling. The terrorists were telling the authorities something . . . simultaneously teasing and taunting in ugly defiance.

"I'm not really sure," the ex-SEAL began slowly.

"Go ahead, Jake," Briggs urged impatiently.

Now Malloy paused, nodded.

"Two *targets*," he finally said. "My hunch is that these bastards are sending us *two* attacks of some sort on Friday night. Just a guess."

Briggs stared at the map of Queens they'd put up on his office cork board eighteen minutes earlier.

"Not a bad guess, I *think*," he judged. "Why two? Why two now?"

"Another guess," Malloy specified. "They want us to

know that they can strike at two different locations at the same time . . . or about the same time. I'm betting it'll be *exactly* the same goddam time."

"Ego trip?" tested Briggs who'd done well in the FBI course in criminal psychology. "Demonstrating their power?"

"Show-off time," Malloy agreed. "It won't be a house of worship or a school. Been there . . . done that . . . these horrors will go for something different."

"How different?"

"Well, if they continue to escalate, and I don't doubt that for a second," the ex-SEAL said, "the targets will be ones that can deliver more bodies."

"We could double the patrols and add bomb-sniffing dogs at both airports," Briggs proposed, "and do the same for the bridges and the tunnel."

Malloy shook his head.

"Not double . . . *triple*," he recommended. "And we'd better brainstorm with the borough president about other possible targets with massacre potential."

The FBI executive winced for a second at the blunt words.

"I feel the same way," Malloy told him. "It's a nasty phrase, but we don't have time for nice talk. This is the biggest borough in the Big Apple, Frank. There must be a hundred targets in Queens to suit those bastards. Hospitals, a stadium, you name it."

Briggs didn't try to do that himself. Instead he set up a conference call with the Queens borough president, the security chiefs at the airports, bridges, and tunnel, the commanders of all the police precincts and firehouses in the threatened borough, and Police Commissioner Jefferson.

"Just ask for any additional manpower or *woman*power you need," Jefferson said, "and you'll get it in an hour.

This deal is time critical. If you have any idea—even a hunch—about what the target might be we must know it immediately."

Silence.

Ten . . . fifteen . . . twenty seconds. Slow and loud.

"Call me or the Task Force, day or night," Jefferson urged. "We're counting on you. The whole city is."

The conference call ended.

"Kennedy first," Malloy said and pointed across the corridor to the briefing room where a VCR, television set, projector, big screen, and slides waited. Briggs accompanied him, and quickly found the slide showing the location and access roads of the large international airport's terminals. Planning ahead, the Task Force had assembled a library of over three hundred slides of potential targets in the great metropolis.

Briggs dropped the slide in the projector, turned on the light beam. As the picture appeared, FBI agent Donna Olsen politely and audibly cleared her throat in the doorway behind them. They turned, saw her left hand held a pink message slip.

"A man phoned while you were on the conference call, Captain," she told Malloy. "He wanted you to know he was coming through town with his brother next week."

She looked down at the message slip.

"On the eleventh or twelfth," she added. "Said his name was Gambelli."

Malloy's face communicated nothing. Neither did his voice a moment later when he thanked her and took the pink piece of paper. He went through the slides with Briggs for the next seventy minutes. When the ex-SEAL returned to his own office he closed the door, carefully tore the message slip into small pieces, and put them in an ashtray. He burned them before he used the handle of a steel killing knife to reduce the residue to powder.

Fine gray powder.

Old habits died hard, Malloy thought as he put away the knife that no other cop in the city kept handy. It certainly wasn't an official weapon—not for the New York Police Department. Even if Malloy explained that it was really a souvenir, he thought, the commissioner wouldn't like it.

He wouldn't believe Malloy either.

The commissioner would be right.

Now the ex-SEAL walked back to rejoin Briggs in trying to develop a defense, to plan where to place extra plainclothes cops, where to add FBI agents, Customs officers with dogs trained to sniff out explosives.

They succeeded in persuading the mayor not to disclose this threat to Queens because there would be a panic. They did not succeed in thwarting Gunther's plan. At 8:19 P.M. on Friday night a bomb that included seven sticks of dynamite blew to bits a car parked beside the Queens borough hall.

At the same time the much larger explosive charges that Arnold had placed three miles away in the movie house dropped the ceiling of the theater on 327 people just as Bruce Willis was gunning down half a dozen villains. 141 people died immediately. Another 102 were carried out to be taken to hospitals.

Police cars, fire trucks, EMS vehicles, vans with crews and cameras from a dozen video news operations, scores of reporters and photographers from local, national, and foreign dailies and magazines.

The sirens were howling . . . the injured crying out . . . ambulance crews and fire teams cursing . . . and journalists dedicated to freedom of the press and beating the

shameless competition yelling and pushing. Not all of
them did that. Only about three-quarters ignored what
their mothers had taught them—the needs of the injured,
and the police, came first. The more-than-aggressive media people were distracting, getting in the way, interfer-
ing, and infuriating.

"Stay back! Get back, dammit!" Malloy shouted.

They did not comply. One grinning still photographer
stepped farther forward to snap a picture of Malloy's angry face. For a second the flashbulb blinded the ex-SEAL.
That raised Malloy's emotional temperature even higher.

"I said *get back*," he reminded grimly.

"What are you going to do? Shoot me?" the photographer defied.

Malloy flipped back his jacket.

The nine-millimeter Glock semiautomatic in his holster was clearly visible.

"Next of kin?" he asked.

Stunned, the man with the camera froze, felt the cop-
pery taste of fear, and retreated three paces.

"You got a bad attitude, Captain," he complained.

"It's getting worse," Malloy reported truthfully.

Fifty minutes later he and Briggs were back in the Task
Force headquarters overlooking Foley Square when the
technical experts called in their preliminary analysis of
the basic features of the two bombs. The explosives used
to destroy the car and the movie theater were dynamite,
almost surely from the same plant.

"What else?" Malloy demanded impatiently.

"These devices were detonated simultaneously, but
not by a timing mechanism," the senior FBI bomb specialist said.

"Radio control? Both on same frequency, right?" Malloy thought aloud.

"How did you know, Captain?"

"Just a hunch."

Uncomfortable with the idea of hunches, the bomb expert hesitated before he spoke again.

"Well . . . I see . . . we'll continue with our detailed studies of these weapons," he announced stiffly. "We should have a full report in forty-eight hours."

"Make that twenty-four," Briggs corrected.

Malloy flashed him a thumbs-up as the telephone conversation ended. Briggs looked at him warily, sighed.

"I suppose you could figure there's bad news and good news," the FBI supervisor calculated. "Bad news is these thugs have radio control capacity, and the good news is we know the frequency they use."

"Don't want to rain on your parade, Frank, but that was good for about nine seconds," Malloy responded. "They wanted us to know they're radio savvy, but they're not dummies. You can bet your pension that these wise guys will never use that frequency again."

It was nearly midnight, and Malloy was tired.

He was even more weary after he and Briggs watched the television news reports of the carnage, then endured several minutes of the mayor, a trauma surgeon at a local hospital, and three religious leaders of assorted faiths discussing the terrible event.

All those dead and maimed . . . and it wasn't over.

It wasn't *nearly* over, Malloy thought as he drove north toward his apartment. He had no idea of what *they* were after, or why Gambelli had called, or where a very important Drug Enforcement Administration agent named Joanne Velez might be.

And he was hungry. When a red light stopped his progress up Eighth Avenue at Fifty-first Street, he suddenly remembered the superb seafood meal he'd enjoyed with her just a few blocks east. The occasion had been their first anniversary—one month after the night they came together. The restaurant was Le Bernardin, French, elegant, memorable.

Looking at the crosstown traffic flowing steadily west, Malloy remembered the fine wine they'd enjoyed with that meal. She'd been impressed that he'd selected a 1995 Batard Montrachet, and so had his wallet. It was too late to drive over to Le Bernardin tonight, the ex-SEAL realized, and he didn't want to go without her anyway.

Where the *hell* was she, he wondered for the thousandth time.

When he got home, his eyes hurt and his mailbox was full and there was a message on the answering machine from his mother. She spoke of his brother's "surprise" birthday party in thirteen days, reminding the former SEAL to bring an appropriate present. She didn't say a word about her concern over her policeman son's dangerous work.

She didn't have to . . . he could hear it in her voice.

Down in the Colombian city of Cali, the fourth biggest cocaine dealer in the world was also concerned about Jacob Malloy's health.

"I think enough time has passed," he told his homicidal chief of staff. "According to our friends in New York, the captain is very busy with a highly efficient group of terrorists. He can't be thinking of us."

"But we can think of him, right—jefe?"

"Have to. Unfinished business . . . and my professional reputation," the drug lord said.

In the global narcotics community it could be very dangerous if other major players thought you couldn't defend your turf or your honor. In Columbia's cocaine world it might be fatal.

"Let's send the captain a present," Eugenio Gomez told his aide and sipped more of the VSOP Rémy Martin cognac. "Something very attractive to show that we respect him. I don't care what it costs."

"We could send The Red Rose. Top of the line, jefe. About $100,000."

"Do it," Gomez ordered. "Do it right away."

The Red Rose reached Manhattan forty-one hours later.

22

"FIFTY-SEVEN KEYS," the big Indian wearing the headset said.

He wasn't talking about a typewriter or a piano . . . an electric organ or the control face of any computer either.

In his world "keys" was shorthand for kilograms. A kilo was 2.2 pounds, and each one was worth a lot of money and trouble. The powerfully muscled Navaho—that was a white man's word, the tribe said Dineh—was manning one of four sophisticated and expensive listening devices that the taxpayers of the United States of America paid for to make this operation work.

They didn't know that.

The people who were being spied upon were also unaware of the eavesdropping. It was entirely legal with a court order and other amenities, but the listeners kept it secret. They weren't a bad lot even if they called the Indian—they tried to remember to say Native American—"Chief" when he wasn't a chief at all.

His older brother was the chief.

He was (a) Thomas Largo (b) thirty-six years old (c) a keen fan of classic country music (d) a highly skilled employee of the Drug Enforcement Administration who had joined the federal payroll some eleven years earlier when he left the Marine Corps.

This operation—like just about all those conducted by DEA's group here in southern Florida where the Cowboys roamed—was a delicate one. It was dangerous because a lot of money was involved. These Cowboys weren't professional football players who worked on the celebrated Dallas team of that name. They didn't herd cattle either. They were quick-on-the-trigger and totally ruthless hoodlums from Colombia. The keys of cocaine were also from Colombia.

The dope was destined for New York City.

When "cut" and packaged for retail sale, the street value of the shipment would be about $2,090,000 at this week's price. Gangsters of other nationalities were also greedy, savage, and routinely homicidal. They were moving in cocaine too, but this particular shipment involved that small percentage of the population of Colombia that was thriving and murdering in the dope business.

The vast majority of Colombians and Mexicans and Peruvians and Panamanians and Burmese and Thais and Turks—Iranians and probably Icelanders and Italians too—had nothing to do with the narcotics trade. They were of no interest to the narrow-minded DEA people who were—for some obscure reason probably rooted in U.S. culture—irritated by the fact that most efforts to smuggle dope in were succeeding and drug dealers in the U.S.A. and abroad were getting richer and more cocky by the day.

By the hour.

Stopping this fifty-seven keys of very pure Colombia coke wasn't going to change the basic situation significantly, but the DEA people would feel a *little* better. With Civil Service wages what they were, that would be a small victory. The object of this operation wasn't to grab the cocaine here but to roll up the whole distribution network in New York.

That was why the smart female undercover agent had been sent down from the Manhattan office to infiltrate this particular group moving the 57 keys, about 125 pounds, up to New York City. She had to be smart, the shrewd and practical Navaho thought. Being pretty, even as attractive as she was, would not save her life.

He listened to her on the concealed microphone again. She was tough and clever all right, he judged admiringly.

Handled herself very well. *Perfectly* so far, and she had to maintain that all through the drive north. They'd be loading the pouches of white powder into concealed compartments in their two cars tomorrow. One vehicle would trail the other by ninety or one hundred yards all the way north, with those in the second car watching for any sign of police surveillance.

Every sixty or seventy miles the dope dealers' cars would switch places. At some places they might leave the main highway just to see if any other vehicle also turned off. The DEA watchers could not get too close . . . or too obvious. From time to time a federal helicopter might take over the surveillance, but not for long.

If it all worked, the woman undercover agent might live to help nail the wholesalers who were waiting for the dope in New York. If anything at all went wrong, the Navaho thought, the DEA might never find the chunks of her body.

It wasn't that these Colombians were worse than anyone else.

It was simply that they were as vicious as the others, and all of them were totally terrible.

Now he heard what he'd been waiting for.

The drug dealers' two vehicles with the fifty-seven keys—and the female undercover agent—would start north at eleven A.M. with an estimated time of arrival in New York at about noon on Friday. It could be an hour sooner or five hours later, depending on traffic and a dozen other factors. Knowing the departure time was more important, the DEA agent wearing the headset thought. That would permit the federal watchers to be in the right place at the right time.

"Cool," Thomas Largo judged aloud.

That word did not accurately describe how a former Russian intelligence colonel was feeling in a CIA safe house in Virginia. The people who were questioning him were still maintaining the fiction that he was their guest, but they weren't smiling as well as they had when he first arrived at the three-acre "farm."

The cover story fed to neighbors was that this place was a discreet drying-out clinic for affluent alcoholics, a fiction crafted to explain the secluded nature of the main house behind trees and the comings and goings of individuals who didn't seem to be related. Some of the people nearby had family members who drank too much themselves, and respecting other individuals' privacy was an unspoken rule in this part of the state.

Not in the safe house, though.

The stakes were too high, and nothing was out of bounds for the "hosts." The periods of questioning were growing longer each day, and the still-but-less-polite inquiries just a bit tougher. The men "talking" with Belkov worked in shifts, three in each team. There was no lovely red-haired woman or any other female among them. That was too bad, Belkov thought.

At least the interrogators had fresh names, he told himself as he reached for a glass of water. Not one of them was pretending to be a Bob or Victor, a change from those decades when so many CIA people used those bland all-purpose cover names. The round-faced leader of this shift was a bald-headed man, about forty, whom the others called Sam.

Sam had a number of talents that the Russian defector respected. One was a face that smiled when the eyes in it didn't—good for intimidating people. Another was a gift for raising the level of threat step by step without raising his voice.

"I think we've gone over that before," he said and Belkov tensed.

He'd been stalling and speaking about matters and people covered weeks and months ago in the material he'd given the CIA courier in the covert meetings in Moscow.

"I'm not criticizing," lied the man with the chilling eyes. "We understand that you're probably tired after your long journey. It was quite a trip, not easy for you. It wasn't easy for us either . . . took a ton of effort and a good deal of money. Not that you can measure everything in money," he continued smoothly, "but this cost over half a million dollars."

Here we go, Belkov thought.

"I appreciate all you've done," he declared.

"Hell, it was worth it. *We* appreciate all *you've* done. Yes, we respect you, Colonel."

This is it, Belkov realized.

As the Americans put it, he was between a rock and a hard place. That saying was one of the graphic American idioms Belkov had come to admire.

The pungency of the phrasing didn't help, of course.

Now they were going to grind him.

All he had—the only thing he could use to protect him-self—was his professional cunning.

He didn't want to pay more than he had to, but he knew that he must pay. The precise price—like almost everything else in the cloak-and-dagger world—could be bargained out carefully. The Americans couldn't be quite sure about what secrets he kept, so they didn't really know what questions to ask now.

It wouldn't be much of a problem for them though.

They'd probe with a thousand questions, about every-thing, hoping for some nugget, some treasure that would justify the entire operation and all the time and money they'd invested. The total was more than twice . . . maybe three times . . . $500,000.

"We've been talking about the past," the CIA ques-tioner pointed out in a tone that was an excellent imita-tion of casual. "Let's take a look at ongoing operations."

"Where?" Belkov fenced.

"We can start with right here—in the United States. Your turf, right?"

The Russian nodded slowly.

He had defected to save his own life, but he still wasn't ready to insure his own future by giving the Americans one of Moscow's agents. He'd thought it out, and de-cided whom he'd identify for the CIA and FBI to pursue.

It ought to work.

The Americans were already tracking this prey.

"There is a covert action unit," Belkov began, "that has been operating here for some time. I was the Control in Moscow for these people."

"How many people?"

"I think the number is *five*. Maybe *six*. They're quite

self-sufficient. Had to be because it's been very difficult to get funds to them. They've managed to raise money themselves."

The three CIA men exchanged glances.

"How do they do that?" the bald American asked.

"They steal it. Armed robberies. They've hit ten or twelve banks, taken over two million dollars."

"On your orders?"

Belkov shook his head.

It was going well. He could see the Americans were buying it.

"They aren't actually our people," the defector reported. "They're not Russians. They're East Germans, a leftover Stasi unit sent to the States before East Germany collapsed. If you've been checking out the Stasi files you may have heard of this team."

"Stasi? Still here? Who are they?" a CIA man blurted.

"*Where* are they?" Sam asked more calmly.

Mirror was safe . . . for a while, Belkov thought.

They'd be satisfied with the Stasi group . . . to whom he felt a much smaller loyalty. They were, after all, Germans and Belkov hadn't forgotten what the damned Germans had done to millions of people. The fact that these Germans in the Stasi team hadn't even been born in the Hitler era could be ignored.

"I don't know where they are right now," Belkov replied. "I can tell you their unit designation, and something about their commander. The unit name is *Omar*."

As Belkov paused, the three Americans leaned forward. He could see that they were interested.

23

"**SON OF** a bitch!" Malloy said as he read the "flash e-mail" from City Hall. It wasn't Mayor Dowling he was cursing.

The ex-SEAL and Briggs didn't pause to discuss the message. They walked swiftly to the elevators, waited impatiently for a car, and descended to the lobby of the big federal tower. They strode directly to the telephone booths.

"Wise guys!" Malloy declared angrily.

He reached into the booth specified in the e-mail, put his hand under the shelf, and found the square of paper Scotch-taped there. In a single motion he peeled it loose to hold it up for Briggs to scan it with him.

Pay up time. We're ready to do MUCH worse. Prepare to deliver on Friday $10,000,000 in used fifties. Pack it in four double-taped plastic bags. Delivery instructions coming. Follow them precisely, or get ready for a LOT more corpses. The streets will run red if you don't obey.

The Beirut Brigade

"They finally came through with their demand," Briggs said. "What do you think?"

"It's not like the other messages, Frank. The borough's not named, and they don't mention what time of day."

"What would that mean?"

"I'd say this is for real . . . the big one," Malloy reasoned. "They want to reduce the risk of getting stopped or caught, so they're giving us less to work with this time. And there's got to be a reason they want the cash in double-taped plastic bags."

"Water?" speculated the FBI inspector.

"Maybe. Why four bags? Maybe they're going to split up the cash and run. Whatever it is, the mayor will insist on getting the cash ready," Malloy predicted. "These are smart bastards. They know he has no choice."

"Not that smart. They just made a mistake," Briggs judged.

Malloy calculated and nodded.

"You mean the damn cameras," he guessed.

"The blessed cameras," Briggs corrected.

Since the bombing of the federal building in Oklahoma City there had been video cameras recording who entered and left this tall slab of U.S. property. Very few people knew that, for the cameras weren't that easy to see.

"We'll try to match the composite drawing of the man who bought the chemicals for the napalm against some face on these videotapes," the FBI supervisor thought aloud. "They made one *big* mistake."

"One may be all it takes," Malloy answered.

While members of the Joint Task Force were very carefully reviewing all the tapes of pedestrian in-and-out traffic in the previous twenty-four hours, Malloy was building another defense of his own. He didn't need the FBI for that . . . just a secure phone line.

It took three calls and some connections left over from his work in the covert operations community to reach the right person at the National Security Agency's heavily guarded headquarters. When the conversation began that person was the wrong person, automatically denying that NSA could do what Malloy wanted.

"Don't screw with me . . . or you're history," the ex-SEAL warned.

"Who do you think you're threatening?"

"A one-star general who's going to be wrecked if these hoods pull this off," Malloy answered. "If the streets up here run red with blood, as they've promised, some of that red's going to be yours. Your career will be dead, General."

General B. J. Warner thought for several seconds.

He'd heard about Jacob Malloy. The word was that he was capable of doing anything . . . and that was just for openers.

"You want *all* the transmitters?" he tested.

"Every one of yours and anyone else in The Family."

"Family?"

"The whole fucking intelligence community including ASA and other outfits you wouldn't send a Christmas card."

The general shook his head.

"You've got a very abrasive personality," he declared.

"I'm getting counseling," Malloy confided sarcastically. "Tell everybody to get ready. When I say GO, everyone GOES. Same time, full power, wide sweep. It's got to be like *gangbusters*. Do you read me, General?"

SEALs weren't quite like other people, the general reminded himself. Yes, the kind of dangerous work they did for the nation required a special sort of individual. Overall, they were a disciplined and effective outfit.

General Warner recognized all this.

And he still detested one arrogant ex-SEAL named Malloy.

"What's your phone number?" the NSA general asked. "I'll get back to you."

Half a minute later he was on a secure line speaking with an admiral in the Pentagon who could answer questions about the Navy's covert operations . . . if he wanted to.

"I'll spare you the dance, Tom," Warner announced. "I'm phoning about a threatening call I just got from a former SEAL up in New York. You know a guy named Malloy?"

Admiral Doherty dodged the question.

No effort . . . it was a reflex thing.

The U.S. Navy didn't talk about SEALs, past or present.

"What did he threaten?"

Warner told him.

"Is this guy sane?" he concluded.

"Most of the time, I hear. I don't know him myself, of course."

More reflex evasion.

"You think I should take him seriously?" the NSA general tested.

"From what I *hear*," Doherty answered carefully, "it might be a big mistake not to. You know what's going on up in New York with those bombings and it could get bloodier. Civilian casualties . . . terrible."

Warner realized that Doherty was being sensible.

Pentagon translation: he was covering his ass.

The admiral was surely taping the whole conversation. That was standard procedure at ONI, and at NSA also. Brigadier General Warner now had to protect himself too.

"We'll certainly do anything we can get authorized to do to prevent civilian casualties," he said righteously. "I'll talk to my boss immediately."

"Good thinking," Doherty responded.

For a moment the general wondered whether Doherty was being ironic. Hell, it didn't really matter.

"*All* the transmitters and ears?" he checked to get Doherty on tape confirming the whole thing again.

"I know it's a big commitment and unprecedented," the admiral began.

The bastard was still protecting himself, Warner thought.

"But I think it could be a necessary precaution," Doherty continued. "Give him everything. From what people say about this Malloy, you don't give him half . . . ever."

"And if this works . . ." Warner thought aloud.

"You'll be a hero," the admiral predicted.

The head of NSA had three stars and no fondness for surprises. He was going to hate this too, Warner brooded grimly.

"I'll see what I can do," he said noncommittally and cursed as he hung up the telephone.

A lot of people in the NSA and other defense agencies wouldn't like this at all. Ten thousand times more civilians would be furious . . . at least at first. He swore again.

Admiral Doherty was smiling. He knew that the situation in New York was critical and the threat was monstrous, but he couldn't help smiling for several seconds . . . in anticipation. He realized that the odds strongly favored the anonymous and skillful bombers who had the initiative, a small brutal team invisible in the New York's sea of millions of people.

The terrorists could attack anytime, anywhere.

That wasn't what made the admiral smile.

Malloy was preparing to stop them . . . in his own way.

It would be unconventional and dangerous and imaginative, the admiral thought. Those were the kinds of things that Jacob Malloy did best.

24

SERGEANT PETER Rocco of the Joint Task Force thought this was a very fine day. First his loving wife had given the opera-addicted New York City police officer a mint-condition reissue of Callas singing *La Traviata* for his birthday. Now this.

"Bingo!" he said as he put the two portraits on Malloy's desk.

One was the composite drawing of the man who'd bought the chemicals for the napalm. The other was a photo taken off the tapes of the federal Javits Building's security cameras.

"Without the mustache and the gray hair . . . it's *got* to be a wig," Rocco began.

He paused to let Malloy make the comparison.

"*Bingo*, right?" the detective asked.

"Bingo!" Malloy agreed and shook Rocco's hand.

The whole Task Force knew about the identification in three minutes. Police Commissioner Jefferson got the news and the two images barely sixty seconds later. Both portraits were immediately transmitted to every NYPD precinct, then to every FBI bureau from Washington to Providence.

Multiple copies were being duplicated within the hour for distribution to radio car crews and foot patrolmen all across this state and adjacent New Jersey and Connecticut. Officers at commercial airports, rail and bus terminals, and tunnels were also given the portraits with orders not to seize the man but follow him until Task Force experts could take over the surveillance.

Unfortunately Arnold—he'd bought the chemicals—was not going to or through any of those transportation facilities. He was staying indoors, working on the two detonation systems for the big charges. Gunther had told him to concentrate on that. The others had already picked out their battle positions, checked them for clear views, and tested escape routes again.

Just as they'd done after the bank robberies, the members of the Omar unit would all leave the area separately. Even though Gunther would collect the multimillion-dollar payment from the city, the others could wait to get their shares from him when they were outside American borders and jurisdiction. He'd already given each of them $300,000 of the cash taken at gunpoint from those Midwestern banks.

And four complete sets of perfectly forged identity papers.

With those documents, and another million dollars apiece from the Big Apple tribute that Gunther would smuggle out of the country, they'd be set and free. They'd be out of the game that hadn't really ended when the Wall came down in Berlin and the Soviet Union splintered. Lots of civilians naively thought it had and they were safe, but the professionals of Omar had no such illusion.

* * *

Some sixty miles south of Tampa, a federal undercover agent whom Malloy missed urgently certainly didn't think she was safe. She was in a blue Lexus sedan with over a million dollars worth of top Colombian white and two heavily armed criminals who had killed 14 people in the past twenty-seven months . . . and wouldn't hesitate to murder 14 or 114 more. The three men in the escort station wagon riding shotgun—actually a pair of Uzis and an M-10 that spat a thousand rounds a minute—had themselves slain nearly a score of men, women, and children.

And two guard dogs hacked up with machetes.

A considerable amount of cocaine was hidden inside the station wagon. The tight-as-a-drum gangsters in both vehicles were edgy and suspicious. Several of the nattily dressed hoodlums rode with hard smiles and one hand just inches from a concealed but instantly accessible weapon.

They'd have been even more tense if they knew of the very small radio beacons that a sophisticated Navaho employee of the DEA had attached under each vehicle to facilitate tracking. He'd wanted to hide listening devices inside the Lexus and the station wagon, but a cautious supervisor had pointed out the risks to the undercover agent and the whole operation if the hair-trigger thugs found the miniature transmitters.

So the sixteen DEA people patiently—well, *almost* patiently—followed and waited and worried about Joanne Velez. When the cocaine crew's vehicles stopped for the night at a better than average motel west of Kissimmee—where the culture was once Seminole but now profitably Disney World plus—the federal agents hoped she could continue to hold off the chief dope mover's sexual advances.

It hadn't been easy.

Her story that she was recovering from a botched abortion had worked so far . . . barely. But Raoul Santamarta was as lustful as he was cunning, and he was beginning to "joke" obscenely about oral sex.

She had forty hours—maybe less—depending on the traffic.

If she could deflect him that long—until they delivered the cocaine in New York—DEA agents could take the whole group from Florida into custody. Pretending to bust her with the others, her federal colleagues would seem to cart her off in handcuffs to a women's detention center.

She'd be out of range of his anger and weapons and sick machismo.

It would be touch and go until the last second.

Santamarta was known for his rages, and the brutal ways he responded to any perceived opposition. In the motel room, she finished combing her hair in front of the mirror. She had to look cool and confident, she thought as she put on her lipstick—a sexy shade of red she'd picked to go with her role as the sister of a big-time Dominican coke operator who was in jail.

The cover story—Russian intelligence professionals would say *legend*—was a good one. There actually was a Dominican narcotics merchant of that name in prison in Puerto Rico. He'd been in solitary confinement for three months, would stay there for at least another six weeks.

Now she saw something in the mirror that caught her attention. There on the screen of the television set was the mayor of New York City. He was talking to the television cameras—as mayors everywhere do. His voice continued even as the screen suddenly Blossomed with pictures of the body bags outside the devastated movie theater in Queens. She didn't see Jacob Malloy, but she didn't have to.

Her stomach knotted as she realized that he was there. The sons of bitches who did this would hit elsewhere, probably soon, and he'd be there too. That wasn't just probable. That was certain.

In a second she urgently hoped that he'd be careful.

She knew that he wouldn't.

Joanne Velez rechecked her makeup in the mirror, turned off the television set, and left to rejoin her homicidal traveling companions for dinner.

25

next morning.

When Briggs entered the Joint Task Force's suite with his coded plastic card Malloy was already in his own office. His brow was furrowed, his eyes red with fatigue.

"You're in early," the FBI supervisor noted, "and you've looked better."

"I've felt better too," Malloy responded. "Of course, you ought to see the other guy."

"What other guy?" Briggs asked as Malloy drained the coffee cup that had sat on the desk before him.

"The profoundly disturbed and fucking antisocial individual who's behind this horror show. I don't know who he is yet, Frank," Malloy admitted, "but I know he's going to look very terrible and very dead when I find him."

Briggs shook his head.

It was contrary to U.S. law and the principles of due process in FBI training to plan to execute anyone. That couldn't happen without a full and fair trial followed by intensely opinionated newspaper columns, loud and stupid oratory in talk show debates, appeals, and then books, television movies, sermons, and sometimes even litigation about legal fees.

That was the decent way to handle lawbreakers, but Jacob Malloy meant to ignore the rules. He had a reputation for "inappropriate improvising," the FBI inspector thought soberly. Before Briggs could continue the dialogue Malloy handed him a printout marked SECRET.

"Just came in from Hanrahan in Washington," Malloy said.

Hanrahan was the chief of the National Security Division of the Bureau. It covered both counterintelligence and antiterrorist operations. This printout was the classified weekly update sent to specialized FBI units across the country.

Briggs read it carefully.

Libyan agents in Texas, Chinese spies in California, Iraqi stooges trying to buy components for nerve gas, some strange leftover team of East Germans who'd been with Stasi and were reported to be still here, a white supremacist force stockpiling automatic weapons and body armor in the Rockies, a small number of pious and misguided immigrants from Palestine trying to buy and export explosives, a militia outfit in the Southwest checking out synagogues to burn.

"The usual stuff," Malloy said as Briggs folded the printout carefully for filing.

"Nothing about The Beirut Brigade," Briggs observed ruefully. "The only unusual thing is that Stasi bunch out there . . . God knows where."

"And She won't tell, so *we'll* have to track them down—if they really exist. No, someone else will go looking for them, Frank," the ex-SEAL corrected. "We've got psycho bombers to catch."

"You think they're crazy?"

"There are a *lot* of loonies out there," Malloy replied. "I'd say the idea of Stasi types wandering around here isn't sane at all, and these bombers we're after have to be around the bend to operate this way. It's wall-to-wall head cases out there, Frank, from sea to shining sea."

"Calm down, Jake."

"Does your mother know you're doing this kind of work?"

There was no point in talking to him now, the sensible FBI inspector decided.

"I'll see you later," Briggs dodged and walked quickly to his own office.

Malloy glanced at his notes, rejected the idea of another cup of the bitter coffee, and looked down at his pad again.

He studied the word he'd written at the top of the list.

Cash.

Underneath it was the phrase "double-sealed bags."

Beneath that—underlined and followed with a question mark—water.

Now Malloy turned his head to study the map on his cork board.

New York City, divided by water, largely framed by water.

Water? he wondered.

Then he thought of Gambelli, and picked up the phone.

He was on the secure line to the Pentagon in half a minute.

"Admiral Doherty's office," a cool crisp female voice said. The woman didn't sound like anybody's secretary, and she wasn't. She was a lieutenant, j.g., who'd been third in her class at Annapolis, very smart, very polished, an admiral's aide and good at it.

"This is Jacob Malloy. I'd like to talk with him—right now, please."

His tone was like steel but the *please* was different.

"May I tell him what this is about?" she asked automatically.

"His birthday," the ex-SEAL answered.

She thought he might be lying, but something in his voice also made her think the admiral might want to speak with this hard person. He was hard all right. That was one thing about this caller she knew for certain.

The admiral was on the line seconds later.

"Who is this?" he asked warily.

"Jacob Malloy. It's a common name."

Doherty laughed as he recognized the phrase.

"I've been expecting you to check in, Jake," he said. "I heard about your call to General Warner. I don't think you made a positive impression there."

"Happy birthday, Admiral."

"You're about nine weeks early."

"Then we can talk about something else," Malloy told him in a swift change of subject. "How about Andy Gambelli, SEAL Team Two?"

"What about him?" Doherty wondered.

"I want him to phone me . . . in the next forty-five minutes," Malloy answered and recited the Task Force's number.

"I don't know where he is."

"You can find him, so let's not waste any time, because I don't have any. He's not far from New York, and he's not alone. He's supposed to be through here tomorrow."

"And you want him today?" Doherty speculated.

"Yesterday would be better."

Malloy hadn't changed a bit, the admiral thought.

"Sounds like you're up to speed, Jake," Doherty complimented.

The ex-SEAL ignored the remark.

"And if he's got *stuff* with him, I want it," Malloy declared.

"What does that mean?"

"You know damn well, Admiral, and he will too."

Malloy was right, of course.

He was almost always right, and—like Gunther—a great problem solver. He was brilliant in planning and leading an impossible attack. Should have stayed in the Navy, Admiral Doherty thought.

"I'll find Gambelli," the Naval Intelligence officer pledged.

"Thanks, Admiral. And happy birthday!"

"You serious about that, Jake?"

"Would I lie to you?" Malloy replied and then there was a dial tone.

Some thirty-one minutes later Chief Petty Officer Andrew O. Gambelli was on Malloy's phone. His voice was unmistakable.

"I got a message to call," he said.

Malloy could hear that Gambelli was being cautious.

He had to establish his identity and authority immediately.

"This is Sting Ray," Malloy announced using his SEAL battle designation. "This is Sting Ray," he repeated, "and I'm ready to go."

For a moment Gambelli was stunned.

This was within the United States, and the SEALs had never fought here. "Ready to go" was the phrase that meant it was time to attack.

Who?

"Where are you? How soon can you get here?" Malloy pressed.

"We're on our way to West Point to give a classified training demo, interservice exercise. This thing in New York? Some kind of test?"

"*Saturday night*," Malloy answered bluntly.

The real thing.

That was the final battle cry before assault.

"Saturday night? Jeezus!" Gambelli reacted.

"Jeezus to the third power. I need you here by four o'clock."

Then Malloy told him where they'd meet.

"And bring all the toys," he ordered.

"We don't have everything with us," Gambelli warned.

"What you don't have you can steal," Malloy reminded him.

Sure, Gambelli thought as the conversation ended abruptly.

Saturday night? Anything goes.

Fast forward. Thirteen hours and ten minutes.

It was dark in New York. The sun was down, but Mirror was perspiring in a telephone booth near Lincoln Center. Mirror was holding the instrument, pretending to speak to maintain control of the situation. This way no one else could tie up the phone when Mirror needed to dial on schedule . . . in half a minute.

It wasn't the Manhattan temperature that was bothering the deep-cover agent.

It was the inescapable fact that something—more than one thing—was going wrong.

The operation wasn't supposed to get untidy like this.

Untidy? The damn thing was starting to unravel like some cheap Chinese sweater. Mirror had been working on a dozen projects for Moscow for years. This one had been simple and routine for a long time . . . from the beginning. Mirror had simply passed messages back and forth, routinely, professionally, following the standard Moscow rules.

They weren't working anymore. Mirror had to know why.

It wasn't neurotic curiosity.

It was something a lot healthier, Mirror's survival.

Time to call. Mirror hung up, dropped in a quarter, dialed.

In another phone booth down in Greenwich Village, Gunther picked up the instrument. He wasn't the least bit warm or tense. He was on the verge of the greatest triumph of his life. *Cool.* He thought it and felt it.

He was leaving all this with a lot of money, and no one to give him orders or meddle in his life. He was going to be free. Early retirement, the Americans would say. Screw the Americans, Gunther thought maliciously.

And the Russians . . . and everyone else.

He'd leave them all a fine going away present, the Omar leader told himself. Then he identified himself as Don. Last week the cover name had been Eddy. It changed twice a month.

Moscow rules.

Screw Moscow.

"Don," the familiar voice began, "I was talking to your aunt, and I hear somebody's been saying bad things about you in Washington. Somebody's spreading lies about you hanging out with some nasty people."

"What people?"

"Drunks," Mirror continued. "I think one of them had some strange Arab name. Funny, huh?"

Omar, Gunther computed.

Some U.S. agency knew that Omar existed.

What else did they know? Whatever it was, it wasn't funny.

"That's ridiculous," Gunther lied effortlessly. "I haven't had a drink in three or four months, and you can tell that to Aunt Bessie. Any idea where this stupid story came from?"

"I'm not sure. By the way, have you been in touch with your aunt?"

"Through you."

"Well I thought I was keeping the family up-to-date by my letters to Cousin Dave," Mirror began.

Cousin Dave was Colonel Belkov.

"But your aunt just asked me to find you. I don't think Dave bothered to tell her."

This didn't make any sense at all.

Belkov was the Control for Omar—a very experienced and reliable staff professional in Russia's foreign intelligence apparatus. If he was aware of where Omar was and what it was doing, it was impossible to believe that "Aunt Bessie"—head of Moscow's operations in North America—didn't.

"You'd better check on this with Dave," Gunther said slowly.

"That's what I thought, but your aunt tells me Dave's dead."

Dead?

Natural causes . . . or another of those bloody purges in Moscow no one heard of until some defector escaped years later?

Was something ugly happening again in Russia's spy services?

Time to get out, Gunther computed.

Whatever it was, he'd be out of range, out of the country, invisible, within forty-eight hours.

"I'm sorry to hear about Dave," Gunther said. "It's scary the way people go just like that."

Like *what*, Mirror wondered.

And how had the Americans—after all these years—discovered Omar? Belkov had never mentioned what the unit was doing, and the man Mirror was speaking to never gave the slightest hint. There were more important things than that to think about tonight, the deep-cover agent realized.

Who in Moscow had been lying?

Why? And was Mirror's own survival threatened now by Americans . . . or Russians?

"I'll see if I can find out more about Dave . . . and the rumor you're hanging out with bad companions," Mirror announced.

"Let me know next week," Gunther said in a voice that sounded a lot more cheerful than Mirror felt.

Why wasn't the Omar commander worried?

Mirror gave Gunther the time and phone number of the booth where the deep-cover agent would call him at ten minutes before noon on Sunday. Seconds later Gunther was walking toward Sixth Avenue. He was proud that he called the street that as die-hard New Yorkers did. The name had been *officially* changed to Avenue of the Americas over a quarter of a century earlier, but only visiting business types or tourists accepted the politically correct suck-up-to-our Latin American neighbors alteration.

Gunther knew this city as well as many natives.

Having studied it, he knew how and where to hurt it. He was ready to hurt it a lot tomorrow. Pleased by this thought, he took a bus north to within eight blocks of his bedroom. A cab would be, could be, a mistake. Taxi drivers might remember a face and a drop-off point. The people who guided the large buses were much less likely to recall any individual who didn't dress or behave strangely.

Descending from the bus without word or incident, Gunther made his way along side streets. When he paused for a traffic light, he noticed two large men reflected in a store window. They were ten steps back, and seemed to be eyeing him. When the light changed he continued, and they were still back there. He turned another corner. So did they.

There was a very good chance that they meant to rob him.

Mug him, in American street parlance.

The word that the FBI knew of Omar had bothered Gunther more than he'd communicated to the deep-cover agent. Beneath his exterior calm Gunther was annoyed, and he was really in the mood to kill somebody—to let off steam. One somebody or two? Two might be better.

Or at least smash them senseless.

He was quite expert at breaking bones and ruining faces, but this wasn't the night for it. If he beat them to death with his hands trained to crack bricks their corpses would pull police to the neighborhood.

That was not an acceptable option.

And if he shattered their wrists, arms, collarbones, kneecaps, they'd still be alive to talk about him. That wasn't practical either. Not now, for tomorrow's operation could not be put in hazard.

Whether they were muggers or not, they were lucky. Gunther had a great deal of experience in "losing" followers, and these two were no match at all. He reached his bedroom six minutes later, thought hungrily about the sexual skills of the loyal woman with the fake Southern accent, and forced himself to focus on packing his remaining clothes into a small suitcase.

He'd already sent most of his garments ahead, as unaccompanied baggage, to a hotel in Rio de Janeiro. He had a reservation there starting next week. Rio was the freewheeling heart of Brazil, which had excellent food, women to match, and no extradition treaty with the United States.

He scanned the four passports and perfect sets of forged identity papers. The rest of what he'd need waited in the office with the panoramic view of the Hudson River. Suddenly he felt the surge of lust again, decided not to masturbate, and took a shower.

He'd take another in the morning, he thought, before he drifted off to sleep.

He wanted to be clean and fit for the massacre ahead.

26

IT WAS one minute to seven in the morning.

Way downtown . . . New York's old City Hall building.

The ten million dollars had reached the mayor's office at a quarter to three on the previous afternoon. It came in an unmarked van that also held six armed bank guards. The vehicle pulled up at the back of the building where the scores of hyperthyroid media people waiting on the other side of City Hall couldn't see it. Though the journalists were well educated and good at their work, they couldn't look through the heavy old structure so they didn't notice the plainclothes cops emerge to load the canvas sacks onto a dolly and roll it inside.

There were eight of the plainclothes officers, and the commissioner of police. All of them and the mayor watched as the mayor's chief of staff and an accountant from the controller's office counted the money—it was in bundles of fifty-dollar bills—twice.

Ten million dollars . . . exactly. The mayor signed a receipt.

Then the chief of staff nodded, and a dozen large plastic bags were placed on the conference table. The terrorists had specified that this money be packed in four bags, but the cautious man from the municipal controller's office had brought extras just in case.

In case four wouldn't hold all the bills.

In case one of the bags was defective or ripped somehow.

In case of who knew what. Accountants are cautious people.

When the bundles of cash were carefully wedged into the large bags, they filled four almost completely. Each of the four was sealed with very strong masking tape. Then, as a precaution, they were sealed a second time with more of the tough industrial tape. The bags themselves were made of heavy duty green plastic that could support significant weight.

The commissioner nodded thoughtfully.

It might take more than one terrorist to carry all this.

How many of them would come to the pickup?

When would the terrorists communicate?

Commissioner Jefferson, Mayor Dowling, and the other public servants at City Hall heard from The Beirut Brigade several times in the next four hours. The first time was at five after eight.

The phone rang . . . the mayor's unlisted private line.

"Got the money?" a man's muffled voice asked.

Gunther assumed they were taping, would try to trace the call, then get a voiceprint to use against him. That was why he spoke swiftly and briefly and used an electronic voice mask he'd bought seven weeks earlier at a shop that sold such "novelty" items.

"We've got it," the mayor confirmed.

"Good. I'll tell you where and when later. Now I've got a little present for you. Right . . . NOW!"

It was a loud present.

Actually, two of them.

Radio-controlled bombs simultaneously blew up a stolen Ford parked next to a gas station near the Triboro Bridge, amputating two fuel pumps and starting a pair of fierce fires, and a station wagon across the street from a mental hospital in Brooklyn. It took forty minutes for a squadron of police to round up the injured and incoherent patients wandering through the neighborhood.

"They want us to know they can still do damage anywhere they choose," Briggs judged when the action reports reached the Task Force. "I'd say they're sending us a message, Jake."

"I'd say we got it."

He excused himself to telephone the general at the National Security Agency's headquarters south of Baltimore. Speaking with undisguised hostility, Warner confirmed that *everyone* was now ready to do what the ex-SEAL had demanded.

"They don't like it," the general said. "They don't like it a bit and I don't either."

"But it's on, right?"

"It's on when you give the word," Warner confirmed bitterly.

"You'll be the first to get it," Malloy promised.

He hung up and turned to the black woman standing beside him.

"You've got the bomb-sniffing dogs working the air and rail terminals?" he tested.

"We've brought in bowwows from as far as Philadelphia and Boston, Captain," she confirmed. "The hounds are on the job!"

He thanked her before he reached for the telephone again.

* * *

A dozen miles north of Wilmington, Raoul Santamarta was also making a call. He was at a roadside booth, twenty yards from the vehicles that carried the cocaine, his armed colleagues and Joanne Velez. They'd driven hard, taking turns behind the wheels so the delivery in New York would be on time.

The wholesalers in New York would be angry if they were late.

That might be bad for business.

Reputation was important in the coke trade, for profits, for customer relations, even for personal health.

Santamarta was speaking with a business associate in Florida, asking him to tell the people in New York that they'd be there by two o'clock and reporting that there'd been no problem on the journey.

"Everything's okay," he assured.

"I don't think so," Diego disagreed.

Then he switched to Spanish to inform Santamarta that he had a problem. A man had just come out of a prison in Puerto Rico where a *certain* woman's brother, *Dominican* brother, was doing time. It seemed that this brother had mentioned that his dear sister, his *only* sister, had died in Mexico, when she was run down by a drunken pimp.

The man in Florida didn't have to spell the rest of it out to Santamarta. The woman seated beside him in the car was a fake. It didn't really matter what kind of fake. Whether she was some sort of cop or just some greedy impostor out to score drugs or cash wasn't important.

She had fooled him, and that made Santamarta embarrassed.

She was a threat to his dignity, his income, his freedom.

That made him furious.

It was too bad he couldn't kill the bitch now, but that

would delay the delivery. This added to his rage. He controlled it.

"I'll talk to her after we see our friends in New York," Santamarta promised.

"Then you can give her a ticket home," the drug dealer in Florida suggested.

A ticket home . . . that meant dismember her *slowly*.

"Good idea," Santamarta agreed.

He returned to the Lexus, and the two vehicles started north again. He smiled at her, and she smiled back. It was clear that she didn't suspect that she was in mortal danger.

Neither did a DEA operative named MacIver.

He *knew* it.

A member of the Florida team working this case, he'd been picked because his Spanish was perfect. He was manning one of the wiretaps, taking the place of the big Navaho who was in a DEA car trailing this load of cocaine. MacIver called his supervisor at once, spoke to him for two minutes. Then MacIver dialed the number of the Navaho's cell phone.

"Scrambler," MacIver said bluntly.

"Go," Largo replied as he hit the button to jumble the sounds.

"They know she's phony," MacIver announced, "and they're going to burn her as soon as they drop the stuff in New York."

"My God! Have you told Washington?"

"Half a minute ago."

"How are they going to get her out?" Largo worried.

"I'm not sure . . . and they're not sure either."

"What the hell are you talking about?"

"I'm talking about *her*," MacIver answered, "and they're talking about all that coke and rolling up the whole distribution crew that's moving it in New York."

"You want to spell this out?" the Navaho asked.

"The D.C. wise men are thinking about what might be the best thing to do. Best for everyone, best for the nation."

"You know what my brother would say? My brother, the chief?"

"As I recall, you usually tell me that your brother would say *bullshit*," MacIver remembered.

"Exactly, and he's *very* smart."

"Runs in the family I guess. Listen, they're trying to figure out how we can grab her just a second after the shipment is delivered. They want it all, Thomas."

"They always do. Don't these big brains realize that if our timing isn't absolutely perfect she's *dead*."

"Calm down, Thomas."

"We've got to do something," the Navaho insisted.

"You just keep up the surveillance, and they'll let you know what to do. They're working on a plan right now," MacIver assured him.

"My brother's right," Thomas Largo insisted fiercely. "Tell them that."

After considering this suggestion for a full three seconds, MacIver concluded that it would not be in the best interest of Joanne Velez or Thomas Largo or MacIver himself—let alone the nation—to tell civil servants four grades higher than any of the three field agents that the Navaho had said *bullshit*.

It might distract them from their planning.

They were actually making a plan as the drug dealers and the DEA cars rolled north—a little faster than before. Santamarta was in a hurry to butcher her. The thoughtful planners in the District of Columbia were not aware of that. What they knew was that her only chance was if the DEA struck with complete surprise—overwhelming force.

So they ordered nine unmarked cars to take up positions near the Manhattan end of the Lincoln Tunnel. They'd follow the drug convoy to the point of delivery. An overhead helicopter would provide intelligence and serve as a mobile command post.

That ought to do it, the DEA supervisors thought sincerely.

Of course, no one could be sure.

There really wasn't much of an alternative, the executives in Washington told themselves. If the federal teams tried to rescue her now Santamarta and his thugs might kill her instantly. She certainly couldn't defend herself, for the role she was playing would be compromised if she carried any weapon.

This was probably her only chance, they said to each other. Even as they spoke, they all thought—they all knew—that it wasn't a very good one.

27

"**WHEN DO** you think they'll call?" Briggs asked tensely.

Malloy looked at his watch, saw it was nearly eleven.

"It's what they're going to say that bothers me," he replied. "These bastards have to pick up all this cash without getting caught or followed—and then get away with ten million dollars when an army of cops, local and federal, is looking for them. They know we'll be covering every way out of town, and they've planned for that."

"You're *sure* the mayor will deliver the money?" Briggs wondered.

"Reasonably sure, but are the terrorists sure? Can they be sure we're not trying to trap them? *Absolutely* sure? They've got just one shot to grab the cash and split."

"And we've got one shot to take them so we better get it right," the FBI inspector worried.

"They've got a plan, Frank," the ex-SEAL reasoned. "Got to be a complicated one. Well, tricky anyway. There'll be surprises . . . more than one. Nothing simple, I expect. Something clever with deceptions and distractions, bells and whistles, God knows what."

"My mother would say we should pray," Briggs said quietly.

"Always listen to your mother," Malloy responded. "You pray and I'll make a call."

He dialed the number of the cell phone on the hip of a petty officer in the U.S. Navy. The man had an automatic pistol on his other hip, a knife that could cut metal or throats, like the one in Malloy's office, and an HK-5 sub-machine gun across his knees.

This was the silenced model refined for covert operations.

It threw out nine-millimeter slugs . . . six hundred rounds a minute.

This Heckler and Koch killing tool was a triumph of fine German engineering, but Gambelli and the seven other SEALs with him didn't care who'd made the weapon every one of them carried. They weren't very interested in who the enemy was either. Right now they waited in this big truck, with their "toys" laid out before them, waiting for Gambelli to hear from Sting Ray.

They knew who Sting Ray was.

He was an expert—like them. He knew how to chop down a fucking tree with an HK-5 if he wanted to, and a lot of other things that involved the "toys." The SEALs were in combat uniforms, their wet suits and water gear stacked nearby.

"Team's set," Gambelli assured Malloy.

"It won't be long," said Sting Ray. "Truck okay?"

"Fine. It's a new thing," Gambelli observed. "We're used to boats, chariots, chutes. First time we're riding in on a goddam truck."

"Piece of cake," Malloy predicted.

"Piece of cake," the veteran SEAL petty officer concurred.

* * *

On the scenic green outskirts of Princeton, New Jersey, where her father was doing something chemical and wonderful at the famed Institute for Advanced Studies, a twenty-three-year-old graduate student and published poetess named Alison Levin was also thinking about cake. She was attached to the university not the Institute, and the baked goods she had in mind was a wedding cake. Her overachieving brother, youngest partner at a powerful and big-dollar law firm, was getting married.

Tonight.

In a remarkably grand and costly hotel in Manhattan.

He'd always been just a bit unconventional—with an I.Q. of 179—so he'd persuaded his fiancée that it would be stylish to wed on a weekday. She agreed, because her father was rich enough to indulge stylish and she hoped that the whole thing might make next Sunday's fat edition of the *New York Times*.

That's why Alison Levin was carefully putting into a garment bag the delightful and utterly up-to-date bridesmaid dress she'd change into at the hotel. Her parents were already there, and now Alison Levin, who'd written a very touching haiku for this special occasion, prepared to follow them in her appropriate "graduate student" vehicle. The green sedan was six years old and, like its owner, very peppy.

Gunther was feeling energized too.

He was about to take a lot of money and kill many Americans, prospects that made him smile as he looked down onto the Hudson River below.

His people had gone over their assignments again and again.

The equipment was all in position. Every piece had

been tested, even the special whistles. Gunther was par-
ticularly proud of these whistles. He knew that the city
police and FBI—possibly even special units of the military—would be mobilized and massed to do everything
they could think of to defeat him.

Think was the key word, Gunther exulted.

There was no way that the Americans could thwart the
whistles.

They wouldn't have any defenses against them because the Americans couldn't imagine that he'd use them.

He was far more cunning than all these dull Americans
put together, Gunther told himself proudly as he eyed a
Circle Line tour boat cruising by on its appointed round.
The fools he read about and saw on television—the
mayor and police commissioner and the people on that
Task Force—would have to accept his superiority in a few
hours.

When he'd be gone with the money.

When the body bags numbered in the hundreds and
the morgues were swamped.

Now he took out and studied the parking lot ticket for
a few seconds. Then he went down to the street and
walked to a telephone booth seven blocks away to make
the next call.

28

"NO TRICKS," Gunther said harshly as he began to speak to the mayor.

Then the commander of the long invisible Omar team grinned, for he was the one planning the tricks and the massacre. There was a point to the mass murder he'd planned so meticulously. It would provide a diversion exactly when he needed one.

"No tricks," the chief executive of New York City promised immediately.

That wasn't entirely true.

He was planning to have a rented civilian helicopter, a police chopper might be too easily spotted, follow the delivery from overhead. That would simply be a prudent precaution, Dowling told himself . . . and the police commissioner.

Jefferson wasn't the least bit enthusiastic.

"You really want to run the risk of spooking these people?" he'd asked bluntly.

"We'll just watch and see," Dowling had replied craftily. "Maybe we'll see something that could help us catch them later."

Now it was a dozen hours later.

The helicopter was ready to ascend, Jefferson was still opposed to the risky idea, and the leader of The Beirut Brigade was on the phone speaking swiftly.

He gave them the number of the parking receipt, location of the lot, description of the gray van.

"Cell phone in the glove compartment," Gunther announced. "I'll give you forty minutes to load the bags in the back, and drive it to 118th and Broadway."

The FBI's best team of tracers worked urgently, straining to pinpoint the phone and place where the call was originating.

"Okay . . . forty minutes from *now*," Gunther said and the line went dead.

The chief of the tracing experts shook his head.

Gunther had phoned using a sophisticated relay box . . . and the call had been too brief anyway.

"Another twenty-five seconds might have done it," Briggs said when the tracers reported.

"He knew that, Frank," Malloy replied. "This is one rabid bunny, Frank. Sick but he knows the game backward and forward . . . and sideways too. This isn't one of those sincere amateurs who blew up the damn World Trade Center. This guy's gone to school."

Briggs suddenly lit a cigarette.

He hadn't done that in nineteen weeks. Smoking was prohibited in the Task Force area, but he didn't care.

"*What* school?" he asked grimly.

"It wasn't Barnard, Frank," the ex-SEAL told him briskly. "I dated a gang of Barnard girls, and not one of them knew dick about covert operations techniques. Maybe one of those creative Montessori schools."

"Why are you so damned cheerful?" Briggs demanded.

"I'm an optimist," Malloy confessed, "and I see the future positively. I'm *really* looking forward to this guy's autopsy."

Briggs puffed on the cigarette.

He felt guilty, and that irritated him.

"You think there's just one guy?" he snapped.

"There are, beyond any doubt, more than one, and they're completely unjust," Malloy admitted. "I'll go to *all* their autopsies, okay?"

The secure phone on Briggs's desk interrupted.

He recognized the hard-edged executive voice of the able man in command of the FBI's local office. He was physically two floors below Briggs . . . and above him in rank.

"Just got a Priority Alert that I'm supposed to share with you, Frank," Donald C. Wicker announced. "This one is Ears Only."

A security classification even higher than Eyes Only.

No written message that might be read by the wrong people, who could be almost anyone.

From sources that would not be identified the Bureau's wary National Security Division had developed information that the Omar group had significant expertise in explosives. There was a definite possibility that the leftover Stasi unit might be carrying out the recent bombings in New York City.

The terminology was pure Bureau talk, but that didn't matter.

The source was the CIA—specifically the specialists so carefully interrogating Belkov—but the Bureau wasn't going into that. This was also unimportant to Briggs. The mystery—the anonymity of The Beirut Brigade—was fading. Of course, it might be too late.

Malloy wouldn't say that, Briggs thought.

He decided that he wouldn't either.

"Any names go with that?" he pressed positively.

"Not yet, but there's a second Ears Only, and *that* comes with a name. *Sort* of a name. Code name—this you don't even mention in your sleep—code name for a deep-cover agent of a major foreign power," Wicker said.

He was using his *important* voice, Briggs noticed.

Well, this was damned important.

"The name is Mirror, and the foreign power is Our Old Friends," Wicker confided.

"The Martians?"

"You said it, not me."

For years the KGB legions had been collectively described in U.S. intelligence circles as The Martians. The cloak-and-dagger professionals who worked in Moscow's renamed espionage agency had inherited that designation.

"Source says that Mirror is The Martians' top deep-cover here—the Number One mole—very good and plugged in big time. There's a chance that Mirror is somehow connected with this Omar outfit."

"You make any sense out of this Omar operation?" Briggs asked.

"I can't talk about it," Wicker answered.

He didn't know either, Briggs realized.

"You're sure this Mirror is for real?" he tested.

"Our friends in The Puzzle Palace," Wicker began with a standard Pentagon phrase for the National Security Agency, "have picked up *several* flash signals to Mirror."

Those were ultra-high-speed transmissions.

Only in recent months had the NSA acquired the very advanced and remarkably expensive gear to pick up those radio messages. The listening and decoding agency wasn't talking about this excellent new hardware because—like any government body in any country on any planet—NSA wasn't about to admit that it hadn't owned such technology previously.

And NSA never talked about anything anyway, Briggs recalled. The staff there probably didn't even say "Good Morning" to each other.

"From what Washington knows, or suspects, about Mirror," Wicker continued, "Mirror's mission is to provide information about both U.S. intelligence and counterintelligence activities. Mirror has been successful for at least several years."

"How successful?"

"*Significantly* successful," Wicker replied.

He didn't really know, and neither did the CIA debriefing experts trying to milk Belkov. The defector was holding back as much as he could . . . maneuvering with the cunning of a Hollywood agent as he tried to get the best deal for his client.

He wasn't just playing for additional points or a bigger percentage of the gross in this negotiation. They were dickering about his survival—and that of a number of other people who probably didn't understand that they were in very great danger.

"Do we know who or where Mirror is?" Briggs asked.

Wicker chose to address the second part of the question.

"Mirror, or Mirror's source, is *inside*."

"Inside what?" Briggs blurted.

"Be very careful," the SAC of the local FBI office told him. "The word is be *very* careful."

"He didn't say inside what," Briggs thought aloud moments later when he summarized the conversation to Malloy.

"Yes, he did," the ex-SEAL disagreed. "You know it, and so do I. *Inside* the great U.S. intelligence community. In one of our army of security agencies this mole—or the mole's source—is looking and listening and stealing on a regular basis."

Briggs nodded . . . barely.

"Could be Ames time all over again," Malloy warned.

The name of the traitor who'd sold U.S. secrets and sources in Moscow to the KGB for $4,600,000 chilled Briggs with acute concern. This time it might not be the FBI's federal rival, the CIA, that had been penetrated.

"That's why this is Ears Only," Malloy said. "None of those smart scared people in Washington wants to run the risk that somebody at the next desk or computer might warn Mirror we're looking for him."

"Or her," Briggs added. "Could be in any agency . . . anywhere."

"Maybe right in your National Security Division in D.C., or the Pentagon, maybe in Wicker's office downstairs or ours."

Briggs tensed and then scowled.

"That's not so funny, Jake," he said. "Not funny at all."

"It wasn't meant to be. I've got something else to say," Malloy announced, "and that's not funny either. I know that Mirror's a lot more important—in the fucking Big Picture, to both Washington and Moscow—than one crew of bombers in New York City."

Briggs nodded again as he waited for the rest of it.

"Assuming that this Omar group's doing the bombing," he said.

"Right, but this is *my* city, Frank, and these bastards are killing a lot of people in *my* city and I'm truly pissed that this Mirror might be able to tell Omar what we're up to and help these very capable and homicidal professionals get away," the ex-SEAL declared angrily.

He barely paused before he continued.

"How does that fucking grab you, Frank?" he challenged.

"I can understand that, Jake."

"And don't humor me because as my good friend, Frank Briggs, just said, there's nothing humorous about this."

He was venting, Briggs realized. Briggs had learned about venting in the applied psychology course, and he'd heard that Jewish people had tempers. Of course, Malloy was only half Jewish and clearly had a temper and a half.

"Go figure," Malloy would have said.

Briggs said something else.

"Nothing humorous. I'm with you all the way on this, Jake," he declared honestly. "I live here too, and I'm totally committed to protecting New Yorkers from terrorists. That's our primary assignment. We take out the bombers *first*. Then we'll do what we can about Mirror, who really belongs to counterintelligence anyway. *Deal?*"

"*Deal*," Malloy agreed. "Now let's bust those bombers."

They were calling in status reports from teams they'd put in possible major targets—big places such as Radio City Music Hall and other theaters, Yankee Stadium and other arenas where there'd be sporting events today, the vast convention and exhibit space at the *other* Javits Building over on the river—when FBI agent Donna Olsen interrupted.

She'd been covering the tie-line to the mayor's office.

"They're rolling," she reported. "Van with the cash just started north, and the beacon in the trunk's working. Our backup cars are following two blocks behind . . . just in case."

They weren't supposed to intervene or try to seize the bombers when the money was passed. The Task Force people were to hang back—out of sight and not threatening—but just about close enough to help if something went wrong in the delivery.

Anything could go wrong.

Everything could go wrong.

This whole setup was wrong, Malloy thought, but he didn't know what he could or should do about it . . . in the next hour. Maybe two. He was sure that was all the time they had.

"Chopper reports they've crossed Twenty-third Street," she announced.

There were seven members of the Joint Task Force in Briggs's office now, gathered to hear the updates.

The unmarked tail cars were maintaining radio silence, and the civilian helicopter that the police were using was calling in only intermittently . . . and on a frequency unlikely to be monitored because it was reserved for fire boats.

Steady progress up Broadway.

Lincoln Center . . . Eighty-sixth Street . . . now 110th.

"Almost there," Briggs said, "and they're on schedule."

The ex-SEAL shook his head.

"What's the matter?" Briggs asked.

"I'm waiting for the tricks. There are going to be tricks, you know," Malloy predicted.

"Maybe not," Briggs replied hopefully. "It could go off clean. Things sometimes do, Jake."

Malloy shook his head again.

"This isn't a Disney number, Frank," he declared. "This is a goddam horror show with real monsters . . . not actors."

116th Street. Malloy instantly visualized the buildings

of Columbia University flanking Broadway, Barnard College on the left closer to the river, on the right dormitories for male students, there was the massive iron gate at the entrance to the main campus.

117th . . . 118th . . . the rendezvous point.

Following instructions, the driver of the van stopped and took the cell phone from the glove compartment.

The minutes went by slowly.

"Nothing's happening," the man overhead with the powerful binoculars said. "I can see it all clearly . . . nothing."

The observer in the helicopter was wrong.

Something was happening.

Gunther was looking up from a vantage point nearby, looking left and right, and up.

And Gunther saw the rotorcraft.

He recognized it immediately as a threat or at least a breach of his terms. He wasn't that surprised. He hadn't really expected them to stick to the agreed procedures. He certainly felt no reason to do so. He never had, and he never would.

And he was ready for something like this.

What's more, it told him he certainly had a right to punish them for this dishonorable behavior. He'd warned them that the streets would run red. Not yet though. He had to collect the money first.

Gunther picked up his own cell phone.

He looked around to see if anyone who might be a policeman might be watching him. Then he dialed the number of the instrument he'd left in the glove compartment of the van.

29

CAT AND mouse.

He'd show them.

Gunther told the policeman behind the wheel of the van to drive across the Brooklyn Bridge, then on to an industrial area he'd scouted weeks ago.

"That's not *it*," Malloy reasoned when word reached the Task Force. "He's playing games."

"What makes you think so?" Briggs wondered.

"Because there's simply no easy way out of there . . . and he doesn't do anything simple anyway. He's moving us around like pieces on a chessboard. I think he's setting something up—the next damn move."

Malloy didn't know for certain. This was his sense of the enemy, and Malloy's own gut instinct.

His gut was right. Gunther was buying time. He had to make sure that his people on both sides of the Hudson were in position—with all equipment in perfect working order—ready to strike. As he ran through his checklist again, he was glad he'd raised the price from his first thought of eight million dollars to ten million. The idiot

Americans deserved this extra punishment, and he'd enjoy the additional cash.

He wouldn't even mention it to the others.

It would all be his. He'd made it possible. The others were just weapons he used to accomplish his goals. Now he was almost *there*. He'd planned it out realistically. He'd always known that the Americans probably wouldn't deliver the money except under both extreme and immediate duress.

Okay. Immediate was now.

The duress he'd prepared for them was terrible and irresistible . . . that stupid helicopter couldn't stop him.

Next step. New directions to the van driver: back over the East River to the World Trade Center in lower Manhattan near the tip of the island. Traffic in the busy streets of the financial area moved slowly.

Farther south on a multilane highway in New Jersey, the cars and vans and station wagons were flowing more rapidly. The stream of vehicles rolling north included the sedan carrying half the cocaine shipment, Raoul Santamarta, and the undercover federal agent. Looking forward to the prospect of butchering her in seventy or eighty minutes, he glanced over at Joanne Velez for a few seconds and grinned. Unaware of his plan but not trusting this homicidal hoodlum at all, she automatically responded with a better-than-fair and totally false smile.

The DEA followers trailed about 110 yards behind. There was a highly principled, intelligent, and angry Navaho in the first federal car. He was making his fifth call on his cellular phone to a senior DEA official in the District of Columbia.

"You can't let them kill her," Largo repeated. "We owe her. You've *got* to stop them."

"We're working on a plan," the supervisor assured him.

"No, you're planning on grabbing the coke—the big bust—ripping up the whole network. Think about *her*!"

"That's just what the New York office is doing right this minute. They're going to run the whole thing."

Then the man in Washington recited the number of the "control" officer in DEA's headquarters in Manhattan. Largo was speaking with a supervisor there seconds later. Three cars back, Alison Levin was singing along with an old Madonna song sounding boldly from the radio of her car—even more aged than Madonna's sassy hit of yesteryear. The head of the young poetess bobbed to the rhythm.

She heard a horn, nearby and behind her. She glanced at her rearview mirror and recognized her favorite aunt's discreet blue Seville behind her. Aunt Dorothy was on her way to the wedding too, and the Seville undoubtedly carried a garment bag with some low-key but chic dress she'd bought with her earnings as a successful stockbroker.

Alison Levin wondered for a few moments what color her aunt's dress might be. Then she waved to acknowledge Dorothy and the Seville. She caught a glimpse of some movement off to her right. There was a snappy fire-engine red sports car in the next lane. The good-looking man behind the wheel, somewhere in his thirties, had seen her wave, and he was waving back as if he thought she'd gestured to him.

Or was he simply joking?

Might be some kind of nut. There were all sorts of weirdos on the roads these days, the poetess reminded herself. Too bad. He had a great face, and the red sports car said something positive.

No, she decided.

She was a with-it free spirit and not a stick-in-the mud, but she'd better ignore this fellow and his lively looking car.

There was the turnoff for New York. She steered her sedan to leave the wide highway, and her aunt followed. So did the man in the red sports car. The traffic was flowing steadily and swiftly. Unless something went wrong, she'd be at the tunnel in less than twenty minutes, at the hotel not much more than fifteen minutes later.

Now back on the eighth floor of a building on the Manhattan side of the Hudson, Gunther phoned Arnold who was waiting four blocks south.

"It's time," the Omar commander said.

"I'm on my way."

Then Gunther spoke to the woman with the fake Southern accent and excellent sexual techniques. She and her teammate were in position a mile from the New Jersey entrance to the third tube of the Lincoln Tunnel, the youngest of the trio under the Hudson to mid-Manhattan.

Howard was also on the New Jersey side of the wide river, tense but confident behind the wheel of a station wagon half-filled with boxes. Boxes more than half-filled with explosives—each of Arnold's carefully constructed bombs equipped with both a radio-controlled detonator and another one.

The other one was the backup . . . the surprise.

"Check your watch," Gunther ordered. "You know how long it takes to drive through the tunnel. Pace yourself. I'll meet you in eighteen minutes . . . *mark*."

Next Gunther recounted the cartons . . . sixteen sturdy cardboard containers with the word "catalogues" stamped on two sides, the rolls of industrial tape, and the labels addressed to one of his fictitious identities. Each with the capacity of four shoe boxes, the cartons would soon be waiting for him at General Delivery in post offices in Fort Lauderdale, Miami, San Juan, Puerto Rico, and Charlotte Amalie in the Virgin Islands.

The *U.S.* Virgin Islands.

Shipped inside the U.S. postal system, the cartons would not be searched. Gunther would send them out from the freight forwarding outfit on the street floor of this building. That firm was an important reason for choosing to rent an office here. The freight company would move nine million dollars. Gunther would have the security of transporting the other million himself in a pair of money pouches and hidden compartments in his baggage.

It wouldn't be searched either—not going within the U.S. Customs perimeter. He'd figured out how to move the money abroad later, slowly, inconspicuously. Within five or six months he'd have it all in another country.

Gunther put on his bulletproof vest, covered it with a gray workman's shirt, and picked up the loosely wrapped package that contained his compact M-10 submachine gun and seven magazines for it. The cell phone was clipped to his belt.

He phoned the money van once more. This time he directed the driver to proceed north to the parking lot of The Cloisters, the grand and medieval branch of the Metropolitan Museum of Art up above Washington Heights. Now Gunther reached for the shoulder bag that housed the remote control, slipped the strap over his shoulder.

He left the office, double-locked the door behind him.

You couldn't be too cautious in this city.

Everybody said there were lots of thieves here.

It was difficult to tell who might be a criminal, he thought.

Gunther himself looked like an ordinary peaceful citizen, the Omar leader reflected, but he himself was on his way to steal ten million dollars and kill six hundred people. Give or take a hundred . . . it didn't matter much in the big scheme of things.

Gunther was almost smiling as he entered the elevator to descend to the street. He had enough control not to, of course. If you did, people might wonder why you were smiling. They'd be more likely to remember you, and Gunther wasn't about to run that unnecessary risk. He might decide that it would be safer to kill such a person to avoid the chance of being identified.

Gunther didn't want to kill anyone now.

That would come later, he thought as he left the building and made his way to the parking lot across the street.

30

EIGHT MINUTES later, astride the powerful motorcycle, halted on a side street near Pennsylvania Station, Gunther phoned new orders to the van driver.

South to Grant's Tomb . . . 122nd Street and Riverside Drive.

Now Gunther studied his wristwatch before he called the mayor again.

"Game's over," the Omar commander said bluntly. "You and your damned chopper are putting a lot of lives in immediate danger."

"What are you talking about?"

"You'll find out in just about *four* minutes," Gunther threatened and once more amputated the conversation before the call could be traced.

He guided the big bike north, saw the stolen black car two blocks from the tunnel where Arnold had parked it. Gunther looked at his watch again.

Fifty seconds . . . it was going to work . . . forty seconds.

At that moment the two vehicles with the drug dealers and Joanne Velez entered the New Jersey mouth of the tunnel. A football field behind her rolled the pair of DEA "tail" cars, with Alison Levin's worn sedan and her favorite aunt's blue Seville cruising right behind the unmarked federal Ford and DEA's Dodge station wagon. The red sports car advanced in the next lane.

"Going into the tunnel," the Navaho reported tensely to the "control" officer now running the operation from DEA's New York headquarters. "When do we move?"

"We're getting units into position, Chief," the supervisor replied.

Largo frowned. The use of "Chief" still bothered him, but the uncertainty of the situation troubled him a lot more. He would have felt much worse if he knew that one of the Omar team was half the tunnel ahead of him in a rolling bomb.

Twenty seconds . . . ten.

Gunther raised the remote control and pressed the button.

The dynamite in the car Arnold had parked exploded.

The sound of the blast boomed over the noise of the Big Apple's traffic. It struck like a club, pulling the instant attention of everyone within blocks. That included the people in vehicles and the uniformed metropolitan employees at the mouth of the Lincoln Tunnel two blocks away.

The plastic bags filled with high-octane gasoline that Arnold had placed in the trunk ripped open, igniting the fuel and splattering it for over fifty yards. Suddenly there were a dozen small fires and acrid columns of black smoke curled skyward.

This attack wasn't to kill or even to frighten.

It was a diversion . . . and it worked.

The Port Authority employees on duty at the tunnel exit turned and started to run toward Gunther's diversion. Seconds later Scott began slowing his sedan just ninety yards inside the third tube. Puzzled and annoyed, the impatient drivers behind him trod on their brake pedals. They'd expected to accelerate at this point, and didn't understand why the opposite was happening.

Now Gunther was racing toward the mouth of the third tube.

Just before Scott reached that point, he reduced his speed even further . . . and those behind him had to do that too. Right at the exit he suddenly slammed on the brakes, twisted the steering wheel, and spun the wagon so it effectively blocked the exit. Two of the vehicles following him rocked as their drivers swore . . . one sedan banging into another in a classic rear-end collision.

Horns blew. Women held children as cars whipsawed to a stop.

Domino effect . . . exactly as Gunther anticipated.

Vehicle after vehicle shuddered to a halt. The drivers didn't shudder or halt. Outraged and frightened, they kept yelling and cursing.

Scott pulled the string that let the spring device raise the sign in the rear window. He pulled up the one inside the windshield himself. Next he carefully set off the grenade to fill the car with blinding nauseous gas. The windows were closed as he jumped out and locked the door.

He ran some dozen yards away from the tunnel.

That was when Gunther swept up on the motorcycle. Scott climbed aboard behind him as they'd rehearsed, and the big bike roared off past the startled Port Authority personnel. They were totally and understandably surprised by all this. They were well trained and knew their jobs, but no one had tried to hijack the Lincoln Tunnel before.

The Port Authority people on the New Jersey end of the third tube were similarly stunned when Gunther's female agent and sexual collaborator—servant would sound vulgar—followed Scott's ritual precisely and plugged up that entrance. She knew Gunther's schedule . . . and how nasty he could be and would be to anyone who was late.

She swung her explosives-packed vehicle out of line, raced ahead at exactly the minute specified, and intimidated her way into the opening. At just that moment, another of Arnold's charges three hundred yards away was set off by remote control. The Omar agent who did that repeated what Gunther had done less than forty seconds earlier. Now Casey did what he'd been told.

The man on the motorcycle was right there for her as this loud attention-grabbing diversion distracted the Port Authority staff. The ex-Stasi agent who'd never be Doris but played the Southern belle so deftly was on his powerful machine before any civil servant could react.

The Omar operatives were gone with a roar.

Now both ends of the third tube were sealed.

Drivers whose vehicles were within sight of the four-wheeled bombs that Gunther had left got out and walked uncertainly to see what was going on.

What the *hell* was going on?

Several preferred what the *fuck* was going on . . . and they generously shared this with anyone within earshot.

They were more than angry when they read the signs.

After that they were very frightened.

News broadcasts, daily papers, all the instant media had reported on the terrorist group whose name was on these signs.

The Beirut Brigade killed people in large numbers.

It was immediately clear that everyone in this tube of

the Lincoln Tunnel was in great danger. Even approaching the bomb cars might cause an explosion.

Stunning shock . . . then something else. From both ends of the familiar underwater passageway fear rolled car by car, yard by yard, human by human. It seemed to move like a flash tidal wave, startling and irresistible. Horns blowing, louder, building. People were shouting and crying . . . accusing and denying . . . some screaming, others groaning. A number looked puzzled because they thought this made no sense.

They were, of course, right.

That didn't help.

Religious men and women, children too, began to pray. A few people told themselves it must be a joke, or part of a movie filming, or perhaps a test. A number of less foolish individuals and several other persons with asthma started gasping in reflex psychosomatic response.

The noise level in the tunnel rose with the emotions.

Suddenly there was an odd silence. For a few moments the only sound was a baby crying. As if it was contagious, a dozen adults began to weep. The vice president of a mortgage company began to shake, and a famously tough football coach stuck his head out of his station wagon window as he prepared to vomit.

The sick and the shouters, the silent and those praying, all faced the fact that every one of them could be dead in a matter of minutes, hours at the most. Could they hold out that long? Would the air supply end, the river run in, explosions crush them and obliterate the third tube of the Lincoln Tunnel?

Why had this happened here and now . . . to them?

Was anyone outside doing *anything* to save them?

Anger joined fear under the Hudson River, and it stayed.

31

"**HIGH EXPLOSIVES** . . . do not touch . . . extreme danger.' That's what the damn signs say," Jefferson told Malloy over the direct line established yesterday.

"Uh-huh. Not bad."

"What do you mean *not bad?*" the commissioner demanded. "This professional estimate doesn't help at all, Jake. You've got to give me more than *that.*"

"I said he'd do some number, and the son of a bitch did," Malloy replied. "Now let's take his trick apart. He's not a one-trick creep, you know. This guy's a star. You say there's some kind of gas or smoke inside both vehicles?"

"That's what the Port Authority people say . . . and so do our cops. We've got eight radio units and an EMS truck at our end," Jefferson reported, "and New Jersey has thirty-two state police and a SWAT team covering their side."

"He's got everybody scared . . . but he doesn't have the money," the ex-SEAL reasoned aloud. "Where's the van?"

"Up at Grant's Tomb on Riverside Drive."

"It's a matter of time now," Malloy said. "He's got

something to do—collect the cash and bug out—and I've got something to do. Take down his whole gang. Who goes first?"

"We've got to get those people out of the tunnel," Jefferson insisted.

Malloy heard a telephone ringing near the commissioner.

"He's on the mayor's private line," Jefferson whispered.

"Put it on speaker," Malloy urged.

"Do exactly what I say . . . or they're all dead," Gunther ordered.

Malloy could hear him quite clearly.

"I can do it in a second," Gunther warned.

Radio-controlled detonators, the ex-SEAL computed silently.

"And tell those morons to keep their hands off the cars. The charges have hair triggers. Here's where you deliver the money . . . within twenty minutes. Your last chance—that's it."

Then he instructed the mayor where the van should go, a pier on the Hudson River in the fifties.

The whole conversation took just under twenty-five seconds.

"What do you think, Jake?" Jefferson asked as soon as it ended.

"He didn't say anything about pulling off the helicopter," Malloy analyzed. "He's not concerned about it anymore. Why? What's he got up his sleeve?"

"We've got to send the van, Jake," the commissioner said.

"And if he can detonate in a second, he has to know *what* second. He has to have a reason."

"For God's sake, Jake, don't do anything to give him one," the tense commissioner ordered.

When Jefferson hung up the telephone, Malloy paused for several moments to consider . . . to compute . . . to remember. As he put down the phone he held he visualized the schematic chart the Task Force had scanned in a survey of possible targets.

Malloy dialed the number of Gambelli's phone.

"This is Sting Ray. After this it's all secure-frequency radio," Malloy said. "The bad guys might be listening to phone talk."

"Yes, sir."

"You got a suit and toys for me?"

"Damned right, sir. And we're ready to go."

"Crank up the truck, and meet me just above where the *Intrepid*'s parked. Five minutes ago . . . got it?"

"On our way, Sting Ray."

Briggs recognized the look in Malloy's eyes five seconds later as he stood up, checked the Glock in its holster.

"Got an idea, Jake?" the FBI inspector asked.

"More like a plan, a plan and a half if you include a call to NSA when I come out."

Malloy paused, swiftly wrote the phone number and the name Warner on a memo pad.

"He's a general," Malloy told Briggs.

"What do I say to this general when you come out?"

"Tell him I asked you to call because I'm busy—and I want full power *right now*. Say it's gangbusters time."

Malloy started for the door.

"You really going in, Jake?"

Malloy nodded, explained his plan.

"If it doesn't work, just throw the bits in the river," he concluded.

"There may not be any bits, just hamburger," Briggs warned.

"You don't like my plan?"

"I hate it," Briggs said vehemently. "It's very clever . . . and I absolutely hate it."

"You got a better one? It's the only one I've got, Frank."

Briggs shook his head, twice.

"If it'll make you feel any better, I hate it too," Malloy confessed and hurried to meet the truck waiting on the river's edge sixty yards above the massive World War II aircraft carrier that was now a floating museum and memorial.

Malloy gave the SEALs orders as he stripped, changed into a wet suit. He spoke swiftly, succinctly.

"I want three operators with full weapons and a radio location scanner to get over to the Jersey side of the river. Not from here, these pricks may be watching. I'm just about sure they're watching both ends of the tunnel."

"Got it, sir."

"I don't care how you make it to Jersey. Commandeer a boat or steal one at gunpoint up at the Seventy-ninth Street Marina," Malloy continued. "On the Jersey side grab wheels—maybe a bus or something civilian—and roll down near the mouth of the tunnel. Don't show yourselves. These hoods may be looking for you."

"Okay to ask who they are, or is it classified, sir?"

"It's classified and these bastards are Krauts, pros from East Germany."

The chief petty officer looked puzzled.

"There is no East Germany, sir. It doesn't make any sense."

"I've been thinking the same thing for years," Malloy agreed. "Now, Chief, I need you to take the other three operators and set up, very inconspicuously, near the Manhattan end of the tunnel. You got the sniper gun?"

"Just got a Barrett .50-caliber, shoots through bullet-

proof glass, accurate with a good scope up to a fuckin'
mile—if you'll pardon my language, sir."

"I grant all of you full absolution," Malloy assured them.

"Now when we find these Krauts, sir?"

"These are bad Krauts, not good ones. Lots of good
ones, they write great music. Okay, when you find these
guys you stop them and make sure they don't get away,"
the NYPD captain told the SEALs. "I don't want any
high-speed chases down the goddam ten-lane Jersey
Turnpike. Somebody could get hurt, volunteers going to
cheer up people in hospitals. Girls' soccer teams."

"Force estimate?" the chief petty officer asked.

"How many bad guys?" Malloy translated. "No idea.
If it's no bother, bring me one for a souvenir."

The unspoken message was immediately understood.

One for interrogation and information.

The others wouldn't be needed so it wasn't necessary
to take risks . . . or prisoners.

Malloy pointed to a weapons sack, bulging, waterproof.

"Toys, sir," Gambelli confirmed and handed him a
small tank of oxygen.

"Big enough, sir?"

"I hope so," Malloy replied.

They all descended from the large truck, looking utterly incongruous in their strange gear in midtown
Manhattan.

"I've got one more call to make before I splash," Malloy said and reached for Gambelli's phone.

"Couple of things, Frank," he told Briggs twenty seconds later. "First, ask Carla to have a pair of bomb dogs
on duty at each end of the tunnel. They don't go near the
cars . . . yet. Second, I need you to get to the Port Authority czars and tell them they've got to turn the damn

air pumps off in thirteen minutes ... and keep them off for another two. Make it two and a half. Just a second."

He turned to Gambelli.

"Climbing rope and grapnel?" Malloy asked.

"I'll get it," the petty officer promised and hurried back into the truck.

"Third, alert Jefferson and our people that I'm sending in some real rough characters to help on both ends."

The SEALS grinned proudly.

"Full cooperation for these guys, Frank. They get things done," Malloy said.

"Who are they?"

"They're feds like you, Frank. Salt of the earth, the sea too."

"You've brought in SEALs?" Briggs guessed.

"The tunnel's interstate, Frank. Federal jurisdiction. National emergency. This is the Varsity, Frank, and we need the Varsity. Any news at your end?"

Briggs hesitated.

"That bad, huh? Let's have it," Malloy pressed.

"You know a man named Harry Holland?"

"He's a pistol at DEA, my lady's supervisor. Is she okay?"

"For the moment. I'm sorry, Jake. Holland's been getting calls from an agent tailing two vehicles loaded with coke up from Florida."

"How bad is this?"

"It isn't very good," the FBI inspector said. "Your lady's in one of the cars, and they know she's federal. They mean to kill her."

"Where's the car?"

"This is even worse. It's caught in the tunnel. So are two cars full of DEA agents. One of them's an Indian who called in."

Malloy thought about his Uncle Max.

"I've got an uncle who used to say if they deal you lemons you make lemonade," he told Briggs.

"What does that mean?"

"It means that the situation is horrible and somebody's got to do something about it, and I guess I'm elected."

"You're going to make lemonade?"

"Shit, no," Malloy replied. "I'm going to turn this mess into something positive. I'm going to use what you've just told me, and you're going to help. You and this Indian. Apache?"

"Navaho. His brother's a chief."

"Great. Here's what you do. Anytime in the next ninety seconds would be all right."

The ex-SEAL spelled it out rapidly.

"You're handling this very well, Jake," Briggs told him when the plan was spelled out fully. "You sound okay."

He heard Malloy sigh.

"I'm fucking terrible, Frank," the ex-SEAL said truthfully and turned to accept the climbing rope and grapnel Gambelli was offering him. Then he attached the oxygen tank.

"Ready?" he asked.

The SEALs replied in unison.

"Ready to go."

It all rushed back to Malloy in a wave.

For the moment it felt as if he'd never left.

"Saturday night!" he said.

"Saturday night!" they answered boldly.

Then they went forward to attack the enemy.

The battle was joined. The war—this special war—had begun.

32

THE POLICEMAN in the van slowed down, aware that he could not make a mistake. He had to find the Hudson River pier that the terrorist on the phone had specified, and he must not be late.

No, that wasn't it.

There—the next one—that was the destination the harsh-voiced man from The Beirut Brigade had specified. The driver couldn't help wonder whether this was the *final* destination where the delivery would be consummated . . . or would the phone ring again with new directions.

Would the transfer go peacefully . . . or would they kill him?

They'd put a lot of people in coffins, the driver thought as he slowly turned off onto the old pier. The bulletproof vest he was wearing wouldn't protect him from these expert killers, he realized. They could murder him in a dozen ways.

His stomach was in a knot, his throat arid.

There might even be some damn kind of bomb in this van. He hadn't had the time—or the orders from the commissioner—to search the vehicle before he boarded it at the parking lot. Why hadn't someone thought about a bomb? Why hadn't he had the common sense to check for one?

Shit.

The telephone rang again.

"You're going to meet two men in green coveralls. Don't look at their faces, or they'll shoot you. Got that?"

"Got it," the perspiring driver answered immediately.

"Move the van halfway down the pier."

The policeman looked ahead, saw no other vehicle. This pier must be one the city was refurbishing. He wondered where the men in the coveralls were, how they'd make their getaway with the bags of money.

He obeyed the instructions.

"I'm there," he reported to his invisible master.

"Leave the motor running. Get out of the van, ten steps to the right, and face south, your back to the van. Then hit the deck, facedown on the pier."

They would come roaring up on a motorbike, the policeman reasoned as he stepped from his vehicle. The two men in green coveralls would jump into his van, and drive away. They weren't going to shift the money to another truck or car here, or now. They must have other wheels waiting with a driver a few blocks away.

But how would they lose the helicopter?

The cop descending from the van decided that wasn't his business. He took ten steps from his vehicle, faced south, and lay down prone on the pier. He couldn't look at the van, but he could listen. There was no sound of any motorcycle or even footsteps.

He heard another noise that he recognized immediately.

The van was moving forward, picking up speed.

It was heading the wrong way. The sound was moving

toward the river. The policeman was so startled he couldn't help rolling over and staring at his vehicle. The door beside the steering wheel was still open. He couldn't see who was driving. The van was going too fast.

Even if it was moving at a tenth of that speed he wouldn't see a driver in green coveralls, or any other garb. There was no one behind the wheel. There hadn't been any mechanical malfunction either.

The van was operating perfectly under Gunther's control.

Radio control.

The policeman suddenly found himself shouting as the vehicle charged toward the end of the pier. He was still yelling at the top of his lungs when it hurtled off the pier and plunged into the Hudson River.

Forty seconds.

Fifty at most.

In less than a minute the van carrying ten million dollars in double-sealed heavy-duty plastic bags was beneath the surface of the Hudson, sinking inexorably to the bottom.

Less than four hundred yards away Malloy was standing on another pier when a police radio car pulled up beside him. The driver said nothing, but the man next to him spoke.

"Captain Malloy?"

"Yes. You got them?"

"Full set. The best. Can I ask what you need them for?"

"You certainly can," Malloy replied and held out his hand.

The sergeant beside the driver—Sergeant Roger Lehecka of the NYPD's burglary unit—was a very intelligent career policeman and a practical one. He was well aware that sergeants who hoped for promotions and pensions would be imprudent to press a captain to answer a question if the superior officer didn't want to.

In this case Malloy wanted to be courteous and candid as his parents had raised him to be, but he didn't have the time. There was a brilliant psychopath—maybe several of them—with bombs and hundreds of people who didn't have much time either. When the sergeant gave him the kit, Malloy said just one word.

"Thanks."

Then he moved to the edge of the river. He put on his face mask. Holding the kit with one hand and balancing the weight of the sack of "toys" attached to the strap around his neck, he submerged in the Hudson. He didn't know that the van with the money was also beneath the surface, less than four hundred yards away.

What he did know was that he had to swim swiftly and hope that the river's current would help him get to the place where he had to be in eleven minutes. If he wasn't there by then, there was an excellent chance that all the people in the third tube of the Lincoln Tunnel would die.

Including Joanne Velez.

And probably Jacob Malloy too.

33

THERE WAS terror in the third tube.

Many kinds—silent and sobbing, swearing and pious praying, clutching loved ones and arguing bitterly, some fainting, a lot of accusing, a heart attack, and a great deal of that fine American sport, blaming the government.

In the gut-grabbing panic some externally strong men tried to hide, a dozen or so people in various tax brackets alleged that the media were to blame for something—the thing that encouraged "loonies and lefties" to do this sort of disgraceful thing to hardworking individuals who paid their taxes and often went to places of worship affiliated with organized religion.

None of those weird faiths, the regular stuff.

The Sunday ones—yes, the Saturday ones too.

None of this Arab or Asian religion that had messed up the sixties and seventies. Nothing far-out like this gang called The Beirut Brigade, which probably wouldn't be doing things here if Washington hadn't gotten so involved in the Middle East peace process.

Whatever that was. When was the government going to get everyone out of this horror anyway?

Most of the people in the tunnel were more sensible, but very frightened. More than a few of those were trying to figure out what they might do about it. Raoul Santamarta wasn't panicked, but he was quite worried about various possibilities. He wasn't about to show that for he had a reputation, an image, in the ultra-macho cocaine world. He was somebody to respect in the dope domain. He'd do anything to protect his "name."

He had to show "cool" even in this acute danger.

"You okay, baby?" he asked Joanne Velez.

His tone was assured, almost cocky, as usual. His face was set in something like a smug smile. Well, all but his eyes. They didn't quite mask what he really felt, the DEA undercover agent thought. The gunman in the rear seat was simply staring ahead stonily and silently. Santamarta had told him that they'd carve up the woman when they made the drop, and he was focusing on that . . . and not soiling his trousers.

"I'm fine," Velez answered as casually as she could.

Even without being trapped between two car bombs, she didn't like tunnels. They always bothered her *somehow*, and she was invariably glad to get out of one of them. Malloy had joked about her dread of tunnels several times before he admitted that his own fear of *something* going wrong in a tunnel was not far from a smothering one.

"They'll get us out, baby," Santamarta predicted. "I know about these deals. It's a kidnap number. *Bandidos* pull them twice a month down in Colombia, other countries too. You pay them off, and they let everybody go home."

She decided to play the insecure female.

"How long you think it'll take, Raoul?" she questioned in her weak woman voice.

"An hour, no more than two to round up the cash."

"You're sure it's money they want?" she asked.

"Got to be. It's always money with *bandidos*. Like that song from the Broadway musical says," he told her with a cynical chuckle. "Money makes the world go round."

"They might be terrorists," she pointed out hesitantly. "I saw on the TV there were terrorists blowing up stuff in New York."

"Terrorists, *bandidos*, same thing," he insisted. "Money . . . money . . . money. Got to be. You don't have any *bandidos* or Red guerrillas in the slammer to exchange. It's fuckin' cash, baby."

We don't really have any *bandidos* shooting up the countryside at all, she thought. This guy's full of crap, Joanne Velez thought.

Then she wondered where the hell Jake Malloy was, right now, when she needed him so urgently. The tunnel was getting to her more and more each second. She had to hold on.

Some seventeen cars back, the Navaho was on his phone, scrambled and urgent. He was asking for permission to bust the dope dealers right away to seize the cocaine . . . and save her. The "control" in the Manhattan office of DEA was still trying to get a "go" on that from Washington.

Alison Levin was scant yards away. She got out of her old car, walked to her favorite aunt's vehicle, and tried to reassure the stockbroker in the blue Seville. She found that it wasn't really necessary. While a 240-pound man in an adjacent Mercedes was vomiting out the window in primeval terror—or was it the ulcer again—her aunt was in decent spirits. She'd just phoned her office. The market was up, both Dow Jones and Nasdaq.

Things would work out, her aunt predicted.

The sister of the groom-to-be shook her head as she returned to her own vehicle. That was when the good-looking man in the red sports car first spoke to her.

"Anything I can do?" he asked.

She looked at him.

A lot of men would have said, "What's wrong?"

This one thought about helping.

"I'm worried about my aunt," she told him. "She's not afraid. She may be in denial."

"I'm scared as hell," the driver of the red sports car admitted without visible embarrassment.

Down in the CIA safe house in Virginia, the late Colonel Belkov—he was *late* to that other intelligence community that continued to behave badly despite the proclaimed melting of the Cold War—wasn't quite scared.

Being a covert operations veteran with a lot of experience and no illusions, he wasn't far from it. He hadn't expected that the Americans would increase the pressure on him so rapidly. He'd expected—well, *hoped*—to dole out bits of information over some months. That was the way it had played out for defectors in the past.

But this was going differently.

It wasn't Belkov's fault, he told himself for the hundredth time. This wouldn't be happening if Omar had limited itself to chores for Belkov and some not too important crimes out in the Midwest. That fucking Gunther had to be responsible for this mess, this heat. The Cold War had almost—well, partly—subsided, and crazy Gunther had found a way to generate enough heat to incinerate Belkov's plan for a reasonable resettlement in the United States.

"There's no reason you shouldn't have a new identity with a secure income—or a lump sum, if you prefer," the senior CIA debriefer had said two days ago, "but we can't concentrate on that until we resolve things with Omar, and Mirror later."

The American interrogator saw from Belkov's face that the "dead" colonel didn't understand the priorities.

"You'd deal with the Mirror matter first, right?" the CIA man guessed.

Belkov nodded, about half an inch.

"We would too because Mirror is a major and strategic agent," the American said. "But Omar has become quite urgent. We have reason to believe that Omar has been killing large numbers of civilians, including nuns and schoolchildren."

Omar was a Deep Black operation, totally covert.

That couldn't possibly continue if the ex-Stasi unit wiped out civilians.

"Bring in the set," the interrogator ordered.

Belkov had been denied access to television broadcasts until this moment. It was a standard isolation technique used by security organizations in many countries to make a prisoner or defector—not much difference in this stage of things—feel powerless.

Now they plugged in a television set.

They didn't bother to turn the dial to find the news.

It was on every channel, live and nasty.

The tunnel, the police cars, the announcer talking of the estimated six hundred trapped inside . . . and the bombs.

"We think those bombs may belong to Omar, that Omar's this Beirut Brigade," the senior CIA interrogator said to the Russian. "From what you've told us about Omar—and the fact no one has ever heard of The Beirut Brigade—that seems more than possible."

"It is not illogical," Belkov stalled.

"Now, *right now*, where is Omar? You ran Omar. You *must* know."

"I can't guess," Belkov said candidly. "According to signal traffic I got back Omar was in the Midwest four or five weeks ago."

Then the interrogator did exactly what Belkov expected.

"*What* signal traffic? Let's take it from that approach. How did you communicate with Omar? It was through Mirror, you said."

Belkov nodded.

"Then if the only person who knows where to reach Omar is Mirror, it is time—it is past time—to change our priorities. Mirror? How do you communicate with Mirror?"

"We've been over this. Coded radio flash signal to and from Moscow. That's all I know."

"We've only been over it eight or ten times," the debriefer said calmly. "We're going to go over this a lot more because a lot of lives may be at stake under the Hudson River at this very moment. I can promise you it will be very unpleasant if it turns out you could have saved those people and didn't."

"I have nothing to do with anything or anyone under the Hudson River," Belkov protested. "I had no idea that any such operation was being considered—not the slightest. It would be totally unfair to blame me for this bizarre action."

He knew the game, and he could see how it was going.

Going faster.

Unfair would be of no interest to professionals on either side, on any side, in any intelligence or counterintelligence *apparat*.

Sooner or later they might decide he was disposable.

He had to make it much later.

The interrogator ignored the childish reference to fairness.

"Let's put aside the Lincoln Tunnel crisis," the interrogator said and turned off the television set. "Do you have any idea—any idea whatsoever—where Mirror might be. What part of the United States? What kind of work Mirror does? In what city?"

Belkov understood that he *had* to give them something . . . now.

He frowned as if he were trying to recall.

"New York," he "remembered" slowly. "Yes, I heard one of my colleagues mention Mirror was in New York City."

The CIA man smiled.

This was progress. There would be more. They'd keep up the pressure—step up the pressure—on this defector to accelerate the flow. They'd milk him dry.

"New York?" the interrogator said. "How about some coffee? We can have some excellent espresso before we continue."

"Espresso would be fine," Belkov said as if it mattered.

While they waited for the espresso, the CIA trio filled the time with small talk about areas of the United States where the defector might be relocated with a new identity and secure economic future.

If Belkov gave them what they wanted.

Everything they wanted, and in a timely fashion.

They didn't say that. It was implicit.

Like the threat of the alternative, Belkov realized.

Carrot or stick . . . or worse than stick.

By the time he was sipping the espresso, the defector was facing the fact that there was a very good chance that they'd hunt down Mirror whether Belkov helped them further or not. They probably had the technology to monitor hundreds of short-wave frequencies, to snatch the flash signal from the air even if it lasted only three seconds.

And they had that massive NSA with its army of technicians and legions of cryptographers operating state-of-the-art computers and code-breaking gear. It was really remarkable that Mirror had been so successful and undetected for so many years, Belkov told himself as he savored the rich black brew.

Mirror was the best of the deep-cover spies, Belkov thought admiringly. Maybe Belkov could divert the Americans from Mirror . . . or at least buy Mirror time. There were thirteen other Russian agents Belkov had in his "bank." In this game, they were his currency.

Better than money.

He'd spend them if and when he must.

Their bulk—their numbers—and their variety would be meaningful to the Americans.

Yes, he could use them, one or two at a time, to help Mirror. They were chips in this game. He'd put them on the table to buy time for Mirror.

More important, time for himself.

Now he finished the powerful coffee, and nodded.

He hadn't known that the CIA could do espresso so well.

34

MALLOY WAS counting on the river charts and the schematics.

They were essential to his plan, he realized as he slipped into the Hudson and began swimming downstream.

It was a risky plan, and he knew the odds were not good.

Not even close to good, he thought as the current moved him faster. There were too many parts to the plan, and every one of them was dangerous. If any one part went wrong the whole thing would cave. Every phase of his operation depended on all the others . . . and luck . . . and surprise.

And smarts.

He had to outwit the shrewd psychopath who'd murdered so many and was ready to butcher hundreds more. Malloy's instinct told him that he really, ultimately, had a single adversary—one brilliant professional who'd plotted this whole bloodbath out with cool expertise.

Swimming and drifting, Malloy raised his wrist to look at the waterproof-to-six-hundred-feet SEAL watch he still wore. He began to push himself harder. He had just a few minutes to get to a small and special destination. If he missed it . . . if he passed it . . . if the river took him away from it, it would all be over.

He had to grab for the metal bar. He had to see it to reach out for it. No second chance, and the visibility ten feet below the surface was limited. The Hudson was getting cleaner, but it was still not clear.

There it was.

A shadow . . . a shape . . . ahead . . . to the right.

All of a sudden he was rushing at it in the current . . . where it should be if he'd calculated correctly.

He was moving too fast . . . too far away.

He was going to pass it.

Now he fought the river as hard as he could . . . then harder. Scott Fitzgerald had written there were no second acts in American lives, Malloy recalled from a novel he'd read at college. There'd be no second chances in the Hudson today.

Panting and gasping, he pushed himself to the limit. He fought the river as if in hand-to-hand combat. He was sweeping by. Suddenly he thought of an undercover DEA agent in mortal danger in that damned tunnel. That added an odd anger to his system . . . to his strength.

Malloy refused to lose.

He certainly wasn't going to let that bastard who ran The Beirut Brigade win. The thought was entirely immature, Malloy realized, but somehow it added something to his effort. Just a bit, perhaps five percent.

He pushed and struggled and battled back. He grabbed out for the murky cylinder he could barely see . . . missed. Now he grabbed out again . . . curled his fingers around something. It felt like metal.

He managed to pull himself closer to the cylinder.

Somehow he hung on, fueled by adrenaline, unsophisticated pride, and nourishing hate. He knew that it wasn't good to hate, and he knew he needed it now.

Hanging on to the metal, he didn't see what was passing behind him at about the same depth . . . sixty yards away. It glided along like a shadow—fourteen or sixteen feet long—definitely not human. Malloy didn't hear it either, but then he wasn't listening for it.

At that moment the police commissioner of New York City walked into the Task Force office that had become the command post.

"You said you wanted me here," he told Briggs.

"No, I said you *ought* to be here and I'm glad you came right away."

"Something's happening," Jefferson guessed instantly.

"Jake's come up with a very interesting plan to save the people in the tunnel," Briggs reported.

"Something wild, right?"

"How did you know?" the FBI inspector wondered.

"I know Jake Malloy. Where is he? What's his plan?"

Briggs looked around as if he didn't want anyone else—not even members of the Task Force—to hear what he was about to say. Jefferson didn't comment. He listened.

"He's under the river now," Briggs began confidentially and went on to explain what Malloy had in mind.

"He assumes that The Beirut Brigade is watching both ends of the third tube. If we send in experts to enter the tunnel to disarm the bombs, the people watching would detonate the charges by remote control. We know they can do it by radio," Briggs reminded.

"What's he want to do?"

Briggs shook his head.

"*Going* to do," he corrected. "Doing right now. In drills to protect possible targets of terrorist attacks, this Task

Force has taken some good looks and done dry runs involving the city's tunnels. Jake remembered what he'd learned about the third tube."

Jefferson gestured impatiently for him to continue.

"The entrances to the tube at both the New York and the New Jersey ends are not the only way that a man—a brave and desperate man—can get into the tube," Briggs said. "About 100 or 150 yards out from each shore there is a small man-made island. It is really the top of a powerful air-sucker to pump fresh air down into the tube. With all those vehicles and carbon monoxide, a constant replenishment of the fresh air is essential."

Briggs paused to look at his watch.

"What the hell is that about?" Jefferson demanded.

"Rescue Company One. It's about Rescue One, Commissioner," Briggs said.

"Fire Department Rescue One?"

"We're having a fire, Commissioner," Briggs told him and pointed at the television set.

A news crew was "shooting" down from a helicopter at the river—as it had been doing, as five or six crews from various broadcast entities had been doing—since the crisis began. The assorted video reporters had noticed a thirty-four-foot cabin cruiser about a mile north of the Lincoln Tunnel. It was difficult to ignore. It was ablaze.

Black smoke was spiraling from two separate parts of the vessel. Men and women were clearly visible, trying to defeat the flames, failing. Now a woman jumped over the side. Another followed a dozen seconds later.

Suddenly a municipal fireboat manned by intrepid individuals whom local tabloids called New York's *bravest*—the cops were tagged the *finest*—chugged into sight. Water cannon were spouting as it moved close.

"Rescue One," Briggs identified. "New York City Fire Department . . . like those people on the burning cabin cruiser."

"It's a fake fire?"

"Malloy considered a fake fire, but he decided the bad guys might figure out it wasn't real so he said use a real powerboat and burn it good. Probably wouldn't cost the city more than eighty grand, Malloy said, and that's a lot less than ten mill. I quote him exactly, Commissioner."

Jefferson tried to make sense of the whole thing.

After twenty seconds of intense thought, the canny commissioner succeeded.

"It's a diversion!"

"Exactly," Briggs ratified. "It's to pull away the attention of the people The Beirut Brigade has watching the tunnel entrances and the river nearby."

"Where the big air pumps are," Jefferson reasoned aloud.

More of the disguised firemen and firewomen were diving into the Hudson. The fireboat kept pouring great spouts from its water cannon. It all looked quite realistic.

"It could work," Jefferson judged warily. "Yes, it's Jake Malloy all right. What's next?"

"More Malloy and more dangerous. In about a minute, he starts up the outside of the pump cylinder—there's a ladder for maintenance people—and I pick up the phone and say *now*," Briggs replied.

"Now *what*?"

"Now two minutes or he's dead," the FBI inspector replied. "As you said, Commissioner, it's pure Malloy."

"And you're going along with this?" Jefferson tested as he shook his head in disbelief.

"Mario Puzo time," Briggs answered. "Jake made me an offer I couldn't refuse. Well, I couldn't think of any other."

"Mario Puzo time?" the commissioner repeated. "You know you're starting to talk like Malloy, don't you?"

Briggs nodded, picked up the telephone, and checked the time on the electric wall clock before he dialed.

"This is Inspector Frank Briggs of the Federal Bureau of Investigation," he announced. "We spoke earlier. Right, the Task Force. Yes, it's time. Now. *Right now.*"

Then he put down the phone and looked at the television set again. The powerboat was still burning. If the ex-SEAL was lucky The Beirut Brigade observers would be watching the fire for the next eighty or ninety seconds.

Suddenly the cabin cruiser's fuel tank exploded.

Big boom . . . big gush of fire.

Every eye for miles—every eye scanning the river and the television coverage of the tunnel crisis—was pulled to the burning vessel. The last of the fire department actors on the craft leaped into the Hudson.

Then there was another major blast.

Even larger and louder. Just about irresistible.

No doubt about it, Briggs thought.

That Malloy had all the luck.

35

IT WASN'T easy.

It would have been extremely difficult even if the time wasn't so short and the risks so great.

All the extra weight that Malloy was carrying—had to take with him—made climbing from the river up the maintenance ladder more than stressful. Damn near impossible would be more accurate, the sweat-drenched ex-SEAL thought for a moment as he reached the third step.

Then he stopped thinking. He forced himself up on what he knew, what his body knew. He had to stop at the seventh step to catch his breath, to let his muscles recharge. He couldn't have come this far if he hadn't continued to work out every day to stay in better than good physical condition. He wasn't one of those body-building types who were proud of their abs and other muscles. This was a habit he hadn't shed when he left the SEALs.

He certainly hadn't expected such a life-and-death test

That was for the fierce young men, years junior, full-time warriors ready for instant assault duty.

He started up again. He could feel the vibration of the

powerful machinery only yards away. Four steps higher, he began to hear something between a hum and a growl. He got free of the oxygen tank, glanced upstream for a second to make sure the boat was burning, and pulled himself, inch by inch, to the top step.

The noise was louder.

It wasn't supposed to be . . . not now.

It should have stopped—he scanned his watch—more than a minute ago.

Until the noise halted completely, until the big air pump spun to a stop, he was stuck out here where he could be seen by the watchers he knew were out there.

If those eyes of The Beirut Brigade spotted him, his entire plan was in peril. The people trapped in the tunnel were all in significantly greater danger than that. The terrorists would recognize what Malloy was doing was an act against them, and they would almost surely react quickly and violently.

Why wasn't the damn pump at rest as promised?

Suddenly the sound began to change.

It took the ex-SEAL several seconds to grasp what the alteration meant, and he sighed. He pulled himself up, peered down into the wide cylinder, and saw what he'd been hoping for so urgently. The big blades that could slice him into slivers were slowing.

Since they normally rotated, day and night, at high speed to pump fresh air down into the tunnel, it took twenty-five . . . thirty . . . thirty-seven seconds for them to stop. He immediately hooked his grapnel to the top of the wide metal cylinder, tested the climbing rope with two tugs, and began to descend into the darkness.

He had to go down carefully but quickly. There was no time to waste, but no margin for error. If he fell and was injured there was no one who could help him. No one would even hear him. Aware of this, he didn't hesitate. Malloy had both training and experience in climbing, up and down, in daylight and total darkness.

He knew from the schematics how many feet down it was from the mouth of the pump on the surface. He also knew from his calculations that he wasn't nearly at the bottom, and the whirling blades would begin to spin lethally again in seconds.

Twenty . . . twenty-five . . . not more.

He moved down the rope more quickly . . . less cautiously.

He had to get away from the deadly arc of those blades at any risk. Now he heard the sound of danger. The motor of the pump was beginning. The steel scythes would be accelerating in scant moments. He had no more time.

It wasn't far to the bottom, he told himself.

He could visualize the chart. It better be right, Jacob Malloy thought as the noise grew and his options vanished into the blackness. He tensed, took a deep breath, and dropped just in time.

Three seconds later the whirling steel slashed the air right over his head, amputating the climbing rope. Now there was no chance for him to escape up the shaft, but that didn't bother him. He'd planned another exit.

Malloy hit the floor of the tunnel. He knew how to take a fall—how to bend his knees and flex his body to absorb the impact with minimum trauma. It was black here on the floor of the tunnel as he stood up, not fully. The ceiling wasn't that high.

He wasn't on the tunnel floor that drivers knew. That road surface was some five feet above his head. Underneath it—running the full length of the tube—was an invisible chamber that no one who rolled by in a vehicle from one state to the other had seen or suspected.

It carried the air pulled in by the two big pumps, releasing it into the upper part of the tunnel through many small openings spaced evenly just above the surface on which the cars, vans, and trucks made their way under the Hudson. It was also useful for men doing certain kinds of routine maintenance.

Bent over slightly to avoid hitting his head, Malloy took a waterproof flashlight from his pouch and flicked the lamp on to get his bearings. He eyed the electric cables that fed power to the many lights upstairs where the vehicles moved. Then he studied the ceiling of this bottom segment of the third tube.

There they were.

Just as the schematic showed, they were set snugly in the ceiling at about seventy-six-foot intervals. He wasn't sure that he recalled the distance between them exactly, but seventy-six feet was close enough. They looked like manhole covers. That was what they were.

They were also his only way into the main part of the third tube where the people were trapped.

There was a problem with these metal disks—a serious one.

Malloy intended to go up into the top section of the tunnel through one of these manholes, but he couldn't open any of them. They could only be opened from inside the main chamber above him. The ex-SEAL had to let somebody above know that a manhole must be opened so Malloy could ascend to help the hundreds of civilians caught between the two bombs.

To disarm the explosive charges.

To get everyone out safely. Swiftly and safely . . . it would have to be done rapidly so the terrorists couldn't try whatever else they had up their sleeves.

As Malloy prepared to bang on one of the manhole

covers to signal that he wanted to come up, Briggs was explaining the ex-SEAL's plan to Jefferson.

"It's kind of complicated," the FBI inspector began.

"Like Jake," the commissioner observed.

"You could say that. Anyway, he said we had to get to somebody inside the tunnel who could be persuaded that this was no gag and had to be done right away. He picked the Navaho."

"What Navaho?"

"There's a DEA team down in the tunnel trailing a bunch of dope guys from Florida, and there's an undercover in the lead car with the coke and the Colombians."

Briggs saw the look on the commissioner's face.

"I'm not making this up, Commissioner," the federal agent said earnestly. "The undercover is Malloy's . . . lady . . . companion, you know. I'm not making that up either."

"I hope not. Now what about this Indian?"

"Navaho," Briggs specified. "Thomas Largo is one of the best people in DEA's office in Miami. Malloy's idea was for me to get Largo's brother on the phone. He's the chief. Speaks Navaho, of course."

"Of course," Jefferson said and wondered why Jacob Malloy didn't do things—didn't think—like other people.

"Malloy's plan is for me to explain the situation to the chief—his name is Peter—and ask him to call his brother on the brother's cell phone. The brother in the tunnel is Thomas," Briggs told him.

"Forget the credits. Can we cut to the chase?"

"Jake wants the chief to speak to his brother in Navaho, just in case anybody might be scanning the cell phone frequencies."

"The Navaho code-talkers," the commissioner suddenly remembered. "Army used them in World War II. I suppose Malloy figures this is World War III."

"Hard to say," Briggs replied. "In any case the Navaho in the tunnel is supposed to open a manhole in the roadbed and let Jake slip in without being seen by anybody watching either mouth of the third tube."

"So you've spelled this out to the chief and Malloy's coming up now . . . or is he inside already?"

"It's a viable plan," Briggs said.

"Something's gone wrong?" Jefferson guessed.

"Just a matter of timing. We haven't found the chief . . . *yet*, so he can't make the call."

"You're not making this up either?"

"We'll find him any minute now," Briggs assured. "The Bureau's got eight cars and two choppers looking for him."

"And who's looking for the money?" Jefferson demanded. "Have you any idea where it is?"

"I know where it *isn't*," Briggs said.

"Ten million dollars . . . what a mess! Okay," the police commissioner of New York City replied irately, "where *isn't* it?"

"It isn't in the van, not anymore," the FBI veteran declared.

He was right.

36

ARNOLD SAW the waterproof light just where he'd rigged it.

Nine feet below the surface of the Hudson, bound to a piling on a pier.

Two and a half blocks south of the office building where Omar's eighth-floor command post offered wide views of the river.

The high ground, traditional favorite of practical commanders even before the Romans went into battle.

The light beneath the surface was a beacon.

Arnold approached it slowly. The underwater chariot he rode—sports model of one created years earlier for underwater demolition teams and frogman units of half a dozen nations—handled sluggishly and moved almost ponderously with its bulky cargo.

Arnold and the chariot had been in position when Gunther stunned the Americans by radio-guiding the van into the Hudson. He'd removed the bags of cash slowly to avoid tearing the plastic, and then he'd inserted each of the four bags into a larger plastic sack of a different color.

He'd lashed them to the chariot, let the current carry him and the craft downriver silently for three hundred yards before he started the motor. Gunther had told him to do that to minimize the chances of being detected. Gunther was good at figuring these things, Omar's burly explosives specialist thought admiringly as he eased the chariot up to the surface just yards from the old pier.

He looked back and forth, then up and along the pier too. No one was watching. Arnold wasn't aware of the burning cabin cruiser upriver. It was pulling everyone's attention, serving Omar and the chariot loaded with money at the same time it met Malloy's needs as well. Even if he knew and thought about the irony of this situation, Arnold would not have been impressed or amused.

Irony wasn't his thing.

He was much better at bombs and discipline, following instructions, getting things done. What he had to do now was to take the cash from the chariot, let the craft slide a few feet below the surface on a strong tether so it wouldn't drift away, and carry the bags up to where he'd parked the dolly.

He freed himself from the wet suit, mask, and tank. Then he packed them in another large waterproof sack that he lashed to the chariot before he watched it submerge. One by one, he patiently carried the four sacks of cash up to the next level of the pier where he'd parked the small truck he'd rented. Gunther had said that Arnold shouldn't steal this vehicle. That way nobody would be looking for it.

Arnold had already placed his suitcase in the rear compartment so he could use the vehicle to leave the city. They might be watching at the airports and rail terminals, Gunther had told him, but there was almost no chance they'd stop every car and truck going out of Manhattan.

He drove slowly and defensively; he couldn't afford an accident now and everyone knew there were some nasty people in this town working out their neuroses behind the wheel. When he reached the freight loading dock of the building that housed Omar's headquarters, Arnold got out and pointed at the dolly beside the man in the dark green work clothes.

That man was the "super" formerly known as the janitor. He saw nothing worth thinking about in Arnold who was wearing a tan work shirt and trousers. Sturdy, mostly polyester, standard garb for men who pushed trucks and delivered light cargo, the tired-eyed "super" thought.

It didn't occur to him that the bags being loaded on the dolly might contain ten million dollars. That was actually fortunate, for if it had he might do or say or look for something that could encourage Arnold to break his neck and put his body in one of the elevator shafts where it probably wouldn't be found for twenty-four hours.

Yes, twenty-four hours would be enough, Arnold judged professionally as he wheeled the dolly into the freight elevator. As it ascended, Arnold did something that was unusual for him. He briefly considered the future. With his million dollars he was going to have a future, a new prospect for a man who'd been busy for years in an aggressive covert action team.

He was going to miss Gunther.

Gunther was interesting, but Arnold told himself that there was no reason making his own choices couldn't be interesting too. It was worth trying, and nobody would be seeking to find and kill him. After all these years of covert warfare that would be restful. He'd considered Tahiti, but people said the French islands were expensive and Bali was fifty percent cheaper and very charming. Arnold had never experienced charming, not a minute from the day he was born.

He might like it, he told himself as he pushed the dolly out of the elevator on the eighth floor. When he rolled the money to the Omar office, Arnold did what Gunther had ordered. He knocked twice, then once, then three times. It was the proper code signal that would get him admission instead of a burst of bullets from Gunther's rapid-fire little M-10.

"Any problems?" Gunther asked automatically as he relocked the door behind the dolly.

"Nothing. It went just the way you planned," Arnold replied.

Gunther didn't even smile. He expected things to go as he planned, though he was never free of the fear—unspoken and haunting—that something could somehow go wrong.

Scott was in the suite too. He was at the window, looking down through the telescope at the mouth of the third tube. Beside him was the odd-looking weapon that was Gunther's backup tool. When it was "fired" no one could see it or hear it . . . no human on earth.

But it could wreck the third tube of the Lincoln Tunnel.

It could bury all those people in seconds.

There was another such device, a twin, aimed at the New Jersey entrance. Now Scott turned and looked at the bags. He wasn't nearly as cold and controlled as Gunther.

"A million bucks!" he exulted with a broad grin.

"Eyes on the river," Gunther commanded curtly. "And keep checking the mouth of that damn tunnel every fifteen seconds. You can celebrate when we're out of the country."

"And the money is too," Scott said as he turned back to watching.

"I'm taking care of that . . . right now," Gunther responded in his "boss" voice.

He joined Arnold in lifting the bags onto a large table. With time short and the stakes high, Gunther slashed the first bag open and began taking out the bundles of currency. The empty shipping containers were stacked neatly at his feet. Gunther pointed, and the two men began to insert the money they'd worked, robbed, and killed so conscientiously to earn.

37

MALLOY TAPPED on the bottom of the fifteenth . . . or was it the eighteenth . . . manhole cover again. And again. He stopped to think and hope and listen. All he heard was the beating of his heart.

This strange thing had happened once before.

He'd been trapped then too—in mortal danger on a SEAL mission so secret that the U.S. government wouldn't admit it ever happened. He'd found a way out, hacked a way out, then. There had to be a way out now.

For a few seconds he "saw" the face of Joanne Velez. He realized that he couldn't afford this indulgence. He couldn't give up either. Malloy took a deep breath before he resumed tapping on the next manhole.

Nothing.

All right, there were many more. He moved on to still another . . . in part out of sheer stubbornness. He'd always been good at that, as his mother had commented wryly so often over the years. He thought about her and his brother's party that he'd miss if he died in this damn hole. Then he tapped on the next manhole cover.

He heard it a moment later.

Clear and metallic.

Someone tapped back, again, and once more after that.

Seconds later Malloy heard the wonderful sound of the manhole lid being lifted. Light . . . he saw a curved sliver of light . . . barely an inch wide but that was enough. It was coming from within the main chamber of the tunnel. So was the grunting that signaled human exertion.

The manhole was open.

Malloy looked up and saw the face of a thirty-something-year-old male who could be a Navaho. Strong features, alert, dark-skinned, yes, he might be a Navaho.

And the man staring down saw the ex-SEAL.

"Captain Malloy?"

"Right," the policeman in the lower compartment answered. He got out of the wet suit as quickly as he could, collected the bag of "toys" and the tool kit that the sergeant in the radio car had given him beside the river, and started up the steps of the ladder from the maintenance chamber.

The dark-skinned man reached down to help him emerge, right beside a dignified black limousine with three very properly dressed Japanese executives in the backseat. Neatly attired and curious and showing no sign of their sensible concern about the danger in this insane American situation, they studied Jacob Malloy as if he were some special effect in a science fiction movie.

They were startled when the ex-SEAL said hello in their native tongue, using about a tenth of the Japanese he still recalled from that undergraduate course at Columbia. They did the right thing. They answered courteously in formal Japanese. The appropriate amenities were observed.

For about nine seconds.

Then Malloy spoke to the DEA agent who'd let him in.

"Son of a bitch," he said.

It wasn't a criticism—just a statement of fact and tension and, in some strange way that somehow made sense, of gratitude.

"Son of a bitch, Captain," Thomas Largo agreed.

They started to walk toward the New York end of the tunnel.

"Better not look at the next fourteen or fifteen cars," the Native American suggested. "We've got two with some real edgy dope guys moving a lot of coke, and they could get nervous if they thought anybody was paying attention to them."

"Those are the hoods who want to hit your undercover?" Malloy asked.

He didn't identify her by name or mention that he cared about her. Neither did Largo.

"The same, Captain."

"Let's deal with them later," Malloy said.

Too bad that the semiautomatic .50-caliber Barrett was outside the Manhattan exit with the small SEAL unit he'd sent there, Malloy thought in a flare of uncivilized hostility. One burst from the heavy B2A1 would rip off the homicidal hoods' heads.

But not now. He followed Largo toward the Manhattan exit. For a second he caught a glimpse of *her* in a Lexus. Joanne Velez saw him too, but there was no flicker of recognition in her eyes. She didn't show her astonishment at the inexplicable presence of Jacob Malloy in a sealed off and besieged tube of the Lincoln Tunnel.

She didn't display any reaction, but she felt a surge of increased hope. Her lover probably had—no, surely had—more ego and much more boldness than a reasonable man needed, she thought, *but*.

But Jacob Malloy wasn't always entirely reasonable.

And if there were any people around who might do the

apparently impossible, he could be one of them. He could also be too damn sure of himself, she recalled. Over-achievers were like that, she thought.

All of this flashed in the seconds it took him to walk by. He was out of sight in moments, out of her view. Other people in vehicles trapped in the tunnel saw him pass with Largo, and wondered who the two men were and what they were doing. A few of the frightened civilians called out questions.

"Fifteen minutes," Malloy responded with a wave.

"What does that mean, Captain?" Largo tested.

"It could mean a lot of things," the former SEAL replied as they saw the mouth of the tube about ninety yards ahead. "That's why I said it. Ambiguity offers possibilities. Possibilities suggest hope. And I'm hoping these people will stay out of my way and off my back until I take my shot at the first bomb."

Now he patted the toolbox, the kit that the sergeant said was first rate. The two law enforcement professionals were some fifteen yards from the car crammed with Arnold's explosives when they heard a groan. It was very near. When they looked they saw that the groaner was female.

In a tan convertible just yards from the bomb-laden vehicle was a woman who might be twenty-five or thirty, Malloy estimated. One other thing was more definite. The size and shape of her abdomen made it absolutely clear that she was eight or nine months pregnant.

She groaned again and grasped her hurting stomach.

"Labor pains," the curly-haired man at the wheel volunteered helpfully. "She's due next week but we though we'd get to the hospital in Manhattan today because she' been feeling funny."

"Good thinking," Malloy said.

"Her obstetrician is Dr. Gewirtz at Mount Sinai," the young husband continued. "He's not going to like this tunnel business."

"I'm not too crazy about it myself," the ex-SEAL confided.

Now he could see the contractions wracking her, and her cries were getting louder.

"I'll take the bomb. You take the baby," he told Largo.

"I'm no doctor," the DEA agent warned.

"Go find one back there," Malloy said and gestured toward the vehicles behind them. "Check out the license plates."

"Maybe we'd better move her back away from *that* car—just in case," the Navaho suggested and nodded at the sedan loaded with dynamite.

"You can't move her," her husband protested.

"It wouldn't matter much *just in case*," Malloy said. "If I screw this up we're all gone, friend."

He paused to open the toolbox.

"I'm not going to screw it up," he promised. "This is a first-class set of burglar tools my pals took from a master thief, and I got an A in bomb disposal. Well, an A minus. That ought to do it."

Largo started back into the tunnel to look for medical help as Jacob Malloy approached the booby-trapped car blocking the tunnel's exit. The gas inside made it difficult to see within, but Malloy could think.

"Gas is to blind us," he reasoned. "They don't want us to study what might be in there. Gas probably is noxious but not poisonous. These bastards are damn good, but getting ahold of poison gas is a much bigger deal than cooking up homemade fucking napalm. *Right.*"

He nodded.

The woman groaned again . . . and again.

"Bomb has to be big—at least forty or up to seventy sticks of dynamite. If they're still using dynamite, which they probably are because they know it."

He studied the back of the car.

"You'd have to be a whistling idiot—a suicidal idiot—to drive around with that much dynamite on the rear seat, and you certainly wouldn't want it next to you if you're driving. *Right.* Has to be in the damn trunk."

He circled around to scan the door of the trunk.

"Radio control's probably somewhere up front, and the bomb's packed into the trunk which these bastards have—being real pro bastards—rigged with some booby trap to take my head off and cave in the whole mouth of the tunnel," Malloy calculated.

"*If* I make a mistake . . . any damn kind of mistake. I don't think so," he declared bitterly as he psyched himself up for the life-and-death challenge. "I'm good with bombs. I'm *very* good with all kinds of explosives. I can do this."

He'd been top man in his class at the explosive ordnance course, the demolition ace in SEAL Team Two. He was a *little* out of practice, Malloy told himself, but he had no choice. There was no instructor or anyone else to turn to, not here, not now.

Time to rock and roll, his younger brother would have said.

That wasn't a phrase Jacob Malloy used.

He suddenly recalled what Free French paratroopers shouted as they jumped in World War II, and it seemed dead right.

"*Merde!*" Malloy called out defiantly.

His mother might not like her Ivy League son saying *shit* in public, even in a flawless Paris accent, but that wa *her* problem. He stepped forward to address his. As he bent over the car's trunk, he took a burglar tool from the thieves' kit the NYPD had given him on the edge of the river.

The pregnant woman moaned, gasped, moaned again. "I think her water's going to break soon," her husband speculated.

"Not a chance," Malloy lied without hesitation or turning his head.

Crouching forward, he pressed his right ear against the trunk lid. You were supposed to listen on the chance you might hear some damn ticking or other meaningful sound. The metal of the trunk lid was cold, and how could he be sure what the hell was meaningful?

One of those damn yuppie words, he thought angrily.

For a moment he hated yuppies and almost everyone else.

Gerbils and goldfish too, he thought as he stepped back to mop the beads of moisture from his brow.

He listened once more, first at one end of the trunk, then another, top, middle, bottom. Shit, he thought. These bastards might have rigged the thing with something silent. He'd have about three seconds—maybe four—before he was blown into nasty pink chunks or even smaller bits.

The burglar kit included a top-of-the-line stethoscope. The previous owner hadn't pinched pennies . . . thank God and all the saints his father's sisters prayed to every day and most nights too.

No time for theology now. Malloy slowly moved the disk end of the stethoscope over the surface of the trunk door. Nothing. For a few seconds he considered whether there might be some kind of pressure fuse inside, or maybe a magnetic gadget that would blow if it detected metal.

Metal like a burglar tool.

The handles of the items in the thieves' arsenal were all covered in ridged rubber, but the blades were steel. They'd do it if the bastards had used a magnetic trigger.

No, they wouldn't. Too risky in traffic. If some other vehicle came up tailgating or even touched the trunk in an accidental bump the driver of the moving bomb would be history. Magnetic was for a booby trap in a building or a minefield, Malloy remembered.

Or thought he remembered.

More beads of perspiration on his face, and the woman was making those noises again. The ex-SEAL realized that pain forced her to do this, but that didn't help his concentration. She probably wasn't even considering his damn concentration, he thought.

That relieved the stress for several seconds.

He saw the insanity of the situation, half smiled, and went back to work. No ticking number . . . no magnetic fuse . . . he ran the burglar tool very slowly around the eighth of an inch space that framed the trunk door.

So far, so good.

He wasn't dead yet.

That was a start, he assured himself as he carefully inserted the tool into the eighth of an inch and began to probe.

He was still alive. Not bad.

Of course, it was going to get worse . . . and the bastards had the ten million. He felt better as he turned his bitterness to them for several seconds. It wasn't adult or mature or Judeo-Christian to hate them so primitively, but he didn't care right now.

Stethoscope to the trunk lock. Nothing.

Here we go.

"Wish me luck," he said to himself as he moved to insert the tool in the lock.

"What?" Largo asked.

The DEA agent had returned, was right behind him. Malloy didn't turn to look.

"Shut up and watch what I'm doing," he said and slid the burglar tool into the lock.

He cautiously probed for the back, then turned the pick left, more, more. Nothing. He took a deep breath before he began to turn it right.

He felt something move.

"I *think* I'm about to open this damn thing," he told Largo. "Could be booby-trapped. Any last words for your loved ones?"

The Navaho wasn't frightened.

"Do it," he said.

Malloy applied just a *little* more pressure, and the lid of the trunk began to rise. He caught it immediately. It was open about three inches. Holding it firmly, he bent lower to look inside.

"Hell's bells and small fishes," he said.

"What does that mean?" Largo asked.

"It means you'd better hang on to this trunk lid really tight if you don't want a very loud noise," Malloy answered.

"Booby trap?"

"At least one, but I think I can fix it if you make sure the lid doesn't go up any higher."

Now Jacob Malloy took a pair of wire cutters from the burglar's kit and stared into the trunk for several seconds.

"Saturday night!" he said and reached in to sever the thin wire covered in red rubber that ran from the lid to something farther back in the trunk.

There was a green wire too, but Malloy's instincts said to cut the red one first. He could have easily been wrong . . . even more easily dead. He wasn't.

"Maybe I got it right," he told Largo.

Slowly—slower than that—he raised the lid a foot.

Then a yard . . . then all the way.

He was coated with sweat. Largo saw the drops on his face.

"Kind of humid in here," the Navaho said in a matter-of-fact tone.

Malloy stared at the bomb inside the trunk.

"Nice job, Captain," the DEA agent judged.

"I've still got *that* to take care of, so pay attention. You're going to do the other one," the ex-SEAL said and nodded back toward the New Jersey entrance.

"I don't have any experience with this. I don't think it's a great idea."

"It's a lousy idea . . . and I should have gone to med school . . . and you'd probably make a fine state senator . . . but we missed our chances. The damn clock's running, and there probably isn't time for me to do both cars."

Thomas Largo looked very unhappy.

"You can say son of a bitch now if you want to," Malloy told him.

The Navaho shook his head.

"You curse a lot, Captain."

"Only on weekdays," Malloy replied. "Now watch carefully."

He pointed to the square packages, two of them, wrapped in bright blue plastic, with wires connecting them.

Then he heard the woman cry out again.

"You find a doctor?" Malloy asked.

The DEA agent pointed back toward the convertible. A trim youngish man—the good-looking driver of the red sports car that was near Alison Levin's vehicle—was leaning down and speaking.

"He says she's got a while," Largo reported.

"Let's hope we do too," Malloy responded and took another pair of cutters from the kit. He paused to test the two square packages with the stethoscope. Then he frowned.

"My mother told me there'd be moments like this," he quoted from a lyric he recalled.

"That's an old song?" the Navaho tested.

"Older than both of us. Here we go again."

In another ninety seconds he'd cut two more wires.

"The next line of the song is *what do we do now?*" he recalled. "Now we go for broke."

A cautious man would have stepped back, but Largo advanced closer so he wouldn't miss the smallest detail of the process.

"You're nuts," Jacob Malloy complimented.

"Finish it, Captain."

The ex-SEAL reached into the trunk, felt all around each of the two packages for any surprises, and finally lifted out one of them. He handed it to Largo who put it down and reached out to accept the second one. Malloy dried his damp hands on his pants legs before he gave it to him.

Suddenly Jacob Malloy smiled.

"I was just thinking that I was planning to update my will last week . . . but I was too busy," he explained.

"Next week, if I don't blow up the other car," Largo replied.

He pointed back toward the New Jersey exit.

"*Right*," Malloy agreed and gave him the tool kit. "On the way back tell everybody to get out of their vehicles and be ready to run . . . to run like hell."

"When?"

"When you've finished taking down that other bomb," the NYPD captain answered. "Half run out this end, the rest to New Jersey. I'll check out the people nearer to New York. Everybody goes when you hit the horn on a car up near the scenic Garden State. You toot twice, I'll answer twice, and it's derby time."

The thoughtful Navaho pointed at the pregnant woman yards away.

"What about people who can't run?" he wondered.

"Someone else will have to carry them. Go!"

Thomas Largo went. So did Malloy.

He went to the convertible.

"We've got a problem, Doc," he said to the physician.

"I think she'll be okay if we don't move her till an ambulance arrives," the doctor reported.

"That's the problem," Malloy confided. "We've got to move her and everyone else. In the language of Aeschylus, it's bug out time."

"How are we going to do this?"

"If God doesn't find a way, you and I will, Doctor."

The curly-haired physician looked at him silently for several seconds before he remembered.

"I've seen your picture in the *Times*," he recalled. "You're Dr. Malloy's older boy. One of my patients is a reporter who says you're . . ."

"Crazy? I think that's an exaggeration, but I'm not sure a normal regular guy would come down here to save your ass, Doc."

The logic was irrefutable.

"You've got fifteen minutes to get her up," the ex-SEAL told him. "Max? Maybe twenty, but I wouldn't count on that. You and I and her husband can carry her out as best we can. I'll be back before then."

Malloy walked swiftly down the third tube, pausing to alert everyone as to what was coming. Almost all those in this half of the tube reacted sensibly and affirmatively. A couple were nearly hysterical but not really negative. The man in the middle of the heart attack abstained from comment because he was semiconscious. Three men in an adjacent truck marked Perfect Plumbing volunteered to lift him when the horn sounded and cart him to daylight.

"Sure," Raoul Santamarta responded. None of the other drug crew in either vehicle said a word. They got out, looked up and down the third tube warily to make sure this was no cop trick, and waited.

They didn't like it down here. The tunnel was starting to get to Malloy too. He could feel the pressure building within him. He'd finished disarming the bomb and was still damp and tense. He swallowed to relieve the stress, then swallowed again.

It didn't help much.

He moved his arms back and forth. That didn't ease the pressure either. In a minute or two his breathing would begin to get just a bit labored. It had happened before when he was on a secret SEAL mission in a secret SEAL submarine that wasn't even on the U.S. Navy's list of commissioned vessels . . . and when he'd led his unit through a sewer on another operation that nobody talked about either.

Now, it was time to get the hell out of here, Malloy told himself. He looked at his wristwatch, SEAL issue. Tritium gas trasers one hundred times brighter than other night-viewing timepieces, charged to run for up to twenty-five years, tempered mineral crystal cover, Swiss quartz movement, and who cared.

How long was the Navaho going to take?

Maybe he should have taken that suggestion he see a shrink about this. Malloy didn't want to consider why he hadn't done so years ago. Nothing unusual about that, he told himself. He was just like a lot of other people. He knew he wasn't perfect, but he wouldn't, couldn't talk about it.

He'd be panting in two minutes, maybe sooner.

Was Largo in trouble? Couldn't he beat the damn bomb?

Malloy forced himself to make his way back toward the New York end of the tunnel. He'd managed not to look at Joanne Velez a minute ago, or club the thug beside her, the former SEAL reasoned, so he should be able to control this too. He could do it. There was the convertible with the groaning woman in labor right ahead.

Less than half a mile away, Gunther wasn't making any sounds of distress at all. He and Arnold were finishing the packing of the money. No one knew who they were or where they were; where they and the cash were going or how they'd get there. Aware that he'd beaten all the federal and local police and other stupid government forces mobilized against him, Gunther was in the best spirits he'd enjoyed in years.

Robbing banks was *nothing* compared to this.

This was being reported around the planet.

It was his greatest triumph, he judged.

"Hey, they've got dogs down there," Scott announced. "Take a look."

Gunther went to the telescope to peer down at the mouth of the third tube. He saw three German shepherds and their police handlers.

"Bomb dogs, but they won't be any problem for us," Gunther calculated. "Arnold and I are taking the boxes downstairs to the freight forwarders now. Keep an eye on things till we get back."

With Arnold's stolid assistance, Gunther completed

the packing and sealing of the cartons, checked the address labels.

"All correct," he said.

Then they began moving the boxes labeled "catalogues" to the dolly so they could complete the next phase of Gunther's plan. In twenty or twenty-five minutes they'd be gone, and all those American morons in the third tube would be buried.

38

THE WOMAN'S cries seemed to be more frequent.

And even louder, Malloy thought as he stepped up to the convertible. Her husband grasped her right hand tightly, his entire face a mute appeal for someone to do something and do it now.

"She should be in the hospital," the physician said earnestly. "She needs help."

"We all do," Jacob Malloy replied and looked hopefully toward the other end of the tunnel.

"I can see that. You're not breathing right, and you're shaking. You'd better sit down, Captain," the doctor advised.

Malloy shook his head impatiently, refusing to acknowledge what was happening within him. The pressure was getting worse.

Then he heard the horn behind him . . . just barely.

It was a long way to the Jersey exit but the signal from the DEA agent was clear.

Two toots. Malloy leaned into the convertible.

"Get her up," he ordered and pressed the horn twice in the agreed response.

The three men had a difficult time raising the pregnant woman. Nine months? She looked like twelve, Malloy thought as they gingerly lifted her. He opened the door beside her, found that easing her out was a major undertaking. She was making a whole range of sounds now, some shrill, some guttural, all hurting.

It took almost a minute and a half to get her to her feet . . . sort of. Malloy's strength was under her left armpit, the doctor's beneath the right, and her husband helped too . . . sort of. She tottered and they propped her up . . . and she stumbled forward a few steps. Then she tottered again, her weight nearly dragging her down.

But the three men fought back, advancing foot by foot to the car that had held the bomb. They maneuvered her around it, caught their breaths for several seconds before they pushed and pulled ahead.

She was out of the tunnel.

So were Malloy, her husband, and the physician whose name the NYPD captain hadn't even asked. Dozens of police near the mouth of the third tube saw them advance blinking into the dazzling daylight. So did millions of people watching live television reports of the astonishing crisis.

One of them was an FBI inspector named Briggs.

He'd been holding a telephone for some forty minutes . . . open hot line to the headquarters of the National Security Agency.

"All the transmitters. This is it," he said to Brigadier General Warner.

Warner kept his word. Within seconds every cell phone frequency in the New York metropolitan area—everything for sixty miles around—was jammed. A large number of people—some both rich and important—were furious. Stockbrokers and their customers, politicians, journalists calling in stories, law-abiding citizens talking to mail order services or sharing gossip with friends and relatives, television and advertising executives who had colorful new jokes—clean and other—to impress colleagues or clients near and far, call girls right in the middle of booking "dates," and ticket agents at sixteen airlines took this interruption personally.

It was an outrage, and Jacob Malloy didn't care.

He was trying to cut communications between the commander of The Beirut Brigade and that man's observers watching the mouths of the third tube. People were pouring out both ends. Malloy was convinced that the leader of the terrorists would try to do something to stop them.

He'd have another weapon.

Malloy couldn't guess what it was, but he was sure that he had to buy enough time for everyone to rush out on foot. How much time would be enough time? He opened the pouch of "toys," took out a standard SEAL HK-5 automatic weapon Gambelli had provided. Without thinking, he checked the weapon to make sure it was "ready to go."

He was. He felt a lot better outside the tunnel.

Then he felt even better than that. There she was, running toward the exit. The cocaine crew was only steps behind her. People coming out were cheering as they emerged. The drug dealers weren't.

Not when they saw the armada of radio patrol cars and scores of police. Santamarta instinctively assumed this must be some kind of trap. *She* must have set it. He'd *do* her—right here. He reached under his silk sports jacket to draw his pistol. He swung it quickly to take aim.

He did not kill Joanne Velez.

He didn't even hit her.

Alison Levin came charging up from behind at full speed. *Maximum warp* in the terminology of the *Star Trek* television series she'd enjoyed as a child, she was running for her life. She wasn't thinking about a new haiku at the moment, just escaping with the garment bag that held the dress for the wedding.

And some damn fool was blocking her way.

She collided with Santamarta, knocking him off balance as she sprinted out into the sunshine. The chief of the cocaine convoy saw his shot go wide. He didn't know who had banged into him, but that didn't matter. He was sure to get the bitch spy with his second shot.

He wasn't paying any attention to an ambulance parked twenty-five yards away. Someone in that vehicle was paying attention to him. The rear doors flew open. There weren't supposed to be guns in ambulances, Santamarta thought for a second. A second was all he had.

There was a man in some kind of camouflage outfit crouched behind an unusual-looking weapon on a tripod. Santamarta had never seen a twenty-eight pound, .50-caliber Barrett before. He had barely a moment to study it before a petty officer attached to SEAL Team Two squeezed the trigger.

All of a sudden there wasn't any Raoul Santamarta, and the bodyguard who'd been with him in the Lexus was just a body. The other members of the drug gang unanimously decided—without even taking a vote—to run back into the tunnel. As they took cover behind the cars a ragged stream of noncriminal civilians hurried from the third tube.

Malloy turned to give Gambelli a thumbs-up approval. "Anytime, Sting Ray," the petty officer called out loudly.

No one else was emerging, but that didn't mean the

tunnel was safe. All of Malloy's instincts told him that the terrorists weren't finished with the third tube. They'd do something when they learned that almost everyone—all but the surviving cocaine carriers—had broken free.

At that moment Gunther and Arnold returned to the eighth-floor observation and command post. "We've shipped the cash," Gunther said. "Time to go." He was surprised when Scott turned from the telescope and pointed down.

"They're out," he said in a stunned tone. "Hundreds of them. I don't know how they did it, but they're out."

"You were supposed to blow the whistle, dummy," Gunther raged.

"When you gave the order," Scott reminded him, "and you weren't here."

"I'm here now, dammit. Blow the damn whistle, pick up your stuff, and get out of here. I'll tell our friends in New Jersey to do the same."

He tried, but all the cell phone frequencies were jammed. Gunther told himself that the woman and Howard weren't as stupid or rigid as Scott. They'd seen what happened too, and they must have phoned for instructions. When they couldn't get through they would attack.

The weapon was already aimed at the mouth of the tunnel, and now Scott turned on the electric power. It didn't make any sound. Then he reached inside his shirt, found the whistle on the cord around his neck, and raised it to his lips.

Still no sound . . . none humans could hear.

It was a trick dog whistle that canine ears would register but not people.

Canine ears and the sound detectors that Arnold had concealed in each of the cars that blocked the tunnel exits. Malloy had been wrong about one thing. There was a second bomb in each car, hidden under the rear seat.

This was Gunther's just-in-case surprise.

Scott blew into the whistle, and forty-six sticks of dynamite exploded. The identical charge in the booby-trapped vehicle at the other end of the tunnel erupted in a massive blast when the woman who wasn't Doris anymore blew into her whistle.

Both entrances collapsed in landslides of concrete.

Gunther had hoped that the tube itself might cave in and a million gallons of river sweep through it to drown people and vehicles alike. He didn't have time to find out.

"You can go ahead," he told Arnold. "I have to set the timers here."

The timers on the incendiary charges that would burn this whole office and all traces of Omar, perhaps cremate the entire building. That might distract or confuse the police below even further, Gunther thought. It would at least tangle the traffic with fire engines tying up the nearest streets, more minutes for Omar and more frustration for the cops who were already so thoroughly outwitted.

Loyal Arnold didn't leave at once. He stepped forward to help Gunther make sure there'd be no obstacles to the blazes when they erupted. Neither of them peered down, so they were not aware of what the bomb-sniffing dogs were doing. At each end of the tunnel the four-legged detectives were frozen, staring up at the windows from which the sound triggers had come.

A lot of people were looking at Malloy—some at the site and about seventeen million on TV screens around the world. When the network reporters identified him as the hero who'd done the impossible, almost everyone reacted with admiration. One earnest individual who'd been watching the extraordinary events for some time leaned forward to get a better view.

The Red Rose was looking for Malloy.

Ignoring the attention, the ex-SEAL guessed what the dogs were communicating. *Probably* communicating ... well, *possibly*. Long shot but the only shot.

"Unless I'm crazy those dogs are saying we ought to search up *there*," he said to Briggs who'd just arrived with the mayor to "comfort" the civilians who'd faced tragedy, and to address the press.

"I could use some uniforms," Malloy continued.

"You're going?"

"Nothing else to do," Malloy replied. "You can kill the jamming, and let my SEALs on the Jersey side know what their target is. Those dogs of theirs must be pointing too."

Then he turned to Gambelli.

"You coming, Chief? It's party time."

Briggs shook his head. Gambelli simply picked up the heavy .50-caliber and followed Malloy.

Across the Hudson, the woman with the fake Southern accent—and several others—was setting another time-delay fuse in a seventh-floor apartment. The building's main charm wasn't the routine 1980 architecture. It offered an excellent view of the mouth of all three tubes of the Lincoln Tunnel.

She patted the sound machine.

"The damn thing worked," she said approvingly. "Let's split, Howard."

The two Omar agents checked and rechecked ever room to make certain that they weren't leaving any evidence of their activities or identities behind. All they re ally needed at this point was the $300,000 Gunther had given each of them, and their sets of forged passports and Social Security cards.

Driver's licenses too—Americans took them very seriously. The former Stasi operatives went through the list again as **Gun**ther had drilled them time after time. "The devil is in the details," he'd said. He ought to know, she thought as they left the apartment.

It had taken a bit longer to get out than she'd expected, but that could hardly matter now. With that in mind she was in excellent spirits as they waited for the elevator. Someone seemed to be holding it on the fifth floor—the usual crap you faced in urban living today, she reflected.

When they got to the lobby she automatically glanced left and right as she'd been trained to do. So did muscular Howard who'd taken the same course and endless reminders from obsessive Gunther. They did it again when they stepped out of the apartment house into the sunny afternoon.

It was a beautiful day, and a million dollars was waiting.

Since grim Gunther wasn't here to stop her, she began to hum.

She was still humming when a small truck marked PSE&G pulled into the parking area where Howard had left the motorcycle. She'd seen the letters before, something to do with the local electric company. She kept humming as three young men came out of the truck.

They looked very fit, and they were wearing outfits that didn't seem quite relevant to the electric company. Their garb reminded her of combat coveralls. The HK-5 automatic weapons they carried went well with that theme. The fact that the guns were German didn't make her or Howard any less tense.

Responding viscerally, Howard drew his pistol.

The three young men reacted swiftly and peculiarly.

"Saturday night!" they shouted and charged.

Howard raised his weapon. They fired theirs immediately and accurately. As Howard fell, they swung their rapid-fire guns to cover her.

"I never killed a lady before," one of the young men said calmly.

She got the message.

"If you've got a piece, put it on the ground . . . slow," he told her bluntly.

His grammar wasn't that good, she thought, but his shooting couldn't be faulted. She obeyed his instructions, and set down the small suitcase crammed with cash beside her handgun.

"None of this was my idea," she announced hopefully.

Two of the tough young men looked at each other, shrugged.

They weren't the least bit interested.

She could talk to Sting Ray.

He'd told them he wanted one to speak to, and they were bringing one.

Cool.

Back on the Manhattan shore of the river, Arnold was leaving the building where Omar had operated. As he walked out into the street an NYPD patrol car was gliding by on its appointed rounds. Arnold made a point of not looking at it. It was passing by when the driver paused in picking his teeth to glance out.

He needed to find a public toilet to urinate.

He wasn't seeking the man in the wanted poster, and was quite surprised when he recognized the face.

"It's the perp with the bombs," he said as he slammed on the brakes.

He still had to urinate, but he concentrated on pointing with his left hand and drawing his gun with his right. His partner had his own weapon halfway out of its holster as he rushed out the other door.

Omar's explosives specialist had no idea that *someone* had created and distributed a poster with his big-featured visage. Arnold was aware, however, that two armed policemen were coming right at him from only yards away.

"Halt!" one of the cops shouted.

Arnold rejected this suggestion. He dropped into a shooter's crouch as he drew his own nine-millimeter pistol. He shot the cop who'd been driving twice in the chest. Gunther had warned Arnold and the others that NYPD officers wore bulletproof vests, but in the heat of the moment the explosives specialist forgot.

One second, one error.

This mistake saved the policeman from death. He was knocked back into the side of his own vehicle by the impact, but he lost his lunch instead of his life. As he threw up, his partner fired back at Arnold.

His partner wasn't that fine a shot. One bullet hit the bomber just above the right knee. Another missed altogether, and the third smashed away a meaningful piece of the left side of his jaw.

Despite the pain, Arnold thought of Gunther. He had to warn the Omar leader that the police were here. Arnold squeezed off another round as a warning to the officer who'd shot him. As Arnold hoped, the cop retreated behind the radio car.

Arnold was dripping crimson as he reentered the building.

"Hey?" the superintendent said at the sight.

No time to reply.

No need to anyway.

Arnold was limping as he headed for the elevator. The excited policeman who'd shot him was already on the radio with the news. He insisted on repeating the address of the building twice.

"Hurry up, dammit!" he ordered. "My partner's shot. Officer down! Officer down!"

The NYPD responded swiftly. Units were on the way from the nearby tunnel mouth in seconds. The lead car saw Malloy ahead, pulled up with the report. He boarded the RPM immediately.

Seven, eight, ten cars, sirens screaming.

The sounds cut through the afternoon like a spear. The unmistakable noise was audible even up on the eighth floor as Arnold banged on the door.

"Cops!" he told Gunther seconds later. "Don't know why, cops downstairs."

He lurched against the wall, dripping blood on Gunther's right shoe as he passed him.

"We've got about two minutes," Gunther told Scott.

He was optimistic, an unusual trait for a career cynic. The radio cars were already pulling up, men jumping out with guns at the ready.

Officer down? They knew what that meant.

The cop who'd been driving looked up from the sidewalk, pointed at the building. It wasn't difficult to follow Arnold. The red stains set out the wounded bomber's route very clearly.

To the freight elevator.

Malloy and four unforms boarded it as Gunther and Scott prepared to leave the office.

"Top floor," the NYPD captain guessed. "They'd want the best view of the tunnel."

He pressed the button numbered eight.

"You take Arnold down," Gunther told Scott and watched them go.

It wasn't concern for the explosives expert that motivated the Omar leader. He didn't want to be seen with the visibly wounded man whose face some cop already knew from the firefight. The other two could make it or not. They weren't his responsibility now.

They entered a passenger elevator seconds before Malloy and his uniforms emerged from the facing cargo cab. The police scanned the corridor. Gunther was already walking toward them. He was neatly dressed, hair combed, the shirt covering his bulletproof vest pressed and unstained.

He was carrying what looked like a sample case.

Gunther was confident that there was nothing in his appearance that would interest any cop. He began to walk toward them in an even stride, radiating business as usual.

Not quite.

Malloy looked him up and down carefully.

Down. There they were.

Three drops of Arnold's damn blood on his shoe.

The Omar leader saw the gleam of recognition in Malloy's eyes.

Gunther wasn't aware that Scott and Arnold were staring into the muzzle of Gambelli's awful .50-caliber downstairs. What he did know was that the commander of Omar wouldn't show a trace of fear to the Americans.

Yes, he'd seen this one.

Captain Nobody . . . thought he was hot stuff.

He didn't scare Gunther.

"Aren't you going to say something clever or patriotic?" Gunther taunted defiantly.

For a split second Jacob Malley tried to decide between "Screw you" and "Saturday night!"

Either would be wasted on this psychopath, he realized.

Gunther was reaching for his pistol when Malloy spoke.

"Have a nice day!" he said and shot Gunther four times in the forehead with the HK-5.

The son of a bitch had vowed the streets would run red.

The blood pouring out onto the industrial floor here wasn't quite that dramatic, but it would have to do.

39

THERE WERE still a lot of people at the mouth of the third tube when Malloy returned. One of them was the mayor, who paused in his oration to eleven television crews to shake hands with "this fine officer" and laud the ex-SEAL as "a credit to the force. Yes, truly one of our department's heroes."

"I owe it all to my mother and father," Malloy told the surprised media folk who knew him.

Then he pointed at the FBI inspector.

"And the feds," Malloy added. "They deserve a lot of the credit. The FBI and some wonderful people at the National Security Agency, and another branch of our outstanding intelligence community."

"At least you didn't say God Bless America, Jake," the police commissioner of New York City noted a minute later when Malloy was out of range of any press.

"I thought of it," Malloy lied, "but I'm leaving that for Frank Briggs."

"He tells me your friendly SEALs killed some guy in New Jersey and grabbed a woman with a sack of cash," Jefferson said.

"The Lord works in mysterious ways."

"And the maniac who ran this terrorist mob is dead, right?"

"I did that *myself*."

"Don't push it, Jake. You'll probably get some kind of medal, and I'm told they want you down at the White House."

"Prayer breakfast? I love prayer breakfasts," Malloy declared and looked around for the pregnant woman.

"Off to the hospital. Her husband said to tell you her water broke," Jefferson reported.

Now Malloy pointed at a man standing beside Alison Levin.

"The lady had a fine physician," he said. "That's my dad's word. Physician."

The good-looking man talking to Alison Levin was using other words.

"That was very brave of you to knock that gun away," he told her. "You saved that woman's life."

"Glad I did, but I don't want to lie about it," she replied. "I was scared silly like everyone else, and I was running to save *my own* life. Poets don't lie, you know."

"We were all scared. I'm a doctor, and I was as frightened as anyone else," he confessed.

"You're the obstetrician who helped her?"

"I'm really a pediatrician, but I did my best."

He held out his hand to introduce himself.

"Mark Mintzer, M.D., at your service. And I really dig poetry."

She looked at him thoughtfully.

"I've got to get to this wedding," she said and hefted the garment bag that held her dress. "You really good with kids, Doctor?"

"I'm good with taxis too," he replied and took the bag from her. She waved to her aunt who joined them.

Malloy watched them go, until he saw Joanne Velez. She was speaking with a senior DEA official from the New York office.

"May I cut in?" Malloy said and shamelessly kissed her.

"This is Captain Malloy," she explained some twenty seconds later to her supervisor.

"I've heard. See you later, and don't worry about the coke. It'll keep in *there* until somebody digs those goons out."

"Not me," Malloy announced. "I'd leave them there till Hanukkah. That's a Hebrew thing."

"I've heard of that too," the DEA supervisor declared and departed to speak with Thomas Largo. Malloy talked with him a few moments later.

"Not bad," the cochief of the Joint Task Force complimented.

"You weren't so bad yourself, Captain."

Now a familiar voice called out from behind Malloy.

"Keep in touch, Skipper," Gambelli said.

And all the hyper young men in battle dress chanted in unison.

"Ready to go! Ready to go!"

Malloy waved at them as they prepared to enter their large truck. He stopped to hand the pouch of "toys" to Gambelli.

Now they shook hands.

As the SEAL unit rolled away, Jacob Malloy rejoined a pretty DEA undercover agent who looked just splendid despite too much flashy makeup. They began to walk away from the Lincoln Tunnel.

"Nice job, Jake," she said.

"So you noticed?"

"I noticed you before you turned out to be some kind of unreal hero," she assured him.

"Saved your butt, didn't I?"

"Saved the entire carcass," she agreed. "I hope you're not going to keep reminding me of this."

He smiled and took her hand as they walked.

"I think we need a serious talk," he announced.

She stopped walking. So did he.

"I . . . you and me . . . back in the damn tunnel," he began.

"What's on your mind, Captain?"

"Our . . . well, I really wasn't planning on institutionalizing this relationship so soon, Jo, but I see I have to," he announced. "I know you don't want me to remind you, but you might be in a body bag if I hadn't—you know—done my bit."

"Your hero bit, right?"

"Dammit, Jo," he protested. "I've got to look after you."

At that instant she saw something glitter in a third-floor window, off to the left. She immediately reached inside her lover's jacket to seize his Glock semiautomatic. Without a word she spun, took aim, and fired twice.

Something metallic dropped just before someone fell out of the window. As the someone descended Joanne Vellez fired twice more. Two hits. Now the DEA agent took Malloy's hand and led him to the corpse.

Female, rumpled skirt up above her knees.

There was a striking red rose tattooed on her right thigh.

"From your fans down in Cali, I'd bet," Velez guessed correctly.

Before Malloy could respond she said something else.

"Who's got to look after whom, Jake?" she challenged.

"We can negotiate," he answered. "You're going to love my mother. How about dinner at Le Bernardin?"

"When?" she tested warily.

He offered her his best boyish grin.

"After we negotiate," he answered.

They went up to the apartment house on West Seventy-ninth Street, and they negotiated three times. As a result, they didn't get to the fine French restaurant until lunch the next day.

The man who sent The Red Rose to New York didn't get to negotiate at all with the seven macho individuals who came to his home at four A.M. on the following Monday. Though the drug lord had not invited them, they entered easily with the cooperation of two of his most trusted bodyguards who sold him out for ninety thousand dollars and a kilo of cocaine.

Six of the intruders had Uzis, and the seventh, who had a mean streak, carried an automatic shotgun to obliterate the target's face. None of the seven said a word, not a curse, not an obscene insult, nothing to indicate who'd sent them. It might have been any of five other narcotics tycoons who'd heard a rumor that this new ruined corpse planned to betray them to the Drug Enforcement Administration. Story was that the damned DEA would kidnap them to be flown to Miami for trial.

The tip about this intended treachery was said to have come from New York where some loose-lipped cop drank too much about a month ago. This account reached the intrepid Colombian police right after the person who sent The Red Rose was buried. Then an unofficial inquiry was made to the DEA supervisor in Cali, and he promptly relayed it to higher authorities in Washington. Efficient federal executives there bounced the question to the DEA chief in Manhattan.

Joanne Velez brought the matter to Malloy's attention that night as they waited for the elevator in the gracious lobby of the stylish apartment house where the ex-SEAL's mother was honoring her other son's birthday. Captain Jacob Malloy saw the undisguised suspicion in her face as she spoke.

She told him about the Cali killing and the rumor.

"You know anything about this, Jake?" she challenged bluntly.

"First I've heard," he replied and shook his head. "Must be a terrible blow to his mother."

"Screw his mother," Velez told her lover.

"She's too good for me. Actually this doesn't *entirely* surprise me. I didn't know the man but the word was he had lots of enemies. People say he was one bad dude."

She stared at him.

"I can see it in your eyes," she accused as the elevator door began to open. "There's something you're not telling me."

The uniformed elevator operator recognized her last sentence. He'd heard a thousand well-dressed women utter those words in this lobby. Now he wondered what else she'd say to the judge's famous son whose handsome face had been all over television.

Joanne Velez didn't say anything on the ascent.

She was too damn security conscious to talk about this in the presence of an unidentified "civilian" who might be anybody and tell what he heard to anyone. She was silent until they stepped from the elevator, heard its door close behind him, and the former SEAL reached for the bell of his parents' apartment.

Then she said it.

"This Cali deal has Jake Malloy all over it," she declared.

"Some other Jake Malloy," he said with a straight face. "It's a common name."

"I love you, Jake, but this is just *crazy*. Do you have *any* idea what the mayor will say when he hears about this?"

She saw that gleam in his eyes again.

He wasn't the least bit uncomfortable.

"Who'd tell such a wild tale to the mayor?" Malloy asked. "Your boss here wouldn't defame a law enforcement officer in the city cops, and you *know* those biggies in D.C. won't get involved in what could be a very hot international dispute."

She had another question. It wasn't any nicer.

"Do you know what you unleashed in Cali? Killing this one guy won't be the end of it," she predicted. "There'll be retaliation and counterretaliation . . . stiffs all over town."

Malloy pressed the doorbell again.

"I've never been to Cali," he said evenly, "and I have no contacts there. Hell, I don't even know the area code."

She was facing him, not the apartment door, when his mother opened it. A fine-looking woman of about sixty with a simple expensive hairdo, she was wearing her good pearls for the party.

"It's going to be a bloodbath, Jake," the DEA agent predicted.

"Mom, I'd like you to meet Joanne Velez," Malloy said calmly. "I love her very much."

The federal narcotics agent turned, froze, and blushed.

She hadn't done that in a long time.

"Oh, my God, I'm sorry, Judge," she blurted. "I had no idea. I'm really sorry, Judge."

"So you're the lady who used my son's gun to save his life," the jurist replied with a warm smile. "My husband and I thank you. Please come in."

"She's packing her own piece now, Mom."

"No shop talk now, Jacob," his mother replied serenely and stepped back to admit them to the bustling birthday party.

Joanne Velez entered first so she didn't hear the judge's postscript to her son.

"And no more wiseass remarks, Jacob. You're too old for that."

Aglow with her best hostess smile, the judge began to move forward to introduce her son's significant other. Now she paused for a moment.

"I don't mean to be a prying mother, Miss Velez, but what was that bloodbath remark about?"

"About thirty—maybe fifty or sixty—killings in the next month or two," the DEA agent said and tried to speak calmly as she summarized the report from Cali.

"Are you suggesting that Jacob might possibly have indirectly caused the demise of the gangster who twice sent assassins up here to murder him?" the judge tested.

"That man and dozens of other gangsters."

"All drug dealers?"

Joanne Velez nodded.

"So since he's dead, the person who ordered Jacob's murder won't send up any more hit men or women to attack my son?"

"Yes, but that doesn't excuse—"

"How could it?" the graying woman with the good pearls broke in quickly. "As a judge, I couldn't condone killing any individual—let alone dozens—even if they were the scum of the earth."

Scum of the earth?

Joanne Velez didn't know quite what to say.

That made it easy for her lover's mother to continue.

"I can't believe that Jacob would be involved in such a thing. He didn't learn that kind of behavior from us, you know. I've always been against the death penalty myself."

For two or three seconds the DEA agent thought that she saw a look—something like the one her lover had shown when they got off the elevator—in the older woman's eyes. This look wasn't *judge* or legal due process at all. It was naked *mother* . . . and a half.

More like three-quarters, that primeval.

"I know you've opposed the death penalty, Judge," Joanne Velez said, "and I know you've never had a case reversed by the Supreme Court."

"How do you know that? Have you been checking me out?"

The federal agent nodded.

"You bet," she said. "It wasn't hard. I care about your remarkable son, and I'm a detective."

A bit amused by the candor, a lot pleased by the caring, the judge couldn't help smiling.

"A *very good* detective and a woman of great integrity, I'm told," she responded.

"Who told you that?"

"A friend of mine who runs the Department of Justice in Washington."

"The attorney general? You asked *her* about me?"

"You're a detective and I'm a mother. Rank has its privileges right?"

The DEA agent looked just a little shocked.

"Your mother would do the same thing, Miss Velez," he graying woman in the pearls said pleasantly.

"Did you check her out too?"

Malloy's poised, very poised, mother let that one go

by as she nodded toward her tall, trim husband ten yards away.

"Come meet Jacob's father," she invited and led her son's beloved across the long room.

"I'd like to introduce Miss Velez," the judge told her spouse in a delightfully light and charming voice a long way from multiple homicide. "There are three things I should mention before I leave you to your own devices and go to mingle with other nice people."

"Only three?" Dr. Malloy asked.

She gave him a very warm wifely smile, and ignored his question.

"First," the surgeon's wife of many years continued, "Jacob says that he loves her, and I don't think that's just because she saved his life. Second, Jacob tells me that she's carrying a gun—well oiled and fully licenced no doubt—in her legal capacity as a federal agent."

"I can't wait for the third, dear," her spouse announced.

"Third, she comes highly recommended as a very good detective of the highest principles, and I think she knows a lot about you already. Get her some champagne, will you?"

Moments after the judge strolled off to do her hostess duty, Dr. Malloy flagged down a passing waiter and took from the young man's tray two glass flutes aglow with sparking pale liquid.

"Shall we drink to Jacob?" the surgeon asked as he carefully gave one glass to Joanne Velez.

"Anytime," she said and they clinked champagne flute before they sipped.

Delicious, of course.

It was no surprise that the judge had chosen qualit wine.

"My first name is Joanne, Doctor," she said, "and I tal

your son—the one who brought me—quite seriously. For the record, he saved my life too and at great personal risk."

She drank a second sip, nodded in approval.

"Danger doesn't seem to bother him, Doctor. Is that a family thing?" she wondered and drained the flute.

"Not on my side," the surgeon replied as he emptied his own glass. "I'm a scientist. Irish but very much a cautious scientist, I keep risk to a minimum and the patients go home by cab not casket. If my wife's right—and she almost always is—you already know that."

"I do. Jacob does things his way, right?"

The senior Malloy waved for more champagne.

"Since he was five, maybe three. I assume that's what interests you," he said calmly. "His way bothers some people, but he has saved quite a few lives, in his own get-out-of-my-way way."

Two more flutes arrived, and received prompt attention.

"That's good, Doctor," she complimented. "I mean what you said. He has a unique get-out-of-my-way way. He has definitely saved plenty of lives, and filled a few of those caskets too."

"Bad guys?" the surgeon tested.

"The worst," she admitted. "He's a hero all right, but not a simple one. Your son is *some* piece of work, Doctor. Say, what are we drinking?"

"Schramsburg from California. My wife won a case in a bet on a football game in January. She's quite a piece of work too."

It figured, she thought.

A mother who was a noted judge who bet on football games, just right for Jacob Malloy.

A father in the life-and-death world of neurosurgery who said he avoided danger, and probably meant it. Pure Jake Malloy.

"I could tell your wife's quite a piece of work, Doctor," the DEA agent confided and finished off the remaining champagne in her glass. "And I can see you're crazy about her."

"We're a romantic family. Come meet my other son," the surgeon urged and gently took her elbow.

Some nine minutes later Dr. Malloy met his police captain scion at the table half-covered with mini-sandwiches of Scotch smoked salmon.

"I like her, Jacob," the surgeon said.

"Me too, and I think she hit a home run with Mom. I don't know what she said to Mom, but the good judge is really beaming."

"That's probably because this is your kind of woman, Jake, and I suspect there aren't very many of those."

"What do you mean, my kind of woman?"

The surgeon ate half of one of the fine smoked salmon treats before he answered.

"Your brother was boasting about how brave and tough and clever you are," the doctor said and paused for another bite, "and he talked about how savvy you were to bring in the SEALs. You know what she said with a perfectly serious face?"

Jacob Malloy shook his head.

"*What* SEALs? She thinks like you do, Jacob. She wouldn't even admit SEALs were there. She's smarter than hell, and she loves you. I'd grab this one, Jake, and hold on tight."

Malloy didn't ignore his father's advice. When they returned to Joanne Velez's apartment, he grasped her hand firmly as they sat down on the comfortable couch.

"There's something more I should have told you," he announced. "Actually two things."

She nodded.

There was never just one thing with Jacob Malloy.

"I'm not saying that I had anything to do with *something* that might—hypothetically speaking—have led to any deaths in Cali," he began.

Hypothetically speaking was a nice touch, she thought.

"But I can certainly see why a reasonable person might be bothered if some other individual did that, even to solve a very serious problem," he continued carefully.

"What are you saying, Jake?"

"It could be a possible solution to the problem," he reasoned, "but it probably wouldn't be the only solution."

He was trying to meet her halfway, she sensed.

"Of course," he added, "such a solution might also deal with the *second* matter. If that individual's life was in danger—hypothetically speaking—experience has shown that the person's nearest and dearest would also be at great risk . . . on an ongoing basis."

He was saying in his own but totally clear way that killing the drug lord who sent The Red Rose might save her life too. He was right. She didn't like to admit it and what had been done in Cali—hypothetically speaking—was terrible, but Malloy was right. There were a dozen moral and legal questions that could be debated, but he was, bottom line, right about the absolutely real threat to her survival.

His solution had been quick and dirty . . . and practical.

And he was sort-of-kind-of meeting her halfway.

He cared about what she thought, dammit.

"Jake," she said. "I have something to tell you. It has nothing to do with Cali, and it isn't the least bit hypothetical. America's full of dysfunctional families, but that's not my problem."

"I don't understand," he told her.

"Jake, my problem is that the Malloy family and especially the son named Jacob are too fucking functional."

"I could try to tone it down," he volunteered.

"It wouldn't work," she answered.

They both rose and embraced, and he held her tight just as his father had urged. That seemed to work fine.

Two and a half miles away, sixteen employees of the Federal Bureau of Investigation were also working well. They were skilled agents of the Counter Intelligence Division who had never heard the name Mirror, but they had no need to know. Some were on rooftops and others in those inevitable vans in a security perimeter around Mirror's residence, and a few agents were, equipped with a court order and very expensive state-of-the art gear, in Mirror's apartment.

The NSA had finally pinpointed Mirror, and since internal security belonged to the FBI it was the Bureau's experts who were meticulously bugging Mirror's apartment and setting up the phone tap. They nodded when a careful search of every item in the flat—actually three searches because Mirror had hidden the transmitter and onetime use code pads so well—exposed the spy gear.

As they photographed every page in the pads, another team was starting a not-too-close surveillance of Mirror. The federal agents stayed back to minimize the risk that the surely wary and highly professional Russian deep-cover operative might spot them.

Kid gloves.

That was the official word on dealing with Mirror.

In the language of Wall Street takeover strategists, Mirror was now "in play." Contacts, communications methods, the whole bag were the FBI targets. There was absolutely no rush about it. Mirror might be milked for years.

Of course, neither Joanne Velez nor Jacob Malloy were aware of this operation or even that Mirror had been identified. They had their medals coming—hers from the Attorney General of the U.S. and his from that person who appointed the A.G. and lived in a big white house at 1600 Pennsylvania Avenue in Washington.

By the rules of this game, that should be enough for them.

Certainly no one in the "intelligence community" would tell them about the additional teams of specialists who at three A.M. that night would, in janitorial garb, bug Mirror's office in a tall federal tower downtown.

The one that housed the FBI and the Joint Task Force.

The manual was very clear.

Neither Captain Malloy nor Agent Velez had a "need to know." They weren't even aware that Mirror had been identified, and neither they nor anyone else in any U.S. police or security organization knew that there was one Omar operative still out there or where he was.

Casey had left the apartment house in New Jersey about ninety-seven seconds before the SEALs arrived. He was rolling south on his big motorcycle when the young men in combat coveralls shot down Howard and captured the woman. Casey was still free.

Nowhere near New Jersey.

Casey was in a bus heading south from San Antonio. He had reluctantly abandoned the powerful bike, and even more sadly dropped his favorite sawed-off shotgun down a sewer. In a perfect world, he thought, he could keep both. However, he still had his anonymity, very good forged identity documents including the passport he meant to use to cross into Mexico, nearly $300,000 in cash, and his freedom.

He was free of all of them, including that grim Gunther.

This wasn't nearly a perfect world, the ex-Stasi agent thought with a smile, but it would do. He smiled again when the immigration officer at the border waved him through into Mexico. The Mexicans were a friendly people, he'd heard, and $300,000 could throw off enough income for the rest of his life.

It was going to be all right.

Peaceful, Casey thought. He'd like that.

WALTER WAGER is an internationally-renowned master of the thriller. Three of his exciting, fast-paced novels have been made into blockbuster movies: Telefon, Die Hard II, based on Wagner's *58 Minutes*, and Twilight's Last Gleaming, based on *Viper Three*. Some of his other novels include *Otto's Boy*, *Designated Hitter*, *Sledgehammer*, and *Blue Leader*. His articles on travel, the arts, and other topics are regularly published in newspapers and magazines throughout the United States. Wager and his wife live in New York City.